Paramaribo!

NIGEL RYAN is the author of *A*
of *The Scholar and the Gypsy* and tran
mysteries. He was educated at Amp.....ai and Oxford, and for at time
taught at Eton. His distinguished career in broadcasting includes stints
as Editor of ITN News, Vice-President of NBC News and Director of
Programmes at Thames Television. He lives in London and Versailles.

LUKE ELWES's 'Hide and Seek' provides the cover image for this
book. His work can be viewed at www.lukeelwes.com.

For Jay
with love
Nigel

PARAMARIBO!

a novel in two parts

by Nigel Ryan

Starhaven

©Nigel Ryan 2012
ISBN 0-936315-36-9

STARHAVEN, 42 Frognal, London NW3 6AG
in U.S., c/o Box 2573, La Jolla, CA 92038
books@starhaven.org.uk
www.starhaven.org.uk

Typeset in Berthold Baskerville by John Mallinson
Printed by CPI, 38 Ballard's Lane, London N3 2BJ

PROLOGUE

Every eye inside the long distance desert bus was fastened on the last minute passenger.

It had been on the point of continuing its journey from the tiny desert border post into the capital when a frontier guard signalled it to wait. A ripple ran through the knot of onlookers, which seemed to have emerged from a hole in the barren earth all around, as two soldiers using their rifles cleared a path for a man in a white suit.

The bus was the first civilian vehicle to be allowed into the newly proclaimed Republic, sealed off from the outside world since the army coup in which the royal family had been massacred, the British embassy sacked and a state of emergency proclaimed. It was 1958. Lurid accounts had leaked out of vigilante groups set loose by the new Revolutionary Council to round up enemies of the state, and the tall man, with his neatly pressed jacket draped around his shoulders, had an air of easy authority as he sauntered towards the bus with his armed escort, hands crossed lightly in front of him.

Until then the only outward signs of the new regime had been the black, red and green design of the Baath Party flag hanging limply in the early morning heat beside a weighted pole that passed for a frontier, and posters of the new Leader with staring eyes pasted round the dusty entrance to the little border hut. An official in a crumpled suit with a Party armband had stamped REPUBLIC diagonally across the royal insignia on the visa in Sam Cork's passport. Outside, sentries stood about fingering their rifles uncertainly, like wasps in the sun disturbed by something they did not understand.

When the soldiers followed the newcomer up the iron step into the bus, the watching eyes inside were hastily averted. He made his way down the centre aisle with a look of amused disdain. Pausing at the row where Sam was sitting, he turned to his escort. One of the empty coat sleeves brushed against Sam's hair.

Sam looked up. His eye picked up the glint of metal. It was then that he realised the man was wearing handcuffs.

He caught a glimpse of a sallow but distinctly European profile and carefully parted hair, black enough for the stranger to pass at first glance for an Arab, despite his exceptional height. He was in his late twenties, roughly Sam's own age. Something about the long nose and the jaw line – or perhaps it was the half smile – seemed to strike a chord in Sam's memory, but he could not place it. He noted, too, the slenderness of the wrist bones clamped together, another echo. When he turned to get a closer look, one of the soldiers was blocking his view. Then the trio was swallowed up among the passengers, children and packages at the back.

With a roar the bus set off again, charging down the unsurfaced track like the hardy iron mongrel it was, sending up a poisonous spiral of black dust into clear blue desert air. The machine was little more than a collection of spare parts; only the Morris engine remained of the original prewar model. In colonial days buses travelled in pairs for safety. Now only half the fleet of six was still in action. One had been cannibalised for spares. Two had been burned out in the previous week's bloody revolution. The Armenian in the next seat told Sam Cork that in the event of a breakdown the Moslem passengers would trust to Allah, but added, good Christian that he was: 'Unfortunately, Allah is not a very good mechanic.'

Sam knew all about the burning of the buses. It happened when a crowd, intoxicated with revolutionary fervour, took it into their heads that the Crown Prince, the assassinated king's uncle and heir, was trying to make his getaway by bus disguised as a woman. Forty people had died in the blaze including an English nanny to the royal family. Her death not only made headlines in the London evening papers, it had also wrought a seismic change in Sam's life. The following morning his boss, the editor in chief of the Universal News Agency, had called him into his office, he assumed to discuss the obituary of the dead monarch that he was writing. The editor was in the middle of a telephone call and the interview lasted less than a minute. He put a hand over the mouthpiece as Sam appeared.

'How soon can you leave?'

'Where for?'

'Didn't my secretary tell you?'

'I don't believe so.'

'The Middle East. Baghdad. She will give you the details…'

It didn't do to get a reputation for being uncooperative. The previous summons had come four years before when Sam had declined a first assignment to Oslo, hoping for somewhere more glamorous. Instead he had been sent to Obituaries, a bourn located behind a frosted glass door marked Obits which he shared with an elderly alcoholic, from which there was reputed to be no return.

'Of course. Absolutely. Right away.'

'Can you speak languages?'

'A little French and Spanish but not Arabic, I am afraid.'

'That should do fine.'

With which the editor turned in his swivel chair and resumed his telephone call.

Sam's remit was to fill in as the agency's correspondent until a local replacement acceptable to the new rulers could be found. Current resident correspondents had had their credentials revoked on the grounds that they were creatures of the old regime, and some nationals even imprisoned. It looked like being an open-ended assignment.

The desert route was the only way in and the bus was full. Civil airports were still closed. The railway had ceased operating long before with the end of colonial days; stretches of abandoned track followed the desert road for a short while after the frontier. Where it finally disappeared into the sand, the bus swung away south across the dunes to face the heart of the desert.

All afternoon the bus heaved like a tanker in a rough sea. Despite the rocking motion, Sam had the sensation of endlessly standing still. Time lost its significance – he had long since stopped looking at his watch. He was aware only of the heat. Hot sand found its way into his mouth and nostrils. Slowly it grew hotter. Then the landscape became flat once more, a face without features, leading into infinity. It was a journey with no horizons of time or space, with no means of measuring progress. Sam felt his identity slipping away. He had no idea how long it was before night fell.

Darkness brought no relief from the heat. Several times he turned to see the manacled prisoner sleeping between his guards. Once the man was gazing out of the window, his face reflected back in the glass, as if he was intently examining himself. But the first spontaneous spark of recognition had gone. He was a stranger again.

It was daylight when they reached the former RAF staging post built earlier in the century to protect regional imperial interests, now a desert anachronism. The ill-fitting Mao uniforms of a Chinese trade delegation that had just landed at the military airstrip looked out of place beside the regulation khaki of the local garrison inherited from their onetime British overlords. Stretching his legs on an Aldershot-brown veranda, Sam surveyed the whitewashed stones and regulation flower-pots of his army childhood. A morning mist was dispersing; the air smelled of hot creosote. Inside the wooden bungalow an Arab cook wearing a Catering Corps cap badge was serving bread and tea with condensed milk, a leftover of the contract to supply breakfast to the bus company's travellers – another legacy of Pax Britannica.

Sam's eye lighted on the bungalow opposite where a khaki-painted Humber staff car had drawn up beside another poster of the Leader. Through an open door Sam could see an officer making a telephone call; the line was bad and the man was shouting in Arabic. Sam's gaze shifted to the car waiting a few feet away. There were three passengers in back. The one in the middle, sitting between two guards, was the prisoner from the bus. The manacled man looked in Sam's direction. Their eyes met.

Sam stood there, unable to move.

The other smiled, and suddenly an echo from the day before became a roar in his ears. It was the unforgettable smile that long ago had been part of his daily life; a conjuror's smile that combined mock astonishment with delight, a *Hey Presto! Ladies and Gentlemen!* that seemed to be inviting your applause for the trick just performed and promising an even more amazing one to come. It was undimmed either by the passage of time or by its wearer's predicament.

'Otway!' he gasped.

There was a clatter of army boots as the officer, having finished his telephone call, hurried down the wooden steps, climbed into the car beside the driver and gave an order. As the car moved off, a cry rang out; it resounded against the timbers of the barrack walls, bringing back with it yet another echo:

'Paramaribo!'

Sam's lips shaped the strange yet familiar sound as if by repetition it would yield up its meaning. It was not just the word itself, but the tone that had caught his ear: it was not a cry of distress but of triumph: a war cry.

'Paramaribo!' The cry was repeated, muffled by growing distance.

As he stared at the diminishing spiral of dust on the horizon, a mantle of pain seemed to descend on Sam's shoulders. He could not at once explain it – somewhere there was an element of shame, and worse, a burden of unexplained guilt. He was aware of a fenced-off area of his past guarded by sleeping demons that he did not relish disturbing.

He was too absorbed to do more than register the arrival of an old taxi encrusted in dust, and the spidery figure of a girl in a straw hat who climbed out, leaving the door open, and began making frantic enquiries.

As the bus set off on the last leg of its journey into the capital, Otway's war cry still rang in Sam's ears. Paramaribo! All at once the jigsaw began to fall into place. Like the lifting of the morning desert mist, his mind went back, suddenly clear, to the scene a thousand years ago where he had first heard it, and where he had made his first encounter with betrayal...

THE OLD SCHOOL

It was strange, like a dream. He had never left home before, except to visit his grandmother's house. He had followed his parents into a drawing-room smelling of dogs, with windows thrown open onto a grass lawn where boys were playing a game with a white rubber golf ball. He took for granted the grown-ups – a big-boned man who did not smile and a woman with a baby voice – whom he assumed to be like the other grown-ups he had known: friendly, if distracted.

There was an overweight child with spectacles to correct a squint, several years younger than himself, whom the woman introduced as Stanley, adding quickly: 'Thompson – my eldest – is in the Navy. At Dartmouth, you know.' His ear picked up pride in her voice. Stanley squinted back vacantly, giving nothing away.

There was a shout from the lawn and the white ball hurtled towards the open window and rolled into the room. He picked it up and offered it to a boy with tousled hair, out of breath.

'Chuck it!'

The boy caught it, and turning to run, asked: 'Can you play minia-ture cricket?'

'I don't know.'

'Do you want to be in our team?'

He did! He did so indeed! In a minute he was placed in the deep field, with the single mysterious instruction: 'House and statue are boundaries.' Intoxicated, he thought: I am part of the team. Suddenly school was all right.

Once he stopped the ball. For the most part he watched, living each moment with his team. Once he let the ball past and found it in the bottom of a grass bank at the feet of an old stone figure. Once again scampering to stop a run, he collided with a seemingly gigantic person between whose feet it had come to rest. Taking him for a master, he said: 'Oh, sorry, sir.' He looked up, following the line of the legs, as long as stilts, interrupted by a pair knock knees, then a long thin body at the apex of which he found the face of a boy only a few years older than himself, staring at him intently. It was quite unlike any other boy's face he had known: the slick black hair and expression of frozen surprise reminded him of the conjuror his grandmother once hired for a Christmas party. Under his arm the boy carried a bright green book. Again he said: 'Sorry!'

A silence followed, then a smile, friendly but mysterious. Then quite distinctly, the word: 'Paramaribo!'

There was no mistake. And no clue as to the meaning. There came another shout. 'Come on new boy!' Quickly he threw the ball. When he turned back, the apparition had gone.

'Who was that?' he asked.

'Oh that's Otway. He doesn't talk to boys who aren't in his hut. He's writing his autobiography.'

'What's a hut?'

He didn't know what an autobiography was either. But already it was a question too many.

'You'll find out,' said the tousle-haired boy.

Wondering how he would find out, he turned back to the game. But the spell was broken. He caught sight of the French windows; memory returned. He ran into the drawing-room.

'You're not allowed in here,' said the baby voice. 'It's out of bounds for boys.'

'Please, where are my mother and father?'

'They've gone home,' said the baby voice.

Ice seized his heart. 'But they haven't said good-bye.'

'You were having such a lovely game they didn't want to disturb you!' The voice went on: 'Besides, I'm your Mummy now.'

Looking back it made him think of a death at sea, a passenger washed overboard and no body left behind to mourn over. His mother had simply vanished. And then, of course, there was his father – but that was different. He was used to his father being absent. His father did not really count.

It was like a dream. But it was not a dream…

1.

It was summertime and cobwebs stretched between the nose and eyebrows of the old stone figure half hidden in the undergrowth. Moss covered the martial epaulettes on each shoulder. The gently crumbling features had an air of resignation and battles long ago. To the boys of Illbury Hall it was known only as the statue. Nobody ever asked of whom. It was part of school life, accepted without question: when everything is new, everything is normal.

The statue looked across a formal lawn that ran up to the French windows of what had once been a country house, behind which was a watching face. The face belonged to an eight year-old boy. At home he was Sam. Here he was Cork. It was just another part of the newness. But just in case, by way of insurance to protect his identity, he had traced the letters SC in his breath on the window-pane.

His attention had been drawn to the window by a gunshot. A dozen rooks were wheeling in the sky, a union protest without a leader. Split into factions by the high tips of the twin wellingtonias marking the farther edge of the lawn, they reformed in a ragged circle over the statue. As he watched his initials fade, there was another shot. One of the rooks dropped from the circle and dived straight into the glass pane a few feet from his face. There was a muffled thud as it fell back, throwing its wings into the air with a frantic beating motion as if, too late, to ward off its brute's end. It lay twitching in the mown grass. Deeply impressed, Sam watched the pulse of its heart grow weaker against the grey black feathers.

A far-off voice was calling.

A burly man with a shotgun under his arm appeared from somewhere, gathered the bird and slung it into a bag without pausing to check if it was still alive. He strode away, limping a little. Sam had been a secret witness to a grown-up act of violence he did not understand but which seemed somehow indecent. The image brought another to his mind, a picture of a naked man and woman shown to him by his older cousin which he equally had not understood and which seemed to him to have more to do with violence than with love.

The voice was calling again, this time louder, and recognisable. It was calling his name. Suddenly he became aware that the rest of the class had turned round and was looking at him.

'Cork! Do you hear me?' There was a snigger from the other boys as, cupping his hands to his mouth, the headmaster boomed with feigned joviality into Sam's ear: 'CORK! DO – YOU – HEAR – ME?'

'Yes, sir.'

'What are you doing?'

'There was a dead bird, sir!'

The hands were cupped again: 'I – SAID – WHAT – ARE – YOU – DOING?'

'Don't know, sir.' And indeed he did not.

'Then I'll tell you what you were doing, Cork. Slacking! You were slacking, Cork!'

There was a hush. The class knew the code words.

'Wait for me under the clock in the Long Hall, Cork.'

Offenders were dealt with at the end of each class. The punishment itself – a few stinging swishes of a grotesquely large leather strap – was not the worst part. Before that there was the Gethsemane of waiting, watching the minute hand creep towards the hour of execution, willing it simultaneously to fly forward and hold back; and the guilty hope that there would be another victim to share the ordeal.

But for Sam, this first time, the worst part was the sense of betrayal: his father and mother, whom he had always trusted absolutely, had omitted to inform him that the world was not a place where justice held universal sway. Childhood until now had been an unspoken conspiracy to ensure his success, engineered by parents and aunts he had always believed to be infallible and immortal. He had been a protected species in a world without end where friendly gods presided and being good brought love and material rewards, and where if all else failed he could get his way by wheedling.

It wasn't like that at Illbury Hall.

Without warning, life had become a conspiracy for his downfall. Each day he woke in a strange country where they spoke a foreign language. Iron tongues summoned the boys to their duties: the anvil clang of the hand-bell for class, the hymnal toll of the big chapel bell for prayer. Fierce alien gods had replaced nursery ones. The incentive to be good in order to please had been replaced by the deterrent of punishment. Minor infringements earned black marks, recorded with outsize full stops against the offender's name on a list behind a glass frame on the notice board in the Long Hall. Seven black marks in a week drew Illbury's maximum sentence – a visit to the clock. Certain individual offences led there automatically – these included Slacking (in the classroom), Shirking (outside the classroom) and Falling Short (a catch-all charge that could be levelled at all times).

For distraction as he stood by the clock there were the names in gold on the Honours Boards to stare at. There were three boards, for Cricket, for Rugby and for Scholarships. One name appeared on all three, its gilded lettering outshining the others for its brightness as well as its length: *T. Canterbury-Black*. This was the headmaster's elder son, now a grown man at the apex of human achievement in the heroic world of Sam's imagination.

The Gethsemane ended when Mr Canterbury-Black – Mr C-B to the boys – came striding powerfully (the boys reckoned he could knock out Joe Louis easily) down the long tiled corridor to inspect the day's catch, flexing his huge hands in preparation for the task ahead.

'What are you here for?'

That first time a ray of hope, that there was a way out, flickered and flared for a moment. New boys soon learned better: this was foreplay, all part of the game. Whatever the answer, there was never a reprieve. At Illbury sentences were invariably carried out in full.

Silence was no defence. 'I asked you a question. What are you here for?' the voice boomed.

'You said slacking, sir.'

'*I* said? *I* said slacking? And what do *you* say, sir?'

The boom turned to thunder; the eyes bore down like fire through horn-rimmed spectacles. The best answer was capitulation, to avoid the futile endgame that led only to checkmate. Like most beginners Sam tried a delaying gambit.

'Don't know, sir.'

'Don't know sir? Don't *know* sir?' Thunder rolled down the tiled corridor for all to hear. 'Don't know what slacking is, you mean? Here's a boy who doesn't know what slacking is!'

A mirthless guffaw was echoed by sycophantic sniggers. Fear of more public humiliation, or an increased sentence – worst of all, the 'double dose' – stilled further resistance. The march to the study followed in silence, broken only by footsteps on the tiled floor. On the summer air, through open classroom windows, the crack of heavy leather at work reached the steps at the foot of the wellingtonias where, still as a silent mourner, the unmarked statue stood unnoticed in the undergrowth.

Little had the eight year old Sam known, as he took his place with high heart at his first morning Line-Up to call out 'S. Cork, Eagles' that he had placed his foot on the first rung of the great Victorian ladder of public service. Illbury stood for the Old School values designed to usher in a new world order.

Each Sunday in the school chapel Father Becket, a tall pale priest, himself a blend of piety and patriotism, expounded this new order: it was the nation's historic mission to shape the destiny of a Christian world, and Illbury's to shape its leaders, tomorrow's Mandarin class. The boys were divided into Hawks and Eagles to encourage the competitive spirit, weed out the weak and bring forth the strong. Under Mr Canterbury-Black's eye and arm, the groundwork of breaking down the old order began. The transition from nursery to classroom was immediate and absolute, and through rules of thumb the boys were taught unquestioning obedience. If in the process justice was at times a casualty, it was a small price to pay: the Empire needed soldiers.

No one at home had told Sam about the new world order. At first he thought there had been some mistake. It would be put right: it always had been, up till now. Meanwhile all his waking thoughts were taken up with the business of survival.

The blackest patch in Sam's timetable was Mr C-B's Latin class, a labyrinth of iron rules that had to be obeyed, by the end of which, as often as not, a Slacker was to be found waiting by the clock. In Latin fear so paralysed Sam's mind that he could not remember declensions he knew perfectly well. Fear was only a starting point. Fear would lead elsewhere too, to a spiral of shame, self-hate, guilt and beyond: but of these darker declensions he as yet knew nothing.

At least Latin had rules. Catechism seemed to have none. The Juniors were taught by Mrs C-B. She came to class escorted by Flo, an ageing black Scottie bitch, official mascot of the Hawks, widely feared for its foul breath. (Ebb, the white male, had retired as mascot of the Eagles after developing a taste for biting boys.) In Catechism Sam was introduced to concepts foreign to the nursery God of Love. He knew about Heaven: here were Hell and Limbo and Original Sin, strange and sinister as algebra. Then there was Mortification of the Flesh, which he understood to mean that you could strike bargains with God: offer up a gobstopper and He would get you off a whacking.

If Mr C-B was implacable, his wife was unpredictable. She rattled her keys like an impatient animal swishing its tail. Her long powder-blue robes reminded him of the Mother Superior at his sister's convent, but the light in her eyes was fire, not warmth. When not rattling keys, her fingers drummed nervously on her desk as she waited for answers: 'Cork, what is the Holy Ghost?'

Sam selected a phrase he had heard his father use and piped up with self assurance: 'Not the foggiest, ma'am.'

The drumming stopped. The face filled with blood, as if about to burst. The headmaster's wife advanced on Sam, gobbling. 'Heathen! Little Heathen!'

He felt the weight of the sentence upon him. Heathens went to Hell – or was it Limbo, which was bad enough? More serious still, he had made a powerful enemy.

Day's end was marred by a final black spot. Shortly before lights out, there was the sound of short heavy footsteps followed by a squeal of feigned delight as the boys pretended that the stout woman who had come to embrace them was a welcome substitute for their mother. Ever since his first night at Illbury, Sam had recoiled from this impostor's smell as she held out her flabby cheek for obeisance. Each ritual peck yielded was a Judas kiss, a betrayal for which he hated himself.

On the first night he said: 'Goodnight, Ma'am.'

'Ma'am in class. Mrs C-B everywhere else. Although you can call me Mummy if you like.'

The day after his debacle with the Holy Ghost the school trunks were unpacked and checked against the school list. Sam's, packed by his mother, was found to be short of the regulation pair of nail scissors; he overheard Mrs C-B saying to Matron: 'No wonder. What can you expect from a Protestant?'

Sam was aware that his mother was not a Catholic. She had married one, and part of the bargain had been to bring up the children in her husband's faith. Until now this had seemed of no importance. Now it was different. It was bad enough that he had heard it said that Protestants, like Heathens, did not go to Heaven, but to Limbo forever. Worse, the criticism suggested that his mother could err, a notion that had never crossed his mind. That night as Mrs C-B marched towards his dormitory he summoned his courage, put on his dressing gown and slippers and headed for the lavatory on the landing. He locked himself in and stood listening. Footsteps sounded on the stairs, heavier than Mrs C-B's. A shadow cast by the landing light appeared on the frosted glass of the door, grew huge, remained there, motionless. Sam held his breath, listening to his heart. He waited. So did the shadow. He opened the door and looked into the face of the headmaster.

'Why didn't you turn on the light?'

'Don't know, sir.'

'And why haven't you pulled the plug?'

Aghast that an inspection might now take place to reveal the unused lavatory bowl, he could think of nothing to say.

'Don't know, sir.'

Another voice broke in. 'He knows perfectly well. He was trying to avoid me. I saw him as I came to say goodnight. Sneaking out, deceitful little Heathen…'

The next night Mrs C-B walked past Sam's bed without pausing, saying only: 'I don't kiss Heathens.' After a week she relented, and the rite resumed. Sam resorted to Mortification of the Flesh. He devised a set of rules to ward off the contagion: by taking a deep breath as Mrs C-B entered the dormitory and holding it until she left, the good-night kiss would not count. It was his first act of resistance, albeit passive, against the new world order.

After lights out, he felt it safe to lower his guard. In his dormitory bed he learned the habit of mourning. Each night he grieved for his mother as if she had died. He had set up a shrine to her in his mind and faithfully kept vigil before falling asleep, reliving the intoxication of her presence, the exquisite unfailing surprise of her kisses. Then stifling his breath so that the other boys could not hear, he consoled himself with the comfort of tears.

But even the night was not always safe. The younger boys' dormitory was at the back of the school. It looked on to a copse surrounded by wire and out of bounds to boys. Just visible inside was the dark outline of a pump house containing the school's electricity generator, which emitted a throbbing sound into the night, the heartbeat of a sleeping monster. But while the monster slept, guards kept watch. Talking was forbidden after lights out, and Matron regularly roved the corridors, listening for Shirkers. During Sam's second week the dormitory door burst open and Mr Canterbury-Black's monotone filled the room: 'Who's been talking in here?'

Sam was mesmerised by the huge strap in the man's hand. He did the only thing he could think of. He feigned sleep. Braver than Sam, a boy said: 'Nobody was talking, sir.'

'Matron reported talking. Somebody was talking. Who was it? I am waiting.'

There was a silence. Two boys backed up the first: 'I didn't hear anything, sir.'

'I shall wait here until the boy owns up. I am warning you. Unless he does, I shall beat the lot of you!'

That night Sam made his acquaintance with raw injustice as, with the line of frightened boys, he submitted his bared behind to receive punishment for a crime that had not been committed. Innocence was no defence. It was all part of the breaking-down process.

By mid-term Sam had almost forgotten the lanky boy he had met on his first day. The 1939 summer was a hot one and, lying on rugs spread about the school lawn, the boys of Illbury were tackling the day's ration of six sweets with the option of a sugar gobstopper resembling a snooker ball that changed colour as you sucked.

Sam listened to the Miles Magister trainer plane overhead, part of something known as Rearmament. Now and then he stole an upward glance and wished the machine would do something more exciting than circle sleepily above the wellingtonias with a drone like old Mr Bloomer's mowing machine on the cricket pitch.

Another monotonous sound of scales coming from a distant piano told him Mr C-B was out of harm's way giving a music lesson. The perils of morning class were safely behind; cricket was next. The problems of the classroom lay beyond the horizon of thought. This was the Good Reading hour that followed lunch, and the brightest patch of the day was beginning.

Not that the actual reading was much fun: for reasons he could not fathom the exploits of Captain Biggles of the Royal Flying Corps, the Great War flying ace, were not classified as Good Reading. Nor were *Death Pack* or *The Beano* comic, currently serialising a battle involving giant squids. Open before him at page one was *Upwards and Onwards* by The Wandering Parson, which he had picked from the Good Reading shelves in the hopes of aviation, only to find the subject was pastoral work in the Himalayas. There were no pictures; as he stared at the solid print his thoughts, leaving the wandering parson earthbound, glided up to the cloudless skies where Biggles patrolled with his ailerons glinting in the sun. Though uncertain what ailerons were, it was with them that until time for cricket Sam's fancy took flight. This was the hour of his private world.

Overhead the Magister's engine had suddenly cut out and the machine had gone into a soundless dive.

At the controls Biggles was clearly in trouble. Scanning the skies, Sam could see no sign of the von Stalheim circus or any other enemy machine, though he knew war was about to break out.

What could be up with Biggles? In a flash Sam understood: his old war wound was playing him up! Fighting his way across the sloping floor of the plunging plane, Sam managed to grasp the joystick. 'Pull boy!' said a faint voice. 'It's all up to you now...' Sam heaved with all his might and all at once the plane began to level off. At the same moment its engine sprang to life. The day was saved.

'Well done boy!' said Biggles. Turning from the controls, Sam read the silent message in the older man's eyes.' England needs men like you!' He reached out and handed something to Sam that also glinted in the sun.

Across the lawn other boys looked up from their reading as the Miles Magister's engine picked up, unaware that the boy now unwrapping another toffee was the nation's youngest holder of the Distinguished Flying Cross.

The Magister swooped low over the upturned faces and seemed to graze the tips of the wellingtonias as it headed west towards Roman Hill, where in preparation for war, mysterious rolls of barbed wire were being installed.

In the quiet that followed the aeroplane's final pass, Sam scented danger. The scales had stopped. A name, not his, was called. Then more silence, broken only by the rustling of sweet papers. Next, out of the blue, came the familiar frightening crack of C-B's strap, followed by a piercing and prolonged yell: not of pain, but of outrage. A man's voice rose to a bellow. Thunderstruck, the boys looked at one another. The sounds were repeated; there was a crash – falling furniture? – a scuffling noise, more shouts, heavy footsteps; silence. Moments later the figure of Otway, running with knees raised and arms pinned to his sides, burst through the French windows on to the lawn. He circled the recumbent boys once, then again, before disappearing into the house. It reminded Sam of a rain dance he had seen on the school cinema.

Clearly the matter could not end there. At Illbury, punishment was accepted in silence. The boys waited for the next move. It came at Line-Up before supper as a boy called Kettle was being sent to the clock for wetting his bed again. 'Puppies have to be house-trained,' intoned the headmaster. 'And you should all know that at Illbury we have medicine for boys who are not house-trained. And for those boys who shirk their medicine' – a pause – 'there is a double dose!'

All eyes turned on Otway. Half a head taller than the boys to either side, Otway stood, chin in air, grinning with every tooth in his head. The headmaster raised a hand to adjust his spectacles, peered and looked away. Was it a defeat, or could he not see? Illbury was divided into two camps that night: one said Otway was a wet, the other a loony. One of his peers called him 'Loopy Kate' to his face. Otway put his face into the other boy's, squinted and rolled his eyes into the back of his head until all that showed was a pair of all-white globes.

Sam did not know which camp he belonged to. But he recognised that, like himself, Otway was an outsider. The difference was that Otway seemed to have no fear. Otway held a secret key to survival.

2.

Kettle was the other new boy. For a time Sam and he eyed one another uneasily. Thrown together by adversity they had to decide whether to compete or form an alliance. It was a question of survival.

Kettle began with an edge. His uncle was a baronet who lived at Kettle Hall and was something in the city. But his most glamorous asset was that his father was dead, and not just dead, but killed in an airship disaster, bequeathing to his heir the mantle of heroic violence. Like the other boys, Sam had seen cinema news reel pictures of the wreckage of the R101 airship burning in northern France, with shadowy figures running past and passengers jumping to their death. Kettle also possessed a two-foot long model of a submarine in which his dead father had served as a naval officer, with propellers powered by clockwork and Royal Navy markings. Along with a group of admiring boys, Sam had watched it circling the school swimming pool twice before running out of power. It lived beside his tuck box, in a long wooden box, built by a cabinet maker, under his bed.

Kettle's moment of glory came with the arrival of a new curiosity to do with the coming war, in the shape of a barrage balloon tethered to the ground, designed to ensnare low-flying enemy bombers. Boys returning from school walks reported a colossal folded eiderdown being driven to the military camp at Roman Hill on the back of a truck. Sightings of its gradual inflation were reported daily. Excitement was hard to contain when it slipped its moorings and appeared in full view, low on the horizon during Good Reading, trailing its wire tether across the fields. Half filled with air, its crinkled pachyderm's outline reminded Sam of Babar the Elephant after eating a poisoned mushroom. As resident expert, Kettle was consulted: he declared it to be almost as big as the R 101. An army truck came up the drive bringing a team of men in khaki. The runaway balloon was recaptured.

For those first few weeks Sam was left to follow in Kettle's wake. But Kettle's edge did not last. He was a whey-faced child with a stammer and an ill co-ordinated body unsuited to ball games. His inability to master reading and writing held up classes and increasingly antagonised the other boys. Discovered holding a pen in his left hand, he was made to conform to the orthodox Illbury method. The remedy did not improve his literacy, but instead coincided with the start of another trouble, lethal for his standing: he began to wet his bed. A week after its first appearance, the balloon made another, ascending in the sky behind the wellingtonias, fully inflated and attached to its tether, again in the Good Reading hour. This time Kettle was not consulted. Lying a few paces away from Sam, he was the only boy who did not look up. Sam knew why. Had he done so he would have been confronted by the spectacle of a sheet hanging out on to dry on a line outside 'A' classroom for all to see. It was his own, a Flag of Incontinence placed there on Matron's orders as a warning to all bed-wetters. Sam could feel Kettle's gaze turned on him, pleading. With a twinge of shame, he avoided the other boy's eye, unsure that he could afford the luxury of compassion.

On the school front, Sam could hear the drumbeat of another kind of war, more real to him, growing daily louder. In war you had to pick your allies with care.

By mid-term, Kettle had a more serious crime to answer for. His stammer was holding up English Recital. Recital was the brightest patch of the week. The English master had dashing looks with a pencil moustache and a way of springing into the classroom like Errol Flynn in *Captain Blood* alighting from the rigging. His smile was like the drawing of a sword, his teeth a flash of steel. Mr Allbright had never been known to send a boy to the clock. He had an incentive system of his own by which, once the class could recite the poem on the school syllabus between them, he read them stories by Sapper from the adventures of Bulldog Drummond.

For a score of golden minutes each week, the English class inhabited a world where Captain Hugh Drummond DSO, thirteen stone of solid muscle and not an ounce of superfluous fat, moved as silently as a cat (a trick picked up in '17 in No Man's Land), dealing out justice to fiends and Bolsheviks. To help him, he had a gang – all first class sportsmen and white clean through. He also had a vice-like grip (he had once strangled a young gorilla) and could do the hundred yards in a shade under ten seconds. He had a lazy grin and blue eyes that could, however, turn to chips of ice in an emergency. The enemies ranged against him were mostly foreigners with a yellow streak, including filthy stinking Lascars who ran unspeakable rackets. Sam did not know what a racket was and did not think he had met a Lascar, but Drummond knew what they were up to, because he was a master of disguises and could move undetected among the great unwashed. Drummond's arch enemy, Carl Peterson, was also a master of disguises, but Drummond always knew him because of his telltale habit of drumming his fingers on his knee.

At first, loyalty to Biggles prevented Sam from transferring his allegiance, but since he prized physical strength above all other virtues and had a limitless taste for violence it was only a question of time: he was soon a main-line Drummond addict. Such was Sapper's lure that boys rehearsed each other in the prescribed school text outside class. Mr and Mrs C-B beamed when visiting parents heard the boys reciting stanzas from 'The Lady of Shalott' in the corridors. Mr Allbright was considered to have a special touch.

As the readings of Drummond progressed, Sam noticed a curious development. In the early days Drummond's powerful build naturally brought the form of Mr C-B to mind in the leading role. But the association with Mr Allbright's voice did its work; gradually the mantle of Drummond passed on to the English master's shoulders. At the same time, Sam became a member of his gang, one of the Breed of tall upstanding Englishmen who were white clean through and played cricket for their county.

Soon he became aware of other changes, too. The first one dated from a visit by Mrs C-B to inspect classroom fixtures. Until then, it had never crossed Sam's mind that the reading from Bulldog Drummond was unauthorised. Mr Allbright had reached the point where Carl

Petersen had injected Drummond with a paralysing serum and his evil associate Irma was advancing on him with a look of unutterable hate in her eyes.

Sam did not hear the classroom door opening behind him. There was scarcely a pause in Mr Allbright's voice as, without looking up from his book, he went on:

> Out flew the web and opened wide;
> The mirror crack'd form side to side:

Mr Allbright's eye, catching Sam's, seemed to bore into him: 'How does it go from there, Cork?' There was a movement behind him and turning, he saw Mrs C-B standing in the doorway, pausing to listen: 'Don't mind me.' Sam rose to his feet, scarcely heard himself saying:

> 'The curse is come upon me!' cried
> The Lady of Shalott.

He could read the relief on Mr Allbright's face. A secret signal had been given and Sam had responded. He was an accomplice. It was not exactly a crime, more a code exchanged between secret agents in No Man's Land. With a thrill he realised that this was The Game and he was in on it.

That evening the change in dramatis personae was completed as he became aware that the villainous Carl Peterson had begun to assume in his mind the physical appearance of the headmaster, while the seething fury in Irma was interchangeable with the false warmth of the headmaster's wife. The idea was too dangerous to share with the other boys. But once planted the seed took hold in his imagination, and there it quietly grew.

For mid-term recital, the text was Lord Macaulay's 'Horatius at the Bridge', abridged for schools from seventy stanzas to twenty-five, each boy to recite one learned by heart. If all went smoothly there would be time enough to hear the outcome of Drummond's final encounter with Peterson, left at the last reading with Petersen holding a lavish party in his airship over London with all the most important people in England about to drink his health in secretly poisoned champagne.

The new boys were to begin. The stumbling block was Kettle, whose stammer was growing daily more pronounced. Originally the trouble was with his S's, but it soon began to affect his M's and P's. From sibilant and plosive it spread until, like a horse refusing a fence, he was liable to take fright and came to a halt at any word starting with a consonant. Once stuck, all attempts to cajole him into speech were vain. Kettle stood struck dumb. Sitting directly behind him, Sam had grown accustomed to staring at the blue vein running through the putty coloured ears that projected from his head as if straining to catch his forgotten lines. Or any lines. Outside class, boys gathered in groups to rehearse him. They pulled his ears and called him Leaky Kettle. They learned his lines for him, and put up their hands when he was called.

Mr Allbright was a kind man. 'Recite it for him, Cork.'

When Mr Allbright asked Sam a question, his mind did not go blank. He was ready with the opening stanza which anyone might be called on to recite:

> Lars Porsena of Clusium
> By the Nine Gods he swore
> That the great house of Tarquin
> Should suffer wrong no more.

Sam's own bit came next:

> By the Nine gods he swore it
> And named a trysting day
> And bade his messengers ride forth
> East and West and South and North
> To summon his array'

Difficulties could arise if he was asked to explain 'trysting' and Sam had no idea of what an 'array' was – perhaps, like ailerons, something that glinted in the sun – but Mr Allbright avoided trick questions.

All in all Sam felt reasonably confident when the big day came.

The class fell silent as Mr Allbright bounded into the room. There was a buzz of excitement as the boys caught sight of two books he laid beside the chalk marker on the high desk, each with a slip of paper marking the place. He picked up Macaulay's *Lays of Ancient Rome*. The buzz became a groan when Mr Allbright announced: 'Kettle will start.'

Reluctantly, Kettle stood up. His chair scraped slowly against the floorboards until it came to rest against Sam's desk. A thin voice filtered through the class-room:

L-Lars P-Porsena of C-Clusium...

Barely audible, the voice dropped to a whisper:

By the Nine Gods he swore.

Then it came to a stop. There was another sigh, followed by silence. Kettle stood paralysed. At that moment the class-room door opened and Mr Canterbury-Black walked in.

Sam watched the pulse beating in the vein in front of him. Like a sunrise, the pasty white translucence turned steadily to red. Still there was no sound. Mr Allbright had risen to his feet. Mr C-B strode heavily into the room and stood in front of the class. He waited. So did Kettle. Nothing happened.

Then Mr C-B picked up the fat volume of Sapper's *Four Rounds with Carl Petersen* lying open on Mr Allbright's desk.

'Is this the text?'

'No indeed, headmaster.' Mr Allbright deftly handed the older man the volume of Macaulay in his hands. With a grunt Mr C-B opened it where Mr Allbright had marked the place:

'Go on, Kettle.'

Full scarlet now, Kettle stared on into space.

'So why haven't you done your homework, boy?' The voice was quiet at first; then getting no answer, seemed to rattle the window-panes. 'I am speaking to you, Kettle!'

But Kettle had lost the power of speech. Mr C-B turned to Mr Allbright, standing uncomfortably beside him.

'The class knows the penalty for slacking. Unless it can recite the whole poem there will be no midterm holiday. I shall deal with Kettle later. Proceed!'

There was a cold in Sam's stomach. He could hear the false assurance in Mr Allbright's voice as he said: 'Who knows the next bit?'

Sam half put up his hand, thought better of it and pulled it down again. Mr Allbright gestured in his direction. Then Sam realised that the master was looking over his head, behind him, to where another boy, arm in air, had sprung to his feet.

'Otway. You next.'

A voice Sam recognised began to declaim:

> By the Nine Gods he swore
> That the great house of Tarquin
> Should suffer wrong no more

As Otway came to his own set lines Sam's head seemed to empty; but he was not called on. Otway never faltered. Instead his words gathered space, skimming easily through to the next stanza.

Nor did the voice stop there, but went on, without hesitation.

There were long verses concerning warriors with Latin names including false Sextus who wrought the deed of shame, Tolumnius with the belt of gold, and Astur of the fourfold shield, that Sam was sure were not there when the class had stumbled through the first reading. Far from stumbling, Otway's voice soared up and on, gaining resonance as it went. Ten stanzas, twenty, and still the words poured out. Sam turned to see Otway's arms cartwheeling in gestures of ever increasing flamboyance. In the classroom fear gave way to wonder, and when Otway reached the exciting bit with the bridge where out stepped brave Horatius, the Captain of the Gate, each boy was on the edge of his chair.

> Four hundred trumpets sounded
> A peel of warlike glee
> As that great host, with measured tread,
> And spears advanced, and ensigns spread,

Rolled slowly towards the bridge's head,
Where stood the Dauntless Three.

Mr Allbright had settled on the window sill and was listening as intently as the rest of the class. In the middle of the classroom Mr C-B stood stranded like a dreadnought bereft of steam. Otway was unstoppable. As false Sextus was seen approaching, his voice took wings.

A yell that rent the firmament
From all the town arose.
On the house tops was no woman
But spat towards him and hissed
No child but screamed out curses
And shook its little fist.

Battle was joined, violence linked arms with melodrama. Stout Lartius hurled down Aunus, Herminius struck at Seius and clove him to the teeth, while at Picus brave Horatius darted one fiery thrust. Classroom 'A' was transfixed. And beside the Dauntless Three there now stood a fourth, in the shape of Sam Cork.

A cheer went up. Then behind Horatius, with a crash like thunder, its timbers loosened by the townsfolk, the bridge to Rome fell into the river; and with it fell Otway's voice, as brave Horatius stood alone (or nearly alone: now Sam was beside him) with thrice thirty thousand foes before and the broad flood behind. Sam felt his throat tighten as, in shrill treble, Horatius intoned his prayer:

'Oh Tiber! Father Tiber!
To whom the Romans pray,
A Roman's life, a Roman's arms,
Take thou in charge this day!'

So he spake and speaking sheathed
The good sword by his side,
And with his harness on his back,
Plunged headlong in the tide.

Carried away, Sam had by now sheathed his own good sword and plunged in with Horatius. Luckily he could do the breaststroke and even swim under water, though he had never tried it in armour. With Horatius his limbs were borne up bravely by the brave heart within, and the good Father Tiber bore bravely up his chin. On the banks the Romans cheered. Even the foes of Horatius were magnanimous – all but one, who stood out alone: the one who wrought the mysterious deed of shame.

> 'Curse on him!' quoth false Sextus;
> 'Will not the villain drown?'

As Otway spoke the lines, Sam's eyes were drawn to the lone figure in the middle of the room. Still without pause, even it seemed for breath, Otway now came with a fine heroic sweep into the final straight

> And now he feels the bottom
> Now on dry land he stands
> Now round him throng the fathers
> To press his gory hands.

And so to the grand finale of Lord Macaulay's seventieth stanza:

> With weeping and with laughter
> Still is the story told
> How well Horatius kept the bridge
> In the brave days of old.

Otway sat down to a thunderous silence. Then, with a pounding of rubber heels, the headmaster retreated to the classroom door. Half way through he paused to look back at Kettle. Apparently changing his mind, he disappeared into the corridor. As the door closed behind him, a single movement broke the stillness in the classroom: it was Otway raising his arms to utter the cry that Sam had heard on his first day at school: 'Paramaribo!'

A sea of faces turned to congratulate him. Never one to disappoint his fans, Otway accepted the applause with style. While the eyes, still flashing fire, drank in the admiration, the waving arms and magician's smile invited still more. It was how Sam pictured Len Hutton mounting the pavilion steps after scoring 364 runs for England, by far the most important event of the year.

Mr Allbright's baritone broke in to ask: 'Tell me, how did you come to know the whole poem, not just the school version?'

Otway drew himself up: 'My godfather, sir. He promised me ten pounds if I learned it by heart. His name was Horatius. I was called after him: Horatius Ariel Otway, at your service!'

3.

A mystery to do with the coming war that everyone was talking about dated to the summer before. Sam had spent the day with Daisy, his seven year old sister, playing with a neighbour's daughter at the camp where his father was a gunnery major. Owing to a sudden influx into the camp due to a process known as Rearmament, some Other Ranks had been billeted in officers' quarters. The Corks' new neighbour was Sergeant-Major Dayton, a man whose legendary physical strength delighted Sam, and whose barrel chest was covered at Church Parade with Great War medals.

His daughter Sue, a strapping girl of thirteen bowled faster than anyone Sam had yet faced, almost as fast, he was sure, as Larwood. Luckily her aim was poor. Often when he ducked her bodyline deliveries, the tennis ball would shoot past his sister, acting as wicket-keeper, for four byes. These he added to his score. He reckoned that day he had scored his first fifty not out, and by the end of next day would be on the way to rivalling Len Hutton's record.

That evening there had followed a baffling development. As he came back to the house with his sister, their mother called them into her drawing-room to say that she did not want them to visit the Daytons again.

'But why not? We like them.'

'Because they are not like us, dear.'

'Sue is a very fast bowler.'

'Yes, darling. But Sergeant Major Dayton is not an officer, you see.'

Absolutely he did not see. 'He's got the Military Medal! He showed us. And he smokes Players and I'm collecting cards of England cricketers and he has promised me his first Hutton.'

'That is not the point. You might pick up things, things your father would not like.'

'What things?'

Daisy asked: 'Have they got germs? Like Woolworth's?' The Cork children were not allowed into Woolworth's on health grounds, although Marks and Spencer's was considered safe.

'No dear, it's just that, well, they have accents and your father and I don't want you picking them up. Common accents.'

'What is a common accent?'

'They don't speak like us.'

'They do. We can understand everything they say.'

'They're English people!' said Daisy.

Flustered but unyielding, their mother stood up. 'Now I don't want any more talk about it. I just don't want you playing with Sue Dayton and that is final.'

Another event that same day, which seemed to Sam of far less consequence, appeared to absorb the grown-ups. There had been a wireless announcement that the prime minister had landed in an aeroplane coming from Munich and said that there would be no war. Secretly disappointed, Sam had asked his father if, like Hutton, it was good news for England. The major had paused for a moment before replying: 'I shall have to give the matter some thought.'

Next day Sam asked his mother to explain what his father had to think about so deeply she had replied: 'Your father always thinks carefully before he speaks.' Then, hesitantly, she added: 'It has to do with Sudetenland.'

So that was it. 'Where is Sue Dayton land?'

'Mr Chamberlain says it's a far away country of which we know very little.'

Sam asked his father. 'Czechoslovakia,' came the reply from behind the newspaper.

'Is that where Sergeant Major Dayton comes from?'

But his father was absorbed in his reading. 'Not the foggiest,' said the Major.

From all of which Sam had concluded only that there was more to the Sue Dayton mystery than his parents let on. Clearly, she was more than just a fast bowler.

Sam thought about Sue Dayton again during Junior Cricket one mid-term afternoon.

The master in charge of Junior Cricket was Mr Bloomer. Old Bloomer with his harmless shouting and his limp – a legacy of the Somme – turned out to be an ally. Sam had discovered that he had a good eye for fielding, and the word 'Aptitude' appeared in his mid-term report. Only the day before Mr Bloomer had bellowed: 'Well done boy!' into his ear after he had stopped a ball that stung his hand.

In return for his small success, Sam had lavished unconditional devotion on everything connected with the game. By dint of swaps, beginning with the penknife given to him by his godmother, he had collected all but one of the Players Navy Cut England cricketers that came with each packet of cigarettes. He was still short of Hutton, but he had two Wally Hammonds to trade and it was only a matter of time before he would have a full set and the prestige that went with it.

The marks left by the Great War were embedded in Mr Bloomer's mind as deeply as fragments of shrapnel in his body. As the sports master limped through the buttercup meadow with wicket and balls under his arm, he was surrounded by boys eager for tales of blood, violence and espionage. Unlike the major, he had no need for reflection before expressing his views. His own were fixed and forthright. Mr Bloomer was with the War Party. For him Germans were the enemy and appeasers were no better.

When the newspapers showed pictures of Mr Chamberlain in his wing collar returning from Munich proclaiming 'peace in our time', Mr Bloomer was to be seen stumping the school corridors startling passers-by by shouting: 'He'll rue the day! He'll rue the day!' Since then it had become a catch phrase of Mr Bloomer's, leading up to a joke that nobody understood, that the prime minister was really a Frenchman called 'J'Aime Berlin'. The boys were also unclear what 'ruing' might be, but they knew their cricket and understood when, purple in the face, Mr Bloomer told the junior game: 'It's no good running away! You have to stand up to Hitler and knock him for six!'

Since Munich Mr Bloomer had become an addict of the wireless, and war fever was filtered through him down to Junior Cricket in half understood snatches.

'Miss the news and next thing you know there'll be Germans marching up the drive!' The boys responded in full measure to his taste for theatre. Each day they looked out of the dormitory windows, scanning the empty approaches with a mixture of disappointment and relief. Lately Mr Bloomer had made a new discovery: as a result of his monitoring he had found that the BBC was crawling with traitors. This very afternoon he had been listening to the weather forecast. 'It's been the same for a week now. No question about it. Coded messages! 'Anticyclone advancing towards northern Europe.' What does it mean? Troops movements! Secret signal to enemy agents in England. Same code yesterday! They're on the move!'

Awe at the immensity of the conspiracy held the junior game in suspended silence. Mr Bloomer stopped to point to a clear sky: it was a perfect day for cricket. 'Why do you think the wireless said it was going to rain? To demoralise us! Stop the farmers going out to gather the harvest. The Germans mean to starve us to death so we have no stomach for a fight! Bring us to our knees! First it was Sudetenland. Now we've got the Fifth Column on our doorstep! I tell you we must rout them out – and knock 'em for six!'

Placing the mysterious column alongside Sue Dayton Land in a pigeonhole in his mind reserved for puzzles to be considered later, Sam hung with the rest of the boys on the sports master's words. His head, no less than Mr Bloomer's, was filled with plots to smash England: in *Death Pack* secret messages were transmitted by the enemy in code through *The Radio Times*; in *Wavelength Unknown* (unaccountably neither of them Good Reading) a death ray sent from the wireless detonated a bomb by remote control. In each case catastrophe was only averted by astute youthful detective work. In love with glory, Sam longed to show that he was made of the stuff to knock Hitler for six.

His chance came later that afternoon. Last in to bat for the junior Eagles against the Hawks, he was facing the bowling with a single run needed to win. At the other end his fellow batsman was Kettle. A few feet away stood Cash, the school's head prefect co-opted at the last minute to fill in for a sick team member, a foot taller than Sam, like an adult playing with the children, poised menacingly for a catch. Cash was more than merely head prefect. He was captain of the school cricket team, and his name, freshly painted in gold, stood out on the Honours Board below T. Canterbury-Black. Once he had scored fifty runs in the Fathers' Match. Next term he was going on to public school. To Sam he was a demi-god.

The bowler was a chubby splay-footed boy called Jellicoe, distantly connected with the Great War naval hero, better known at Illbury as Jelly. No athlete, Jelly was renowned for his unpredictable deliveries. As he began a curious waddling approach run, Sam hoped for a wide ball attracting a penalty that would earn the vital point without need for him to take action. It was not to be. As Jelly released the ball, it became clear that it was travelling straight, but in an upwards trajectory: so high, in fact, that Sam realised that it might never reach the wicket at which it was aimed, just leaving time for him and Kettle to run a bye before it could be fielded and thrown to the wicket. Alert to opportunity, Sam shouted: 'Run!'

'Go back!' cried the ever cautious Kettle.

'Run!' Sam insisted, accustomed to overruling his sister.

With which he ran. So did Cash. Picking up the ball, he hurled it with all his force at the wicket to which Sam was heading. Sam felt a blow to his head as the ball bounced off him and bounded towards the stumps. He kept on running, reaching sanctuary a split second before the bails fell off.

A cheer went up. The Eagles had won. And Sam had done it.

'Well played, Cork!' they shouted. 'Well done boy!' shouted Mr Bloomer.

Then there was another cry: 'Sir! Look sir! Blood!'

Putting his hand to his head, Sam felt something damp. A lump had begun to form. Deeply impressed, he looked at the blood that spurted on to on his fingers. A hush fell over both teams. They looked first at Sam and then at Mr Bloomer. The old warrior's face turned crimson as he limped towards the knot of boys round the stricken Sam.

Waving them aside, he inspected Sam's wound. 'Report to Matron, boy. Tell her I sent you. Walking wounded,' he added, not unkindly. 'Steady under fire. Mention in Despatches.' Sam's heart swelled.

Then rounding on the gaping white faces, Mr Bloomer shook his fist in the air. 'Blood! Blood!' he bellowed. 'You haven't seen blood until you've shot your first German! Then you'll know what blood is!'

Half an hour later the whole school turned round in silence at tea and biscuits as Sam, his head swathed in a turban of bandages, emerged from Matron's dispensary. Not only had word of his heroic deed gone before him, but there was an envelope on his plate marked 'From Cash'. Inside was a cigarette card: it was the missing Hutton.

<u>4.</u>

It was all right while the bandage lasted. Sam bore it aloft like a flag of truce, stretching out the period of immunity for as long as he could. He basked in the whispered admiration. He was protected from attack by his rivals. He enjoyed a respite from the authorities.

Now the points of Matron's scissors inflicted tiny stab wounds as they snipped through his stitches, signalling that the truce was over. He winced. Matron had not forgotten that his mother had failed to pack his own pair. No less sharp was the tongue she used to drive her point home: 'If we'd remembered to pack our own scissors we might be entitled to complain. Let's hope your mother has remembered to bring them with her.'

At first he did not understand. He was only conscious that his head felt strangely naked. 'Aren't you going to put on the bandage?'

'Do you want your mother to see you like that?'

He looked at her. 'Didn't Mrs C-B tell you? She'll be here at six. I expect Mrs C-B didn't want everyone else to know she'd been allowed to break the first term no visitors rule. We can't have everyone breaking the rules...'

He hardly heard. 'Run along and brush your hair.'

In a daze he went into his dormitory. He nursed the stubborn shoots with his hairbrush to cover the small scar on his crown, but the bristles hurt and the hair refused to lie down. He gave up and went down to the front part of the building, out of bounds to boys.

Then there she was.

It was like waking from a dream. She was where he had last seen her, in the drawing-room that smelled of dogs from which she vanished a thousand years ago and which he had not visited since. Now she was back – perhaps she had never gone away? She was wearing white gloves and the blue hat he remembered from when she came in to say good-night on her way to cocktail parties, a pretty woman in her early thirties, but in his eyes outside the reach of time, the centrepiece of his universe. He wondered if she was on her way to a party now. Then he realised she must have dressed for him, as if he were a grown-up, too. He was not sure he welcomed the promotion. He had learned to distrust change, all change.

Mrs C-B was there too, wearing powder, lipstick and drawing-room smile. 'Ah there you are, Sam.' He bridled at the bogus trappings of warmth put on for parents, the baby voice and the use of his Christian name, but all was eclipsed in a flash, like a candle in the sun, by the wonder of his mother's presence.

'Well Sam, how are you?'

'I'm all right, thank you.'

There was a silence. Mrs C-B said: 'Sam had a little mishap at cricket. A ball hit him on the head. But he's all right now, aren't you Sam?'

'Yes, thank you.'

Mrs C-B spoke again: 'Help yourself to tea. And Sam...' She had put out her best china teapot. 'I expect Sam would like some sandwiches...'

Sam stood and stared. Together with his Christian name, the teapot and the sandwiches came from another world, where his mother and not Mrs C-B belonged. He could not take it in. For every minute of every hour of every day he had pined for her presence, and now she was there he did not know what to do. He had become used to the emptiness without her. He had grown a carapace around his longing and he could not throw it off at will. It was as if he had become addicted not to the object of his longing but to the habit of longing itself. He watched as if it was a film.

Mrs C-B broke in again: 'Your mother has something important to tell you, so I'll leave you two together.'

When they were alone, his mother opened out her arms:

> Diddle diddle dumpling, my son John
> Went to bed with his trousers on...

It was the jingle with which, long ago, she dried his tears for a cut knee or a disappointment.

> one shoe off and one shoe on...

The tug on the umbilical cord did its work. In a rush the intimacy was back. Sam flung himself at her and held her with all his strength. It would be all right now, he knew. She would make it so. She always had, in the old days.

'And how do you like school?'

Still holding her, he shut his eyes: 'Please take me away with you...'

He felt her stiffen.

'But it's a very good school, and it's a very nice place...'

'I don't like it here.'

'But Sam, we all have to grow up and go to school. Where else would you go?' she wondered. For a moment she was caught off balance. Then, chiding: 'And what about your cricket? And the googly spin bowling you told me about in your letter?' Sensing a weak spot, she pressed home her advantage: 'And how will I manage with you at home all the time, especially now' – her voice trailed off, and she paused, making up her mind, then drew herself up and placing her hands on her rounded stomach, looked him in the eyes – 'now that there's going to be an extra person to look after?'

He knew his mother's blackmail. He always had to behave extra well to get her over a crisis. If she had a headache he had to be a big boy: now there was a baby coming – why or from where he had no understanding – so he would have to be especially good. When he tried to bring the conversation round again to leaving Illbury, she put her finger to her lips, then to his: 'I am counting on you, Sam...'

With that, the subject was banished, and he knew that if he raised it again it could bring on one of her headaches.

So far the baby had little meaning to him other than as an obstacle to his escape plan. Then he understood that his mother had come to tell him that she would not be at home for the start of the holidays. Instead she would be in hospital. There was something about a complication. Even then it was not the scent of danger that troubled him, nor even the disappointment of her absence. What he dreaded most was change: any change.

And then she had to go. Sam did not think his mother unkind; she was just in a hurry, as she always was. There was never time to explain. As the old Humber taxi slowly made off down the drive, wheezing like an elderly sergeant major, she called out from the back seat: 'See you soon darling. Be good.' But the private compact with his mother had always dealt in instant gratification; in the old days bliss was immediate. 'Soon' was part of the new order, 'soon' was the future indefinite, a tense he had not learned at home. 'See you soon...' Blind words uttered under a dark empty sun. He retreated into the shadows of the school corridor. Numbed by her presence, he succumbed in a rush of tears to the familiar agony of her absence. After the tears, a vacuum. In the shadows, beneath the carapace, he felt his heart beating against stone.

Two days later a letter came from his father asking him to be sure he kept a place in his Eleven for the new baby, perhaps even as a googly bowler. There was a drawing of a baby saying 'googly' and a final paragraph:

> My Commanding Officer at Gunnery School was Jumbo Jameson. Jumbo always used to say: 'If you won't let yourself be moulded into form, you'll be pounded into shape.' Old Jumbo was pretty shrewd when it came to human nature.
>
> Love from Papa

Sam tried to picture Jumbo Jameson and wondered if he was as big as Mr C-B. Then he tried to picture his father, but all he could bring to mind was the squeak of shiny boots as he walked away with measured pace into his grown-up world, leaving no footprint behind.

<u>5.</u>

Sam was reminded of the 'complication' when the major came alone in the family Austin saloon at the end of term to drive him home.

'Your Ma,' he explained carefully, 'will be back from the hospital in a few days but the doctor has ordered rest.' The major understood orders. Meanwhile everyone was going to have to be extra helpful.

The house seemed to have shrunk a little but was otherwise the same wooden bungalow for officers' families at the end of a sandy lane of pine trees and army white paint. The Corks', a grade higher than its neighbours, had a front porch and a lawn mown and rolled by Madden, the major's batman. Sam hurried round the rooms, touching familiar objects. Beside his bed where he had left them were *Biggles Flies West* and an Eiffel tower brought back from the Paris Exhibition by his Aunt Olive. In the drawing-room the cat greeted him with a bored arching of its back and fled when he tried to embrace it. Everything was the same. Except that his mother was not there.

On an impulse he turned the knob of her bedroom door and slipped inside. He had not been alone in it since being allowed to sleep in her bed as a treat when he was a small child. Now he felt like an intruder. He looked at the cut glass bottles waiting on the dressing-table. The smell of his mother's powders and scents filled his nostrils, and the room was alive in the soft summer air with her presence. On the dressing-table stood the triple mirror in which, feigning sleep, he used to watch her as she examined herself with her special appraising look, pouting her mouth, trying out a smile, turning her head from one side to the other as if there was a choice to be made, the way she looked when she was buying a frock (Sam always knew what he liked and disliked; his mother never seemed sure.) Next she would remove her make-up with the aid of little face cloths and creams kept in glass pots with silver tops ranged in front of her. Witnessing the secret rite, he noticed that the face in the glass seemed slightly different in reflection. An Irish nanny had once told him dead people went into the wall after death and looked back through mirrors, and he had wondered whether this mirror picture was his mother's ghost image that he was not meant to see. On one occasion he had woken to find her sitting quite still in front of the glass with her hands on her breasts, gazing intently. When the hands moved he saw that she was naked under them, her face expressionless like a dead person. Ever since then he had associated mirrors with secrets.

Sam accepted philosophically the presence of his father's elder sister, there to fill in. Unlike Mrs C-B, Aunt Olive posed no threat to his mother's role. Aunt Olive posed no threat to anyone. A self-effacing figure, neither joyful nor complaining, she lived, when not filling in, with a single guiding passion: the rights of women. Neither Sam nor his sister knew what these could be but they knew that once aroused their aunt had an unexpected core of steel. The most important fruits of her obsession were a succession of holy pictures on Daisy's birthdays of women martyrs to put into her prayer book. The latest was of the massacre of St Ursula and the Ten Thousand Virgins in colour, in which you could see the blood. On the back Aunt Olive had written: 'The Stronger Sisterhood'.

Sam woke on the first morning of the holidays to a familiar volley of sneezes, the signal that the major had reached the bathroom, to be followed later as he came in to breakfast by the squeak of his riding boots in whose shine Madden swore you could tell the colour of your eyes; next came the surprised, slightly embarrassed greeting on seeing his son, as if he had unexpectedly run into a member of his club he thought abroad, or perhaps dead: 'Hello, old chap!' On one front Sam had no cause for concern: nothing about his father had changed.

Then at lunchtime there was a call from the hospital.

The military hospital room had two beds. The major sat on the empty one, a suddenly diminished figure, no longer in command. Round-eyed, Daisy and Sam perched beside him, stricken silent by the instruction not to mention the baby. That it had been lost was understood: quite how or where was beyond their grasp. Their mother seemed as frail as lace, but her linen-white face brightened for a moment at the sight of her children.

Then Daisy had to go to the lavatory. The major took her off, awkwardly, to find an orderly. As soon as they were gone, Mrs Cork patted the bed beside her to signal to Sam to come over. He looked at his mother and she looked at her son; suddenly there were tears in her eyes, and she said: 'Oh Sam...'

At first he was frightened in the presence of a grief he could not comprehend. Then, as he put his arms round her an exquisite peace settled inside him. Her distress played into his hands. Suppressing a secret guilt, he exulted in his gain. The baby was of no importance: what mattered was winning her back. He at once set about exploiting his advantage: 'When will you come home?'

'Soon, darling...'

'And will you play cricket with me? I can do googlies now.'

'Of course darling...'

'Do you promise?'

'Yes. I promise...'

She had promised...

Two days later she was home.

On the first morning Sam woke early, dressed and hurried to his special place in the rockery beside the red-hot pokers growing against the garden fence that smelled of creosote. The sun's rays warmed his feet through the semi-circular pattern of holes in the tops of his sandals, and he could feel the living presence of his mother, asleep behind the drawn blinds of the window a few feet away from where he stood. Suddenly he was all-powerful. He was a poet, filled with love for the whole world. He was intoxicated by a sense of well-being so immediate and so absolute that it was as if he had stepped outside time; and he knew then that he would remember this moment for the rest of his life.

But the blinds stayed down. Captain Armitage, the regimental doctor, called. A portly figure with a twinkle in his eye, he paced the veranda with the major, adjusting his stride to the taller man's, pausing at the turn to emphasise a point. Captain Armitage was part of the old order of things, a point of reassurance, a regular visitor on bridge nights, the major's best man. Now even Captain Armitage could no longer absolutely be counted on. 'Patience. You must have patience,' he told the children. But patience was like his medicines, something alien you had to swallow. Patience was part of a jingle, a meaningless concept in a child's world.

Sam decided to try Mortification of the Flesh. If he could bicycle to the greengrocer and back with Aunt Olive's errands in ten minutes, his mother would get well. 'Wasn't I quick?' he asked, putting the potatoes on to the kitchen table. 'You be careful you don't fall off,' Aunt Olive replied. He enlisted Daisy's support. Daisy shared with him the known fact she had brought back from the convent that if you said ten Hail Marys without taking a breath your prayer would be answered. They raced one another through a decade of the rosary.

Their mother took to sitting up in the drawing-room for a few hours each evening. She played records on the gramophone. Once she played patience with the children (Racing Demon was deemed too strenuous). Encouraged, they embarked on the most ambitious Act of Mortification they could devise: they would count to a million. Sitting in the garden house, they reached the first thousand in three minutes. After twenty minutes their zeal waned.

In church on Sunday Sam tried holding his breath during the reading of the Gospel. He was forced to give up with a sudden gasp in the middle, causing Sergeant Major Dayton with his chestful of medals to turn round from the pew in front.

Three weeks into the holidays Sam's school report arrived with hand-written slips headed 'Application' and 'Progress'. His Cricket report bore a gold star. His mother acknowledged it with an exhausted smile: he would have settled for even feigned delight. He swallowed disappointment. To his relief she turned Catechism over without reading it. She came to Latin. 'Application' and 'Progress' had been bracketed together in ink and two words stood out in the Headmaster's hand like a High Voltage warning: 'Pay attention!' Then came the Headmaster's summary. It ended: 'This boy tells lies. He will not amount to much unless he pulls up his socks.' Mrs Cork read it through. For a moment she seemed to rally. 'But, Sam, you never lie to me…'

A question hung, if not in the voice, in the eyes. Meeting her gaze full on, Sam said: 'No Mamma…' He meant it. The boy his mother loved, the boy he wanted to be, did not tell lies. But he felt the flush burn his cheeks as he spoke. She laid down the reports, suddenly tired. 'Later, when your father gets home…'

She had drifted away once more. There was no place for children in her private world of incomprehensible pain. The dark had descended.

Later that evening listening ears were at the drawing-room door again. They followed the conversation in the room as much from the tone of the voices as from the snatches of phrases filtering through the woodwork.

Their mother's voice was weary, resigned: 'If only he had gone to a normal Church of England school… It's all that religion…'

'And fear of punishment.' Aunt Olive's voice had lost its apologetic note. 'Fear of punishment has not made him good; it has only made him lie.'

'No son of mine is a liar!' For a moment the fire was back in Mrs Cork's voice. 'You must talk to Mr Canterbury-Black. Perhaps we should change schools…'

Cutting in, the major's voice had an obstinate edge that Sam had not noticed before. 'I believe in leaving professional matters to the professionals… and I'm not going to run at the first whiff of gunsmoke. Besides this is no time to be discussing changes… What with the present situation…' And there was more talk about the other complication gathering momentum in Europe. It had become like a tennis rally that was too fast to follow.

Aunt Olive said in her helping-out voice: 'The trouble is, men like war. They are educated for power, privilege and war.'

But Mrs Cork was not to be put off. After a pause they made out the words: 'You could at least think about a new school…'

'Order, Counter Order, Disorder… I have taken my decision and I decline to alter it.'

'Even at the cost of your son's well-being?'

'I have my values…' The major's voice had risen to match hers.

'Your values!' Sensing that her first shaft has struck home, she tried a second: 'I have lost one child. Why should I lose another to your values?' There was a silence, followed by the sound of sobbing. Sam and Daisy looked at each other. A little later, Jack Buchanan's voice singing 'Good Night Vienna' filtered through the woodwork.

In bed that night a single phrase rang in Sam's ears. A new school... Yet another reason to speed his mother's recovery. He counted another two thousand towards his million. Next to divine intervention, Sam placed his trust in cricket: he would woo his mother with googlies. Each morning he got up early to practise with a tennis ball against the fence beside the red-hot pokers, one eye on her window. One day she rallied, even calling out to him across the lawn. The next, the blinds stay down. He decided to raise the stakes: if a million was not enough he would count to infinity.

The household waited on tiptoe. The gramophone was moved into the bedroom. The children tried to read the faces of the grown-ups as they smiled and nodded at the strains of 'Love is the Sweetest Thing' and the new Glenn Miller record 'In the Mood', brought to the house by Captain Armitage.

There were long silent spells. The grown-ups, too, pinned their hopes on a succession of sovereign remedies. After peace and quiet there was music. Then there was the Tattoo.

At meal times and in the evenings Aunt Olive and the major would repeat: 'We must get you well for the Tattoo...', and 'If your are feeling up to the Tattoo...' and 'The Tattoo will get you out of yourself'. Sam had been taken to the Aldershot Tattoo the year before; there was a race between a team of cavalry horses and a team of tanks. Mrs Cork had been with the horses for their tossing plumes and dashing riders, among them a young Polish officer with a duelling scar who had come to the house. Sam was with the tanks. The major declared himself neutral. The tanks broke down and the horses won. That year the army put in a fresh order for 150,000 horses.

Though Sam's side had lost, his mother made up for it by giving him her red leather commonplace book, unused except for her maiden name, Geraldine Winifred Burnes, written inside, for him to keep as a diary. He began by writing TATTOO on the first page.

One Sunday afternoon at the beginning of September, his mother sent for him. She was lying in semi-darkness. He could hear the sound of stillness as he tiptoed into the room.

'Will you run an errand for me on your bicycle, Sam?'

Second to bowling her googlies, there was nothing in the world he would rather do. 'Bring me my bag... There's a prescription somewhere in it to take to Watson's. It's Sunday but he's the duty chemist.' She pulled out a piece of paper folded into a square.

'It's quite old, from Captain Armitage, but it's still good. Wait while they make it up for you and bring it back to me yourself, as quick as you can.'

She smiled, the world's most beautiful woman sending her champion into combat. Sam was already summoning his array, buckling the good sword to his side. She called out as he was leaving: 'No need to mention it to anyone else...'

'Is it a secret?'

For an instant she hesitated. She looked sad. 'Yes... a sort of secret.'

It was enough for her to pronounce the word to invoke the special compact between them. His bicycle flew up the hill to the shops. The chemist was next to the newspaper shop where a billboard announced: PINCER MOVEMENT ROUND POLAND. More interestingly, from the street lamps hung transparent banners with TATTOO written downwards in capital letters, reading the same from both sides.

A bell rang as he pushed the door open, but inside there was nobody to be seen. Four huge glass apothecaries' jars filled with coloured liquids held his attention. A panel slid open in the wall behind him and a pair of eyes inspected him from above a thick black beard. Silently Sam held out the prescription. An arm, encased in a white sleeve, stretched out: fat fingers with black hairs, unlike the ginger hairs of Mr C-B, took it from him.

'Is there a hurry?'

'It's for my mother.' Then, unsure quite why, he added: 'It's secret... A sort of secret.'

A smile appeared in the middle of the beard. 'Well we can't keep secrets waiting, can we?' The panel closed again, leaving Sam alone to gaze at the rows of drawers with inscriptions in gold letters: Peruvian Bark, Citrate of Magnesia, Arrowroot, Rhubarb, Camphor – the kind of remedies Aunt Olive took. Others had Latin names.

A door he had not noticed before opened and the bearded man came in. He had on a white smock, and carried a bottle of pills which he set down on the marble counter. He began writing carefully on a label with a pen. Using gum from a second bottle, he fastened the label on to the bottle of pills, then wrapped it neatly in stiff white paper. Lighting a candle, he heated a stick of red wax to seal the package. It was like a church service. After writing for a short time in a ledger, the man took out a pencil from behind his ear and wrote Sam's mother's name on the package before handing it to him:

'Any more secrets?'

Leaping on to his bicycle, Sam pedalled for all he was worth, counting on his mother to remark on how quick he had been. Unlike Aunt Olive, she understood. It was part of their special compact.

But when he got home she was in the drawing-room with the major, Aunt Olive and Daisy. They were gathered round the wireless from which there came a frail, mournful voice. It was Mr Chamberlain, and he was announcing that England was at war with Germany. What impressed Sam at the time was the major saying 'Damn!' He had never heard his father use a swear word before. His mother burst into tears.

Thinking back later, he remembered the thrill of danger at the wail of the camp's air raid siren immediately after Mr Chamberlain stopped speaking, and the disappointment that it was only a dress rehearsal. He remembered the major leaving for France. In the week before, the camp cinema had shown a newsreel with French fathers kissing their sons as they boarded the train taking them to the Maginot line. Sitting in the garden house afterwards, brother and sister had gazed at each other in awe at the thought of the major kissing Sam. Sam could not recall physical contact of any kind with his father. Then on the platform there had been a quick stiff handshake, a static electric shock of embarrassment passed between father and son, and Sam felt something hard pressed into his palm. It was a half-crown coin.

'For defraying exceptional expenditure,' said the major.

Unclear what his words meant, Sam wrote them down.

Two weeks later he was back at school.

War meant more changes, some exciting. To travel you had to carry a gas mask in a cardboard box slung with string from the shoulder and borne with the thrill of being in on the action. On the straight stretch of the school drive a slalom of concrete blocks had been installed to stop enemy tanks, and a trench dug across the flat fields to either side to prevent Luftwaffe aeroplanes landing. In the school building, stirrup pumps stood beside freshly painted buckets filled with sand and water ready to make short work of enemy bombs. A notice on the long dangling rope of the Chapel bell said in red capitals FOR USE ONLY IN CASE OF INVASION. Another, pinned to the school notice board and headed FOR THE DURATION, explained that the hand-bell would henceforth serve for all purposes, religious as well as lay; the renamed Invasion Bell was not to be touched under pain of expulsion.

The war brought a transformation in Mr Bloomer's fortunes. The school timetable had been amended to include Bomb Drill, at which Air Raid Precautions were taught. Wearing a round tin helmet and an armband bearing the initials ARP, he instructed the boys how to extinguish bombs – sand for Incendiary, water for High Explosive. Mr Bloomer bellowed orders as they lay on their stomachs in pairs, one boy operating a stirrup pump, the other directing the hose onto an imaginary blaze. When Sam asked how you would know which kind of bomb it was, he replied: 'You'll know soon enough if you get it wrong, boy!'

Other changes were more sinister. On the first day back Sam ran down the dark corridor that led to the kitchen to seek out an old ally, the Greek cook. Seeing a dark silhouette in the door frame, he hurried eagerly up. The silhouette became flesh and blood. A voice he knew said: 'What are you doing here? You're not on my milk and biscuit roster, Cork!' It was not the baby drawing-room voice, but Mrs C-B's Catechism voice. 'The kitchen is out of bounds!' As Sam shrank into the darkness, the small plump figure of Stanley pushed past his mother. He held out a slice of bread and honey as if daring Sam to take it, then, still eyeing him, slowly licked the honey from its surface. The departure of the cook was an economy measure, part of something known as the War Effort. It also marked the start of a Pincer Movement on the School Front.

After the initial excitement came a grey dullness. There were his mother's weekly letters to look forward to, but they had become increasingly impersonal, the writing harder to read, and there was no mention of a new school. The arrival of a letter from his father raised then dashed his hopes. It came from somewhere in France in an envelope diagonally stamped PASSED BY FIELD CENSOR. There was nothing about a new school here either, nor of the war other than an anecdote (prefaced with the explanation 'evanouir = to faint') about a French officer with imperfect English who said he had 'vanished' after being wounded. Sam's eye ran quickly to the end of the letter where he knew by now he could expect to find anything his father really wanted to say. The last paragraph read: 'Keep your chin up at school. Remember that "Time Spent on Reconnaissance is Seldom Wasted".'

On the Illbury front the pincers continue to close. Air Raid Drill meant a curtailment of Recital classes, in consequence of the adventures of Bulldog Drummond. Then in mid-November there came a hammer blow: the English master had volunteered to join the Finnish forces fighting against the Russians and would be leaving at once for something known as the Karelian Isthmus. In addition to expert cricketer, Mr Allbright acquired an overnight reputation as a master skier and deadly shot, capable of picking off Russians while travelling at full speed in the snow.

As the school was assembling in the Long Hall to await the car to take Mr Allbright to the station, Sam was summoned by Matron. Her manner was brisk, not unkind, as she told him to brush his hair and change into his Sunday suit. Though the obstinate tufts at the back of his head refused to lie down, she passed his appearance without a word. He went downstairs to join the other boys in time to see the old station Humber wheezing up the school drive. A passenger got out. It was Aunt Olive.

She had come to tell him that his mother was dead.

6.

The train was blacked out. Strips of plaster covered the windows and by the dim wartime lighting it was difficult to make out the station names, written up in extra small letters to confuse German parachutists and spies.

Sam didn't cry. He stared at the black-out precautions, looking for the way out. There had to be an explanation. A solution. There was a mistake. She had promised to watch his googlies. At one stop the other occupants of their compartment, soldiers in uniform, got out. When they were alone, Aunt Olive told him that his father was coming home on compassionate leave for the funeral. Daisy was already there. She had made a black crepe armband for Sam to wear. He was still looking for the way out when they arrived.

It was late night by the time they left the train. The regular ticket collector had been called up and there was a strange face at the barrier. There were no taxis in the station rank. Aunt Olive asked the man for help. He answered: 'Don't you know there's a war on?' They walked home from the station yard.

The funeral was to take place at once, as soon as the major arrived. The children pooled information. Aunt Olive had explained that there had been a haemorrhage, and Captain Armitage was called in, too late. In the street Sergeant Major Dayton saluted Sam: 'You'll be giving a helping hand to your father now?' Normally he would have referred to him as the major. Sam was touched; but he did not know what to say. He was only looking for the way out.

The major came home, a grey, dignified figure. Would he cry at the funeral? Sam and Daisy had established that manly tears were acceptable on certain occasions: in the final scene of *Lives of a Bengal Lancer* when Gary Cooper is awarded a posthumous V.C., his brother officers wipe tears from their eyes. Even so it was as hard to imagine the major weeping as to imagine him kissing his son.

Then abruptly everything changed. The funeral was put off. Instead Aunt Olive would be taking the children to the cinema. Sam was nonplussed. Sharper, Daisy gleaned better intelligence. There was to be a post mortem.

Later that day Sam was called into the drawing-room. A face he remembered was there: it was the black-bearded chemist. He was introduced as Mr Watson: Sam thought the unglamorous name didn't fit him. There was an older man as well, who appeared to be in charge. Mr Watson remembered Sam, too: he had asked about the apothecary jars. The older man looked at Sam with steady blue eyes that made him think of Jumbo Jamieson.

'Did your mother tell you to keep the pills a secret?'

It was not a question of lies, but of loyalty. It was a question of the secret compact, a matter of trust. His mother's words came back to him. 'No need to tell the others…'

'No,' he said.

The blue eyes, kindly, remained fastened on him.

'Mr Watson here says he remembers you telling him it was a secret.'

Sam said nothing.

Much later it would emerge that Captain Armitage had signed the death certificate himself, putting haemorrhage as the cause of death. A new medical orderly at the hospital, part of wartime reinforcements, challenged the finding. No indications of haemorrhaging were discovered and the police were called in. The post-mortem established that death was due to an overdose of a barbiturate prescribed by Captain Armitage. If it was an accident, why the secrecy? Sam's evidence was crucial, but he was too young to go to court, and the chemist's unconfirmed word would be hearsay.

In the end the Mandarin class protected its own. The family's good name was at stake; there were the children to protect. The captain's career could have been ruined by a public amendment of a wrong diagnosis. Nobody used the word depression: depression was a weakness, and will-power was taken for granted, especially now that there was a war on. The police dropped their inquiries. A verdict of Accidental Death was recorded.

At the time Sam was aware of none of this. The only thing that concerned him was the special compact. He had not betrayed his trust. Somehow his mother would honour hers.

A further decision was taken to protect the children. Normal life was to be resumed as quickly as possible. They were not to attend the funeral after all. Instead they would return to school at the weekend, after Sunday Mass, in time to start a fresh week. Did missing the funeral, the formal symbol of grieving, give an added impetus to Sam's secret life, already begun that first day at Illbury when he turned to say goodbye to his mother and she was not there?

After Mass, he ran to his room and collected his half-crown. Then he waited until the house was empty and tiptoed into his mother's bedroom. There were dustsheets on the bed. He sat at the dressing-table and looked hard into the triple looking-glass through which his nanny had once said the dead looked back; but all he could see was the grave and intent face of an eight-year old boy.

A silver gleam caught his eye. It was the tiny antique Turkish hand mirror, almost as thin as his half-crown coin, half hidden under a lace coverlet, which she sometimes used when putting on her lip salve, while he kept secret watch. He slipped his hand under the lace. A moment later the looking-glass was in his pocket with the half-crown.

Years later when he read that the Irishman Samuel Beckett described his life as a quest for a meeting with his dead mother with a view to improving their relations, Sam would think of that day when he had been sure of finding her waiting for him, and began the long voyage upstream in search of her.

7.

High above the statue's head, the twin wellingtonias danced in stately tandem to the winter wind. From higher still came the sounds of the phoney war, Hurricane and Spitfire fighters hurrying urgently across cold clear sky, their martial growl a contrast to the peaceful summer drone of the Magister trainers.

Behind closed French windows the watching face was more with-drawn. Longer and leaner, Sam was growing in other ways, too. A cornerstone of his world had collapsed. He had pulled up the drawbridge to his inner citadel, where his secret new life was taking shape. In front of him lay open the red leather commonplace book with his mother's name in it which he used to record his private account of events.

He was lost in thought. He traced his initials in his breath on the window-pane, watched the letters fade, then turned to stare at the two words on the open page:

DOUBLE AGENT

The problem was, what came next? Vital pieces of information were missing. That morning a man in a brown suit with a bowler hat and leather despatch case had called to speak to the headmaster. Several boys remembered seeing him at Illbury before, after the English master's departure. At the time Mr Bloomer, on the *qui vive* for spies, had declared that he did not like the look of him.

At afternoon Line-Up, the headmaster had made an apocalyptic announcement: the assistant master who had passed himself off at Illbury as an Englishman called Mr William Allbright was not an Englishman at all. He was a German, and his real name was Wilhelm Ulbricht. Though he ostensibly came to England with his family to escape the Nazis, he had omitted to secure British nationality and was found out when his papers were checked. As a result, instead of going to Finland, he had been interned as an enemy alien in a camp on the Isle of Man. The incident was not to be mentioned in letters home. In the meantime there was to be no irresponsible talk about spies.

But once spoken, the word could not be unspoken. The notion that Illbury had been harbouring a spy seized every imagination. Censorship lent wings to rumour. At Bomb Drill Mr Bloomer let it be understood darkly that he had had his suspicions all along.

Sam's diary had a different story to tell. Already Mr Allbright featured in it as a figure endowed with near supernatural strength, remarkably like Bulldog Drummond and, above all, white clean through. One thing was certain: Mr Allbright could not be an enemy spy. There was only one possible explanation: he was a double agent.

Taking up his pen, he wrote Mr Allbright, inserting a B for Bill.

> Mr B. Allbright, master of disguises, moved silently as a
> cat into No Man's Land.

Bulldog Drummond was known to have prowled about at night in No Man's Land in the 1914 War, striking terror into the hearts of the enemy.

> News has just come through that he has made his way
> from No Man's Land to the Isle of Man. On arrival he
> found it to be crawling with Nazi spies. B. Allbright
> passed easily among them, deceiving everybody includ-
> ing his friends at Illbury. What no one knew was that
> the man letting it be thought he was an enemy spy was
> really a double agent.

Sam turned the page to begin a fresh paragraph.

> Another thing they did not know was the nature of his
> quarry. His quarry, at work in the school grounds, was
> none other than Yulowski himself…

When Mr Allbright left Illbury, Sam had reached a point in *The Black Gang* where a Bolshevik with an un-Britsh habit of braining his ene-mies with a rifle butt was about to go to work on Phyllis, Drummond's wife. The Bolshevik's name was Yulowski. Yulowski was one of few people who made Drummond angry. Personally Sam did not much care for Phyllis who always struck him as rather wet, but Drummond did, and Sam accepted that the prospect of her being butchered made him lose his temper. It took five men to hold Drummond down in a friendly scrap. But when Drummond was roused…

Sam had no scruples about plagiarism. With less than a decade of personal experience to draw on, his story lines were lifted wholesale from the masters of suspense. The trouble was, when Mr Allbright left he had taken the volume of Bulldog Drummond adventures with him, leaving the final outcome of *The Black Gang* hanging in the air.

The youthful author sat chewing the end of his pen, wrestling with an early onset of writer's block.

The phoney war dragged on with monotonous reports of reinforce-ments, but no action. For want of bombs, Bomb Drill was replaced by a weekly war briefing with miniature Union Jack and swastika flags to mark the Maginot and Siegfried lines.

Disappointingly, despite a patriotic song hammered out by Mr C-B on the school piano about how the British were going to hang out their washing on it, the Siegfried line remained obdurately in place. Then as March turned to April, more swastikas appeared in Norway. Mr Bloomer revealed that this was the work of Quislings, who now replaced Fifth Columnists as the new enemy to watch out for.

Meanwhile on the Illbury front, a more immediate offensive was building up. Teachers called up for military service were not easily replaced at short notice; a new emergency timetable appearing on the school board included a solid line on Monday evenings of classes all to be taken by the headmaster: Maths, Maths, Latin, Maths. It was one solid Mined Area. To Sam it looked like the Siegfried line.

When in the early summer of 1940 the swastikas at the top of the map suddenly began an advance into France, Mr Bloomer explained Blitzkrieg. Herr Hitler was using the Czech tanks Mr Chamberlain let the Germans have to go through neutral countries. Luckily Winston Churchill had taken over to put a stop to their nonsense. Sam's diary faithfully reflected the party line.

> The Germans knew the Maginot Line was too strong so they cheated and went round. Mr Bloomer says everyone must look out for poisoned chocolates dropped by the Germans, also nuns wearing boots who are really German paratroopers. In England top men at the Ministry are holding their breath as unluckily B. Allbright is too busy in No Man's Land to go to Dunkirk.

There was no mention of Sam's father, waiting somewhere in northern France in the path of the advancing enemy.

> There are also new enemies worse than Quislings called collaborators. They have already sapped France where Mr Bloomer says the Duke and Duchess of Windsor started the rot by fleeing Paris.

Omitted, too, was Mr Bloomer's new joke, 'Gone With the Windsors', no more understandable than 'J'aime Berlin' before it. But included was a single ominous line that acted as a reminder of that other Blitzkrieg closer to home:

Mr C-B has taken over the weekly War Briefing.

'Cork, show me Dunkirk on the map.' Hesitation was fatal. Sam pointed to the Isle of Man. He liked islands.

'Wrong!'

It was a warning shot. At evening Line-Up Mr C-B fired another. He could name a Shirker who didn't know where Dunkirk was.

'Which country does the Isle of Man belongs to, Cork?'

Sam's head swam. 'No Man's Land, sir?'

'No Man's Land sir? No Man's Land? And is that where you come from, sir?' There was a dangerous edge to his guffaw. Sam submitted to the public ridicule in silence. The period of grace earned by the death of his mother had elapsed.

The next event in his life seemed to pass over his head without touching him. The news was broken to him by Mr C-B: Aunt Olive had received a telegram to say that the major had been taken prisoner. General Cash, the father of the head boy, brought the details. The general had a red face to match the band round his hat. Mr Bloomer had let it be known that he was a key figure in the allied Strategic Counter Offensive to be unleashed at any moment. The general had been evacuated from Dunkirk on a destroyer strafed by German fighters and had come at once to Illbury to see his son. He had been invited to give out the school prizes.

He also asked to see Sam. Sam was thrilled to be spoken to by a general in uniform. He noticed that the great man squared his shoulders as he spoke, the way his father did when he was uncomfortable, as if he would have been more at home on parade. The general chose his words with care. Major Cork had been in charge of a unit assigned to hold Calais to the last man as a shield during the mass evacuation from Dunkirk, a few miles up the coast. He had stuck to orders and stayed behind even after the garrison ran out of ammunition. Disobeying theirs, a splinter group had broken out and made their way to Dunkirk a step ahead of the encircling German forces, to be greeted as heroes. 'I expect your father knew what he was doing. Bad luck being in the bag.' He enclosed Sam's hand in his enormous fist. 'Jolly good show!' The general was a jolly man.

The only record of the event in Sam's diary was of the arrival of a general with red tabs on his lapels and a bullet hole in his mackintosh.

Looking back later, he remembered the uneasy reticence of the officers' families calling on Aunt Olive after his father's capture. It was not until after the war that an army inquiry put an end to the polite silence by dismissing charges of mutiny hanging over the renegades and commending their initiative (under the Mandarin code initiative was a virtue that overrode the rules, always provided it succeeded). One newspaper described the major, who gave evidence, as 'the man who lost the war according to the regulations'; another ran a headline THE CORK WHO LOST HIS BOTTLE.

Sam would never forget the major's expression on hearing the outcome. It was as if he, too, felt betrayed. He was a man of his times – the obedient public servant, not just a prisoner of war, but a prisoner of his past. Sam wondered if his parent even had a choice. Had he ever thought to rebel? Did he suffer inner doubts about the Victorian values that had formed his character? Sam would never know. After the report on what became known as 'the Calais Mutiny', the major retreated into an unbroken silence.

Soon after the general's visit Sam had a letter. The envelope was marked RED CROSS above his name and stamped diagonally in black ink OPENED BY HMS CENSOR. It gave him a buzz of importance as it was held up and his name called out at After Lunch Line-Up, when the headmaster distributed the day's post.

Another boy to have mail was Otway; Sam spotted the spring-heeled lope as he approached the headmaster. But instead of handing him his letter, Mr C-B peered at the envelope. It had an Indian stamp.

'And who, pray, is General Sir Horatius Otway?'

Otway stood on one foot, like a stork.

'Sir?'

'Can you explain the sudden elevation?'

'No, sir.'

Behind tortoise-shell spectacles, the coals glowed red. Otway lowered his eyes. The headmaster gave him the letter. Then there were two more, and finally a third, all addressed to General Otway. Boys gathered round as Otway opened the first envelope. Inside was a blank sheet of paper to which was attached a single sixpenny stamp. Otway smiled and stalked enigmatically away.

Sam waited until he was alone before opening his own letter. It contained a lined yellow form with OFLAG 93 printed at the top. Below in separate boxes was a list of headings printed in German and English against which his father had written in block capitals:

ABSENDER/SENDER: MAJOR E.CORK
GEFANGENNUMMER/P.O.W. NUMBER:
OFL436
ABSENTEN/ADDRESSEE: C. CORK

Pencilled in the major's neat hand was the message:

Will write soon with address to write back. Counting on you to captain the team in my absence. Love Papa

Sam read the letter once. Then he studied it for secret codes.

On the second of the headmaster's Monday marathons there was a question in Maths about the cost of a basket of eggs that stumped Kettle. Mr C-B pulled his fob watch from his waistcoat pocket and began counting. Kettle got the answer in time. That seemed to put the headmaster into a jovial mood. He asked what the answer would have been if it had been apples instead of eggs. Kettle didn't know. 'The same of course, fish-face!' 'Fish-face' was safe, reserved for boys in Mr C-B's good books. The headmaster gave a guffaw.

Sam was not called on.

In Long Division the voice boomed harmlessly, distant artillery at the far end of the classroom. Sam had reached the halfway mark unscathed. To come there was Latin, then after the break Algebra, a bad dream in which letters masqueraded as numbers.

Latin class had been translating a story about a treasure guarded by a snake. Mr C-B wrote on the blackboard THESAURUS =TREASURE. Someone else was called on to begin the translation. Sam remembered his father looking something up in a book with ROGET'S THESAURUS written on the spine; for a moment his mind wandered from the text to a scene of his father finding treasure, maybe a snake as well.

'Next word, Cork!' The words exploded like a shell. Sam reached out for a Latin word. Any word.

'Et, sir.'

A pause. A note of derision: 'Ate what, sir?' A suppressed snigger, no guffaw. Sam couldn't say. 'You're guessing, Cork!'

The red eyes turned towards him. 'Cork will finish the translation.' The blitzkrieg had begun. Sam completed two sentences without a mistake. Then just ahead of him, at the start of the third, his eye was caught by a Latin word he was sure had not been there the day before. It danced before him, a demon on a tightrope, making anagrams of itself in the air. He tried to find a way round; it barred his passage. Like Kettle before him he came to a standstill. He could see Mr C-B's hand moving to his waistcoat pocket. Then the bell sounded the tea break.

The sound of chairs scraping against the wooden class-room floor was drowned by Mr C-B's voice: 'We'll find out after the break if Cork's been slacking in Algebra as well.'

It did not take long. As the class began he said: 'Step forward, Cork.' Sam stood beside the high stool with an old Navy Cut tobacco tin containing chalk.

'I'm going to put some equations on the board' – Mr C-B picked up a piece of white chalk and began writing, addressing the class without looking round – 'equations you have all had time to learn...' Now the only sound in the classroom was chalk against slate. Ignoring Sam standing beside him, the headmaster turned to face the room: '...but this time, the answer to each equation will be filled in by Cork!'

Sam picked up a piece of chalk. He stared at the blackboard.

Surrounded by a confusion of numbers and letters, the ranks of missing answers advanced towards him, engulfing his thoughts in a paralysing vacuum. The chalk screeched against the black slate as he began desperately writing in the space at the end of Question 1. From over his shoulder a hand appeared and appended a neat white 'X' against his answer.

'Next question!' The jaw clamped shut. Sam looked at the board, then at Mr C-B. A tic tugged at the corner of headmaster's mouth.

Was this the moment when Sam began to understand that there was no way out? That he had been singled out as prey, and now the hunter was going in for the kill?

He started writing again in the next blank space. Before he had finished a second cross appeared.

'Go on!' Sam stood immobile, as if by not moving he might become invisible, better still, cease to exist in bodily form. The headmaster drew out his watch. 'One minute, Cork!' Sam remained frozen, his eye not on the blackboard but on the tic in the headmaster's mouth. It was a curious relief when the minute was over. The watch snapped shut. 'The rest get on with your home work while I beat Cork.' The class sat stock-still: the regular clocking-in procedure was only by-passed in the gravest cases.

Sam followed the giant strides down a long narrow passageway that skirted the building and led to the front part of the house. At the angle of a corner a door gave on to the main drive. Once past this point there would be no escape. Turning the corner ahead of him, Mr C-B passed for a moment out of sight. The door was ajar. Across the drive he could see the spinney where the school pump throbbed in the night next to a thicket of brambles. Mr C-B was short-sighted. By making a dash for the spinney he could hide, and then...

But even from the prisoner of war camp, the long parental shadow fell across him. Like his father he was trained to obey orders: like him, he was a prisoner of his past, programmed to stay at his post even after his ammunition had run out. The difference was that in Sam's war the enemy did not take prisoners. Even if you surrendered, you were still executed.

With dry mouth he turned the corner. His only hope now was

miraculous intervention. But there was no miracle; and it was only a need to avoid displeasing his absent father that prevented him from crying out as the weapon of punishment rose and fell, and through a crimson mist the voice boomed:

'Double dose for slackers!'

An age later the giant footsteps receded, leaving him alone with a searing pain he thought he could not bear. He crept through the swing door that led to the sanctuary of the boys' staircase and crouched on his haunches. In the dark place at the bottom of the stairwell he felt his foot touch the rock of despair. Then the pent-up tornado began to shake his frame.

There was a sound of footsteps. Scrambling to his feet, he paused, and held his breath.

Then, quite distinctly, he heard a voice saying: 'Paramaribo!'

8.

Sam stared through the darkness. His mind fastened on to the single word thrown to him like a lifeline. He was still too terrified to speak.

'Pa-ra-ma-ri-bo!' said the voice again. The face looking down seemed to be drawing him towards it. It was Otway's. He did not move. 'I have an important message for the boy from No Man's Land.' There was another pause, then: 'This way!' The face vanished. Footsteps sounded on the floorboards over his head. Involuntarily Sam started up the bare black treads. He reached the top in time to see Otway disappearing like the White Rabbit down another flight leading to the kitchen passage; from there he turned towards the French windows of A Classroom. Numb, Sam followed the strange strutting figure. Indian file they crossed the front lawn where the school had gathered for the break. He felt watching eyes following him – the sounds of execution had not escaped listening ears: counting whacks was a schoolboy's perk. Ignoring them, Otway headed past the statue and into the beech wood to the clearing where the older boys had their huts.

A low bough barred their path. The gnarled join where it had been grafted to a long dead beech stump formed an ogre's face with huge mouth opened wide enough to conceal a boy's body. 'The look-out post,' Otway said. He ducked under the bough and beckoned to Sam. 'In case of enemy spies…'

A pair of evergreen bushes stood sentinel across the entrance to the hut. With a ritual gesture like Father Becket saying Mass, Otway parted them, then stooped to lead the way in. Still ashen-cheeked, Sam hesitated, looking at the older boy. Otway turned to execute a bow from the waist. 'Welcome to the AA Hut.'

It was the first time Sam had seen inside a hut. It had makeshift walls of brushwood and logs for half a dozen boys to sit in a circle. A mirror hung by a bootlace from its corrugated iron roof. A notice at the entrance said KEEP OUT – AA MEMBERS ONLY in large letters in green ink. Otway squatted on a log with branches for arms and cleared a space for Sam on another opposite.

Still Sam could only stare. When he opened his mouth to speak, no sound came. But already curiosity was plucking at the corners of fear. On hands and knees now, Otway was clearing the undergrowth to reveal a deep square hollow cavity in the floor, as big as an empty grave. From it he lifted a black tin trunk with a faded P & O shipping label tied to one handle. He opened it and searched inside, his back blocking Sam's view. Pulling out a long piece of paper he turned, holding it to his chest. 'You are hereby invited to membership of the AA Hut. But first you have first to go through the Initiation Process.'

Sam looked at the trunk. He looked at the mirror and the notice. Then, swallowing, he tried again: 'What does AA mean?'

'It's secret. It can only be revealed subject to Ratification.'

There was an awkward silence. Then Otway appeared to relent. 'Except in exceptional circumstances.' He paused importantly. 'First you have to swear the blood oath that you will never reveal our secrets. And once you have sworn you cannot tell, on pain of death. Not to anyone… Hold up your hand if you swear.'

Sam held up his hand.

'AA,' Otway went on, confidentially 'are mirror code letters.' With a flourish, he held up the paper he had been holding. On it, written vertically, were the letters:

A

A

'Now look in the mirror. The letters read the same in reflection.'
Sam looked.

'Next, security procedure.' Otway held up his free hand, palm
towards him, and intoned: 'Paramaribo!'

Mutely, Sam held up his hand. They touched palms.

Otway went on: 'Security Procedure. First you have to say the password Paramaribo! Then the other person has to answer with his personal mirror code. It's Procedure.'

Using a green crayon Otway wrote some more letters.

H

A

O

T

W

A

Y

'H. A. Otway. Horatius Ariel, that's me. Look in the mirror. It reads
back the same. It's my AA mirror code name.' He handed Sam the
crayon. 'You have to have one of your own to be ratified as a member
of the AA hut.'

He watched in silence while Sam wrote:

S

A

M

C

O

R

K

The letters stared meaninglessly back at them from the mirror. The other boy declared, with a touch of asperity: 'That won't do! You have to have a properly working mirror code name before you can be Ratified.'

'Does it have to be your name?'

Otway thought for a moment. 'Real names are best. Some members have mirror Christian names. We already have Timothy and Tom which are mirror words. Cork is no good. Nor is Sam.'

Sam sat downcast on his log while the other boy mused: 'But the rules do not say codes *must* be name codes… You will have to think one up.'

It was all too much to take in. Everything was happening too fast. Sam was still in a state of shock. He needed time to gather his thoughts. From nowhere a question that had been on his mind since his first day at Illbury jumped into his head.

'What does Paramaribo mean?'

'It's a place. In South America. Where I was born.' Sam looked at him with admiration. He had been born on the edge of an army parade ground in Surrey.

Grandly, Otway went on: 'My father moves around a lot. Mostly in the art world. He's in tea at the moment.'

'Is Paramaribo a mirror word?'

'It's a password. It passes through the mirror. It's an important part of the code.' He looked at the letters arranged vertically.

'But the P and the R's and the B are cheating.'

Otway smiled his magician's smile. 'To throw enemy spies off the scent…'

There was another silence. Otway seemed to be making up his mind. Then, voice lowered to a stage whisper:

'AA stands for – ' he paused, leaning forward dramatically – 'ANARCHISTS ANONYMOUS.'

If the words meant little, the manner of their delivery was compelling enough to make his listener's eyes bulge. But before Sam had time to ask what an anarchist was, the bell for chapel sounded.

'All will soon be made plain!' Otway's hand shot up. 'But first, the oath! The AA oath.' And he made Sam put up a matching hand to swear the words once more, this time with new ones renouncing 'Illbury, together with the Devil, Mr C-B and All his Pumps!'

The raised palm closed into a fist. 'Tomorrow we go forth against the Great Array!'

The older boy's confidence was intoxicating. In the space of minutes a wild roller coaster ride had taken Sam from abject surrender to membership (subject to Ratification) of Illbury's most exclusive inner circle. Otway's final words rang in Sam's ears like a pledge as they hurried through the wood, back to reality.

But the fear he had left behind was lying in wait for him in the damp smell of the cement corridor that led to the chapel. It filled his nostrils as he took his place in his pew under the inquisitive gaze of the rest of the school; and it reclaimed him like a policeman's hand on his shoulder as, somewhere behind him, the heavy unseen fingers thumped out the notes of the Illbury hymn:

> Faith of our fathers, holy faith!
> Our fathers chained in prisons dark!

As one, a line of adult mouths opened as one to shape the words –

> Oh how our hearts beat high with joy
> When'ere we hear that glorious word!
> Faith of our fathers! Holy Faith!

– and, as one, closed again as the verse ended, the chins a line of drawbridges raised against him, shutting him out. He looked over to where Otway stood among the Hawks, just another boy now, a year or two at most older than himself, surely no match for the power of adult Authority ranged against him.

That night he mourned at the shrine to the mother who had not come to rescue him. When he woke next morning, the old world was dead. Here the rules were different. At Illbury justice was not just a casualty. Justice was a target. Perhaps this was the moment of lost innocence, when he finally lost faith in the remote figure in shiny boots he had always accepted as an ultimate and benign authority. At Mass he felt himself cringe as Mr C-B strode past him to the altar rails to receive the Communion host from Father Becket. The headmaster's body seemed to fill the chapel, his man's thighs thicker than Sam's waist. As he watched the huge hands with their little mats of ginger hairs pass the Communion plate to Mrs C-B beside him, Sam felt the last drop of his courage desert him. He was ready to pay any price to avoid another beating. He would turn his back on his pantheon of heroes, Biggles, Bulldog Drummond, Horatius, even B. Allbright himself; he would hope they would not see him. He would become a Quisling, a collaborator, a false Sextus. Then when it was all over, he would hide his deed of shame in the dark box in his mind where he kept his bad thoughts, and throw away the key.

Waiting in his locker later that day was an envelope addressed in bold green letters:

CORK – TOP SECRET

He tore it open.

MEETING OF THE AA
To be held in the AA HQ after Evening Line-Up
Those present: Members of the AA
Agenda: Ratification of S. Cork

The note spurred two thoughts: the lifeline offered to him by Otway was not just words, but was backed by action, though of what kind Sam had next to no idea. And then, from nowhere, a memory came back to him. He was standing in the chemist's, waiting for a prescription for his mother. Outside the window was a transparent banner with a word written vertically in capital letters which read the same way on both sides, literally passing through it. TATTOO... A mirror pass word. It was one of the first words he had he had recorded in his mother's comonplace book-cum-diary.

As he committed the magical word to memory, he became aware

of a new resolve that had stolen over him since his encounter with Otway, pushing its way out from under the deadweight of his fear.

At the appointed time, Otway was waiting for him beside the ogre's gaping mouth. He directed Sam to stand by and disappeared into the hut. From inside came a sound of voices. Sam's attention was distracted by a sudden movement in the dry bracken, and he spotted the small figure of Stanley running away. After another minute Otway reappeared wreathed in his magician's smile, topped out with magician's bow. 'You are hereby invited to join the Ratification Meeting!'

Still wondering what Ratification could be, Sam stepped into the hut. A line of boys squatted on the logs at one end. Greatly to his disgust the first he recognised was Kettle, of all boys in the school the least like his idea of an Anarchist.

A modicum of credibility was restored by the presence of the splay-footed cricketer Jelly, from his own dormitory. Apart from clumsiness, Jelly had a reputation for daring. He had first achieved fame by being sent to the clock for blasphemy after spreading a rumour that the pump house in the spinney was haunted by the Holy Ghost. For a bet he had once invited God to strike him dead.

The fourth boy was an evacuee from London with piercing eyes, called Mott. Mott was smaller than Sam but senior in age and class. Sam had once heard his father saying that Londoners were street-wise, and he could feel himself being sized up now with what he took to be a street-wise look.

Otway sat cross-legged facing the others with a green book open on his lap bearing the initials AA on the cover. He began reading with a ceremonial air:

'APPLICATION FOR MEMBERSHIP. It is hereby proposed that S. Cork be ratified as a member of the AA. Those against the motion speak now or forever hold their peace.'

Nobody spoke.

'The Application is granted subject to passing the test of a Mirror Code word.' Otway did not believe in wasting time.

He turned to a fresh page and handed it to Sam with a green crayon. Taking the crayon Sam wrote:

T
A
T
T
O
O

Otway held the writing up to the glass. The assembled Anarchists peered at the green letters. They came back, reading the same in reflection. Otway's black eyebrows shot up. Solemnly he shook Sam's hand. 'Paramaribo!' he said. 'I hereby declare you a fully ratified member of Anarchists Anonymous. You can now be initiated into our secrets.' Turning to the other members: 'That concludes the Ratification Meeting. I shall now conduct Cork's full Initiation.'

The other members got to their feet and filed out. There was no doubt about who was in charge at the AA.

Alone with Sam, Otway came straight to the point: 'First, No Man's Land, then the Initiation!'

It was no longer a question of the old fear of Mr C-B. Sam's new fear was of seeming childish in the presence of the older boy, of losing the lifeline that had been thrown to him. He explained how No Man's Land had begun as a make-believe place for the exploits of B. Allbright, underlining that of course he did not really believe in magic; whereupon Otway's eyebrows went up again: 'Magic,' he said, and there was a sharp edge to his voice, 'is one of our most important secret AA weapons.'

Bolder now, Sam told him about his plans to escape and head for No Man's Land leaving the school in disguise, turning down his school socks at the station so that the porter would not recognise their black and white Illbury stripes. The other boy listened with complete attention, occasionally interjecting a question: 'Do you have an Escape Fund?' Sam explained that his father's half-crown was all he had, and Otway nodded gravely.

Now it was Otway's turn to explain that the letters with Indian stamps were to finance the AA Escape Fund: how by sending a sixpenny stamp to the name at the top of a list, and sending the list on to friends with your own name added at the bottom you unfailingly ended up a millionaire. He had sent some to workers on his father's tea plantation in India, giving himself a high rank, calculating that they would be more likely to respond to a person of consequence. To add weight, he used headed Illbury Hall writing-paper purloined from Mr C-B's study, with *From the Headmaster* engraved below the address. Sam was dazzled: he had never met a millionaire, not even a stamp millionaire. Then Otway explained that unfortunately Mr C-B had begun impounding the letters, while converting rupee stamps into English currency had presented some difficulties.

'However,' and the black currant eyes glistened with secret knowledge, 'there are other schemes afoot.'

He turned to the hole in the ground and pulled out a wooden crate covered with a leather cloth. With a flourish he whisked the cloth off.

Inside was a brand new fleet of miniature fighters and bombers with freshly painted wings and propellers that turned. They were similar to the Spitfires and Hurricanes that patrolled Illbury's corridors between classes, except in one respect: they had been repainted by hand with the markings of the Luftwaffe.

It took Sam a moment to clear his head. 'Are Anarchists on the German side?'

'We are on our own side.'

'Who are you against?'

'Anarchists', responded he older boy tartly, 'are against everybody.' He leaned forward, pausing for effect, and lowered his voice: 'Starting with Illbury… We have, however, a special pact with the Luftwaffe.'

Sam stared back, allowing the words to sink in. He picked up a converted RAF Spitfire, and ran his fingers wonderingly over the swastika on its tail fin and the black and white Northern Cross of the Luftwaffe on its wings.

'We had to ground the fleet at the outbreak of hostilities in case of enemy searches. However, we are assembling strategic forces for the AA Counter Offensive against Illbury.' In solemn BBC announcer's voice Otway explained: 'Conversion work is not quite complete, but we expect it to be ready for our Counter Offensive, due to be launched any moment.' He leaned forward conspiratorially. 'Meanwhile our target for tonight,' he went on, borrowing a current BBC phrase, 'remains Illbury Hall.'

There was no sense in wasting time. Sam had found an ally. Now he would enlist Another. In addition to Otway, there was to hand a Force known to be the most that had powerful of all, and no stranger to Apocalyptic measures.

On his knees by his bed that night he prayed that God would direct Hitler's bombs on to the school and kill the headmaster. It was his first action as newly recruited (and fully Ratified) agent of the AA.

The first direct acknowledgment of his father's capture did not reach Sam's diary until later that week, and even then only indirectly, in the context of – for Sam – an infinitely more important event.

It was laundry day. Sam was waiting his turn at Matron's linen cupboard to exchange his dirty clothes for clean. Mrs C-B was assisting. The two women stood out of sight behind the cupboard's slatted door. Matron clicked her tongue. 'Cork's pyjamas have no name tapes.'

Between the slats he could only make out the back of her head, but he picked up the note of irritation, just as he had when his mother had forgotten the scissors. 'That mother of his…'

'This time it's the aunt. The mother is dead.'

Flustered, Matron rejoined: 'Well, God rest her soul. All I can say is the aunt's no better.'

Sam did not really mind: he had grown his carapace. He was about to step forward when Mrs C-B spoke again: 'But God won't rest her soul, you know. She killed herself. Suicide…'

It was the first time he heard it said. They were talking about his mother. It was impossible, unthinkable. What Mrs C-B said could not be true. If it was, his mother was guilty of a crime meriting punishment beyond comprehension. Father Becket had said in a sermon that suicide was Final Despair, a sin against the Holy Ghost that could not be forgiven. You went to Hell forever and nobody could pray for souls in Hell because they were dead. Then came the worst thought of all: if her soul was dead, it meant she could not be thinking about him. And if she stopped thinking about him, he would die. He shut out the thoughts and shut off his ears.

Sam stepped forward in silence to collect his clean pyjamas, grey flannel shirt, underpants and fresh pair of school stockings with their black and white piping. He stored them in the cupboard beside his bed. Then he opened his locker and took out his mother's little red book into which he had tucked her tiny Turkish mirror.

He turned to where she had written her name in ink inside the cover. With a pencil he drew three neat boxes. In the first two he wrote:

SENDER: S.CORK   P.O.W. NUMBER: OFL 38

Years later when he would come across the diary again in a trunk in Aunt Olive's attic, he would not find it particularly strange that young Sam should have cast himself as a prisoner of war. It was in keeping with his habit of using the events of his daily life as stage props for the dramas taking place in his head. And 38 had been his school number, sewn on with his name tapes, stamped on his possessions, recorded in brass nails on the soles of his shoes.

What he would be unprepared for were the contents of third little pencilled box. The young Sam had drawn it to include the faded ink in which his mother had written her name; with a stab of pain, he read:

ADDRESSEE: GERALDINE WINIFRED BURNES

Like a doctor diagnosing an illness, he would trace the pain to its source. He could see how the diary had become young Sam's means of keeping his mother alive. In the world of the imagination the dead and the living coexist. The only way he had known how to deal with a world which had betrayed him was to create his own version. The alternative was impossible. Besides she had promised.

9.

In June Illbury had its first air raid. It was over in a matter of moments: after the thrilling wail of the siren in the night, some thuds, heavy furniture dropped in a distant room; the fading rumble of engines. Then the dormitory doors were flung open and the boys were herded downstairs into the Long Hall in their pyjamas. Minutes later came the level note of the All Clear.

As the next of Mr C-B's Monday blitzkriegs approached, Sam added his voice to the others in prayers for the Souls in Purgatory; for the Conversion of England; for Deliverance from Famine and Pestilence. But when Father Becket came to the Prayer for Protection from Peril from the Air, he fell silent. He was counting on a direct hit.

Twice more during that week the siren wailed. Twice the school assembled in the Long Hall. Each time the All Clear sounded without an aeroplane being heard. Then on the Friday night the prayer he had uttered with the most fervour of all seemed about to be answered.

It was the strangeness of the sound that woke him, unlike any he had heard before, a discordant hum swelling and fading in uneven waves like a gigantic distant swarm of bees, heading elsewhere. As slowly as it began the sound faded away. The sirens near Illbury stayed silent. From far away in the night came the All Clear. Then his ear picked up the thrill of danger once again: the uneven throaty growl of a lone aeroplane. The next moment there was an unearthly whistle ending in a crash that shook the school and the foundations beneath it; then another, louder still, and another explosion. A third, from directly overheard, began its crescendo of sound to the accompaniment of a man's shout. The whistle reached the level of a scream. There was a thud and the sash windows in Sam's dormitories shook. But no explosion.

Next day the grounds of Illbury were taken over by men in uniform. There was talk of a delayed action bomb. Confined to the house, the boys watched through every window as police, soldiers from Roman Hill, men wearing ARP armbands combed sports field, buttercup meadow and beech wood in line abreast. They left again at nightfall, when a captain with Royal Engineer shoulder flashes came to tell the headmaster that the coast was clear. A stray German bomber had apparently jettisoned its load as it headed home after breaking from the pack. Two bombs had landed near the road several miles away. Perhaps the plane had been hit, and a piece of metal had fallen to earth and buried itself. There was nothing to worry about – certainly no need to interrupt school classes. The Sapper captain saluted and left.

Sam's diary duly recorded the raid, suggesting that B. Allbright had a hand in it. When he came down to Line-Up next day, a crowd of boys had gathered round the war map where Mr Bloomer was pinning up a propaganda cartoon of Hitler and Goering in full uniform eavesdropping on a conversation in a London bus under the heading: CARELESS TALK COSTS LIVES.

At Line-Up the red eyes swept the two lines of Hawks and Eagles. 'False rumours have been circulating in the school, about air raids. As a result of lies put about by a few trouble-makers, parents have been unnecessarily alarmed. One boy has even been taken away from the school. Deprived of his education.' Mr Canterbury-Black believed in making himself clear. 'And I intend to put a stop to it! Illbury has joined the national campaign against careless talk. From now on there will be no mention of air raids in letters home. All written matter leaving the school will be left open to make certain the rule is being obeyed. School lockers have already been inspected to guard against any lies in letters or diaries made up by small boys.' He drove his point home with his hollow boom: 'For them as 'asn't 'eard, there's a war on!'

A guffaw blew away any lingering wisps of doubt about where Illbury's patriotic duty lay; but Sam's mind was already elsewhere. Lockers... With an unpleasant feeling in the pit of his stomach, he pictured his own locker, in which, hidden under the text books, was the red book containing his secret life.

He had to sit through two classes before he could get to it. The wait gave him time to draw up a plan. In mid-morning break he found his worst fear confirmed: the book had been confiscated, together with his mother's miniature looking-glass tucked inside the pocket of its cover.

10.

Sam minded the punishment that followed, but not so much as before. His mother's little mirror had been taken in error and he could expect to get it back at the end of term when innocuous confiscated items were normally returned to their owners. Meanwhile, now that he was no longer alone, the diary had lost some of its importance. Now he had real live allies, even more real than B. Allbright. The nausea of solitary fear had turned into the spice of shared danger. He was part of a band of secret agents operating inside enemy territory. He was a warrior again; he had recovered his shield.

Above all it was exciting. He half believed in the research involving invisible ink, mixtures to impart fatal diseases, laughing gas to render victims helpless, itching powder to make them beg for mercy, a plan to burn the school down by applying a giant magnifying glass to the sun.

Sam was assigned to collect ammunition to stage sabotage raids: gunpowder from pistol caps to make explosions, Deadly Nightshade and poison mushrooms that would produce a nerve gas like the one devised by Carl Petersen to paralyse Bulldog Drummond. He conducted a reconnaissance mission to the pump house where he reported the presence of cans marked Highly Inflammable that could be used to set fire to the school.

Jelly was the designated AA man of action. If a bomb was to be planted, Jelly would plant it: if a frontal assault mounted, Jelly would lead it. His legendary bravery left Sam in awe. Jelly didn't seem to care if the headmaster beat him. Sam did. He was afraid in equal measure of punishment and of the humiliation of being found to be a coward. He clung to the hope that he would never again be put to the test. But most of the time he tried not to think about it.

Otway reserved for himself the task of researching the super weapon and inventions that conferred limitless power on their user: the pill to defy gravity, invisible paint, rays for exploring interplanetary space which could see into the future and read tomorrow's newspapers, a death beam transmitted by remote control on the wireless (as featured in *Wavelength Unknown* and introduced by Sam), perpetual motion, water divining, ways of harnessing volcanic energy or the world's magnetic forces or of trisecting the angle (said to be impossible by the Geometry master, but which once cracked would open the door to the Fourth Dimension and beyond.)

Then there were spells.

Spells originated with Mott. Mott, by-product of the Blitz, had arrived at Illbury with a batch of boys from a London day preparatory school closed down because of bombing. It was unsettling. It was unclear where the evacuees fitted in. They did not have the standing of regular Illbury boys and yet, being all ages, they were they not exactly new boys. It disturbed the pecking order.

The Londoners' tales of air raids gave them a head start over the other boys but, unaccustomed to boarding school, they were soon decimated by homesickness and reduced to red-eyed silence. Smartly striped Illbury school socks sagged down their calves to their ankles. Noses ran; damp handkerchiefs trailed from trouser pockets. Matron was exasperated.

The exception was Mott. His father, a widower, was a senior prosecuting counsel who acted for the crown in the criminal courts. Sir Gregory was a supporter of rod as well as rope, and believed in co-operating fully with the authorities. On one occasion young Mott had come home with a bad school report that earned him a beating; and his father beat him again (with his belt and, according to Mott, grinding his dentures). Mott did not suffer from homesickness. He arrived at Illbury battle hardened.

What he lacked in height he made up for in aggression; he quickly established a fearsome reputation among the regular new boys. Being in their boxing weight he was put against them in the ring where he made their noses bleed. With bigger boys he adopted a separate survival strategy. To deflect derision he invited it. Far from appearing ashamed of his literal shortcoming, he capitalised on it by making jokes at his own expense. By day he recited in an audible mutter 'I will grow, I will grow'. At night he admitted to praying for an increase in stature, if not a cubit then an inch would do. He confessed without embarrassment to his humiliation in Harrods on being sent from the boys' to the children's department to buy school clothes. He only feigned anger when Jelly, on serving duty, handed him a saucer instead of a plate, visibly revelling in the attention. He did not seem to resent the inevitable nickname of Midget, but only larger boys dared use it.

In the assistant masters' Common Room Mott acquired the reputation of being a bit of a card. It was said that he had the makings of a politician. Mott's own ambitions lay elsewhere. Sir Gregory hoped that his son would follow in his footsteps. So did the younger Mott, but not for the same reason. He declared it his aim to become an equally famous counsel for the defence who would one day defeat his father in court and gloat over the look on his face. He adopted an adversarial manner modelled on *The Hand of the Law*, Sir Gregory Mott's account of techniques he employed to ensure that no murderer missed his appointment with the hangman.

The younger Mott practised his own techniques in class using trick questions designed to catch out the masters. On occasion his enthusiasm outran his judgment; he fell foul of Mrs C-B in Catechism class after asking why God created the Devil, and then cross-examining her over her answer. Several times sent to the clock for impertinence, he was described in his first term's school report as clever but subversive.

Mott set about redressing the balance at once. To ingratiate himself with the headmaster he volunteered to sing in the choir, Mr C-B's pet project. Mott had pink and white cheeks and Matron herself was overheard exclaiming that he had the voice of an angel.

Mott first attracted Otway's attention when he found him reading *The Book of Black Magic*, acquired from an occult bookshop with a gift token from his godmother. It had flames on the cover and a chapter on 'Spells for All Occasions'. Otway at once set about cultivating him. Mott was the shorter of the two by a foot, and they made a striking pair as they paced the school corridors discussing the black arts, one with spring-heeled lope, the other on tiptoe to exaggerate his height. Mott soon sealed the alliance by donating *The Book of Black Magic* to the AA library. His first name was Thomas and it was only a matter of time before the letters

T
O
M

M
O
T
T

were being held up to the glass hanging from its shoelace to reveal a perfect AA mirror word.

Sam could not make Mott out. He was unsure where he fitted into Mott's survival policy of oppressing the weak and appeasing the strong. From time to time Sam felt the sharp eyes watching him, like a detective waiting to catch him out.

From all of which he concluded that street-wise people were to be treated with circumspection.

Summer days floated by as Sam grew into his new existence, suspended in a capsule somewhere between reality and fantasy. For some weeks Mr C-B left him alone, and Sam's dark night began to recede into the past.

Near half term news reached Illbury that a distinguished old boy, T. Canterbury-Black, had graduated from Dartmouth and been assigned as a sub lieutenant to *HMS St George*, one of the Navy's Imperial Class battleships now undergoing sea trials at a secret location. He would be coming home shortly on shore leave before departing on a mission that could not be revealed and forming, Mr Bloomer announced in confidential tones, part of a forthcoming Strategic Counter Offensive.

A day or so later there appeared a stocky figure with the broad jaw of his father. Though only nineteen years old, Thompson Canterbury-Black already bore the signs of receding hair. To Sam he looked middle-aged. He sat between his parents at meals and at prayers. He attended morning Line-Up. Mrs C-B took to making loyal references: 'My son tells me you couldn't do that in the Navy...' and 'When my son was head prefect you wouldn't have got away with that!' Sub Lieutenant Thompson Canterbury-Black accepted his mother's attentions with an appropriate modesty, occasionally gravely nodding his assent. On Sunday at Chapel, Father Becket announced that instead of his sermon a certain old boy would recite a poem that was an apt reminder of the values Illbury stood for.

Sam strained forward with the other boys as the younger Canterbury-Black, a head shorter than Father Becket, advanced to the lectern normally reserved for the priest and cleared his throat:

There's a breathless hush in the Close tonight
Ten runs to make and the match to win
A bumping pitch and blinding light,
An hour to play and the last man in.

And it's not for the sake of a ribboned coat,
Or the selfish hope of a season's fame,
But his Captain's hand on his shoulder smote
'Play up! Play up! And play the game!'

The sand of the desert is sodden red
Red with the wreck of the square that broke
The Gatling's jammed and the colonel dead,
And the regiment blind with dust and smoke.

The river of death has brimmed its banks,
And England's far, and Honour a name,
But the voice of a schoolboy rallies the ranks:
'Play up! Play up! And play the game!'

This is the word that year by year,
While in her place the School is set,
Every one of her sons must hear,
And none that hears it dare forget.

This they all with a joyful mind
Bear through life like a torch in flame
And falling fling to the host behind
'Play up! play up! And play the game!'

Afterwards Sam stood in line with the other boys when Mr C-B
announced that there were balsa wood kits for sale of *HMS St George*
which you could make up yourself with glue and a razor blade and
which could go on your school bill. But Sam's motive was more to do
with insurance than with enthusiasm. Even as the square figure left the

lectern, Sam knew he would never quite the feel quite the same about the Honours Board, and the kit remained half-opened in his locker for the rest of the term, gathering dust.

At around this time he began to notice a marked change in his attitude to cricket. Parents' Day was approaching but due to the war and petrol rationing only a scattering of visitors was expected, not enough to make up the usual team for the Fathers' Match. By way of filling in Thompson Canterbury-Black, still on shore leave, had been made an honorary parent for the occasion and invited to play.

To watch the match, Kettle's aunt was installed in a deck chair beside Father Becket, an occasional visitor to Kettle Hall where he sometimes said Sunday Mass in the family chapel during the holidays. Sam sat on the grass within earshot. Otway had applied to be let off watching on the grounds that it was his birthday and his family were coming; for his cheek he had been appointed as match scorer.

The parents batted first. Leading them in was the stocky figure of Thompson Canterbury-Black. He hit the opening ball out of the grounds. A cheer went up. The gangling figure of Otway ran out of the little score box on the far side of the field and placed a tin plate on a hook bearing the figure six.

An hour later, Thompson was still there. The cheers grew thinner as balls pursued by weary fielders vanished into the buttercup meadow and thudded against the wooden pavilion steps. On the scoreboard runs advanced in sudden leaps, ten or more at a time, as the system strained to keep count. There was a stirring of the elders. As a fresh bowler rolled up his sleeves to try his hand against the Goliath at the wicket, Mr C-B rose to signal to the sports master. A consultation took place at the edge of the pitch. Mr Bloomer had a word with Thompson, another with the headmaster. News reached the spectators that, invited to retire, Thompson had politely declined, explaining that he needed the runs to keep up his average for the season; at which point Sam became aware of a further cooling in his love affair with the great Game.

Mrs C-B said something to Lady Kettle and turned to Sam: 'Go and see what has happened to Timothy.' Nonplussed, he stared back. 'Timothy Kettle. Lady Kettle's nephew. Tell him to come and look after his aunt.'

Someone had seen Kettle in the Art Room. Sam set off, pondering the novel notion that Kettle could have a Christian name. He ran the stammering boy to earth in a cubicle in the back of the classroom block, running alongside the school swimming pool. Instead of the familiar crabbed figure hunched over a desk, hand and wrist curled round a pen as he did battle with the twin problems of spelling and ink flow, Kettle stood upright holding a paint brush, now frozen in mid air in a posture that reminded Sam of the picture in the Long Hall of Sir Joshua Reynolds doing a self portrait. Kettle had a startled look on his face, as if he had been caught in the act; but what act? Idly Sam noted that the brush was in his left hand, banned for classroom writing, and wondered if this was the explanation.

He had his answer on the desk between them. On it were two open tubes of oil paint, a bottle of turpentine and a rag. There was also the outline of a large oblong box that Sam recognized. He moved round the desk to get a closer look; the other boy remained blocking his path. Sam was taken aback. It was as if the paintbrush in his hand lent him a new authority.

'I suppose it is all right for you to see,' said Kettle, moving aside. It was the first clear sentence that Sam could remember him uttering.

Propped against the box was Kettle's two-foot long clockwork submarine. Fresh paint gleamed on the hull. A complete transformation had occurred since Sam had last seen it making a circuit of the school swimming pool. A schoolboy of his times, Sam was a keen student of military hardware, from planes to tanks and ships. He recognised the new colour immediately from the naval battle scene on the lid of a jigsaw puzzle in the Games room. What had once been a Royal Navy dark grey had given way to the lighter coloured livery of the German Navy. On one side of the conning tower was a letter U, still wet. Next to it, in a circle of white, was the number 22. On the other side was a perfectly executed outsize swastika. The model of the submarine that Kettle's dead father had commanded had changed sides: it had turned into a U-boat.

'The *U-22*,' Sam read aloud, a note approaching awe in his voice.

'22 is Otway's school number. For his b-b-b...'

The return of the stammer broke the spell. For a moment it was a question of conflicting loyalties. His discovery of Kettle's hidden talent inspired a new respect and went a long way to explaining the link between the universally derided stammering boy and the glamorous, elusive Otway. At close quarters in the Art Room Sam felt a stab of shame. He knew that if it came to holding up English Recital he, Sam, would be the first to harden his heart.

'Birthday,' said Kettle finally. 'It's for Otway's birthday. It's a surprise. Please don't t-t-t-tell…'

From beyond the buttercup meadow a sound of prolonged clapping reached their ears. Thompson must have chalked up his century.

Brusquely, to hide any trace of compassion, Sam said: 'Mrs C-B wants to see you. She says you are to go and look after your aunt.'

'C-could you take it to the AA hut for me and hide it under the floor? I'm afraid the paint is w-w-w-…'

'Wet,' said Sam sharply.

He looked at Kettle. Whatever new wavelength he had been tuned into, Kettle had tuned out again. The blank unfocussed stare was back.

'You'd better go,' said Sam. Kettle went.

Alone, Sam lifted the big box's lid and studied Kettle's handiwork. He took the two-foot long craft in his hands, holding it well away from his body, and looked at the pool.

The temptation was too great.

Another wave of applause reached his ears as he finished winding the submarine's clockwork motor. Keeping one hand on the propeller he jammed the rudder so that it would travel in a tight circle, not straying out of reach. Beside him was a pole with a net attached to it that he had pulled out from under the diving board, ready to perform an emergency rescue. He took his hand off the U-22's propeller and its roar turned to a hum as it settled in the water and described a small arc, leaving a semi-circle of bubbles in its wake.

After one circuit he decided that honour was satisfied. With the aid of the pole he pulled the U-boat in to the side.

A movement caught his eye. He stopped and stared. Sitting on one of the garden benches gathered round the pool, so still that he had not noticed her, was the most beautiful woman he had ever seen. She was dressed in white and wore a pale grey picture hat with a veil like morning mist and kid gloves buttoned to the elbow. She had a languid air and huge slightly slanting eyes. Standing near her, behind the bench, was a younger version of herself, perhaps Daisy's age but taller and thinner, with dark eyes that had the same slant, a strangely long straight nose and thin wide mouth. She, too, wore a wide brimmed hat, which seemed somehow wrong, too old for her years, pulled down over a thatch of fair hair. They looked like a pair of elegant migrating birds that had paused to rest before resuming their onward flight to an exotic destination in another hemisphere – perhaps another planet. They were watching him, the woman with a distracted air, almost a touch of mockery; the girl remote, unsmiling yet intent. It was like being stared at in a foreign language.

The two spectators did not appear to find it strange to see an enemy U-boat with an outsize swastika on its conning tower circling the swimming pool. Perhaps they had other matters on their minds.

Sam hesitated, unsure what to do. There were instructions about looking after lost visitors. Yet they did not look exactly lost or, if they were, they did not seem particularly anxious to be found. He could not imagine them being interested in cricket. In fact they did not look like Illbury relations at all.

He, too, had other matters on his mind. Frowning, he fished the submarine out of the water and checked the paintwork, and returned it to its box.

When he looked up again, the birds had flown.

Clutching his burden, he hurried to the beech wood. The old warrior's sightless gaze was turned away from him, full into afternoon sun as Sam passed, as if he too had more important matters on his mind.

It took only a minute to return the submarine to its new berth in the floor of the AA hut. As he straightened up, Sam spotted the girl again, standing in the doorway. He realised she had been following him. Now she was watching him from under the brim of her straw hat. He stopped. She made no move.

'What are you doing here?' Sam asked.

'Wa-alking.' Like the hat the voice did not quite fit. There was a hint of a drawl, grown-up almost, yet somehow all her own. 'Wa-alking,' she repeated. 'Sometimes I do night walking…'

'What is your name?' Sam asked.

She seemed detached, a bit like himself, an outsider. It was a sort of bond. The silence was broken by a gale of clapping, more spirited than before. Perhaps finally Thompson was out. Sam turned to go.

Behind him the strange voice said: 'Laura…' Then in a single rush: 'Anastasia Maria Helena Laurentina Fitzwilliam.' She made it sound like one word. He stored away in his mind a picture of the girl in the wrong hat beside the other one of a beautiful lady. It took a moment longer to store the words. Like the girl, they did not seem to belong.

Later that day when the parents were leaving, he glimpsed two straw hats through the closed window of a departing car. Waving in their direction was Otway. Even then Sam did not immediately make a connection with the vision beside the swimming pool. That belonged less in the real world of school and more to the world of imagination where his mother was, watching him from somewhere behind her looking-glass, with the same detached air, dressed to go to a party.

11.

So long as the AA Counter Offensive remained an abstraction, the balloon of Sam's fantasy life stayed safely aloft, insulated from reality. In the world of his imagination he was the omnipotent hero with magical powers, free to ensure a Hollywood ending to his adventures.

While Sam dreamed, Otway got down to research on spells in earnest. He spent his spare time closeted in the AA hut with *The Book of Black Magic*, transferring information with his green crayon into the green AA Book. He traced circles with a compass on a fresh page and copied the Great Seal of Baal. He rehearsed incantations under his breath. He drew up lists.

Then one afternoon Otway called an Extraordinary Meeting of the Anarchists and brought Sam's balloon to earth. He announced that his research into the super weapon had borne fruit in the shape of an infallible spell and that the Counter Offensive had now reached the preparation stage. Reality was about to take over from fantasy.

Clearing his throat he read from the AA book:

> To Explode an Enemy by Remote Control and Delayed
> Action. The necessary Preparations must be carried as
> laid down in accordance with the instructions of the
> Lord Godonay...

Details followed of a ritual for burning the victim in effigy by a full moon using a cocktail of magic and contemporary technology. Ingredients included an image of the victim, a personal item of clothing, a feather, church candles, gunpowder and (though whose was not specified) urine and blood.

When the intended victim was announced, it came as no surprise; but at the naming of Mr Canterbury-Black Sam felt the blood draining from his face.

The decision taken, Otway began assigning duties and giving instructions. Jelly's was to be the key role in Preparation. Fireworks had been banned since the start of the war; and a box marked 'Danger – Fireworks' had languished in the glass paned Confiscation Cabinet in the headmaster's study for as long as Sam could remember. Jelly's mission was to break in and steal a supply – but not enough for the theft to be noticed – during the night. Sam's admiration for Jelly's nerve reached a new height, then turned into panic as Otway went on: 'Cork will be responsible for the personal item of clothing such as' – he paused, as if plucking his words from the air – 'Mr C-B's spectacles.'

Sam shrank back into the wattle wall of the AA hut. His legs turned to water. He felt sick. He was being asked the impossible. He knew he did not have the nerve. It was too frightening even to contemplate.

To start with, it was not like home: he did not even know where Mr C-B kept his clothes: and the thought of looking in his study for his spectacles made him blanch with terror. The roller coaster of his mood once again plunged sickeningly downwards. All day he thought about his yellow streak.

Oblivious, Otway personally supervised each phase of the Preparation, strutting busily about. He inspected the plasticine head made by Kettle and pierced the eyes with matchsticks. He pricked Jelly's finger with a safety pin and squeezed the blood into a tooth-mug. Ever pragmatic, when Jelly baulked at supplying urine, he settled for lemonade.

Full moon was a week away. In the days running up to it, Sam avoided Otway's eye. Still no solution presented itself. He dreamed that he was swimming in pursuit of Mr C-B's spectacles when they began to sink. He followed them down until they came to rest on the seabed. They lay there, out of reach, watching him. He gave up, but then in panic realised he had not enough air in his lungs to return to the surface. He woke gasping in terror. The fear stayed with him even after he had forgotten the dream.

Then the day before the full moon he was shaken awake in the early morning by an uncharacteristically agitated Jelly. In his arms he had a cone-shaped firework, the largest Sam had seen, with a label marked Galactic Rouser. He also had something else that made Sam's pulses race. It was a large Panama hat belonging to the headmaster. 'A personal item of clothing,' hissed Jelly in a stage whisper.

All of a sudden the roller coaster took a giddying upswing, Together they crammed the hat into Sam's pillowcase and the firework into Jelly's, and were back in their beds before the dormitory woke.

'Paramaribo!' said Otway, picking up the Galactic Rouser and turning it over. On the reverse side was written:

LIGHT AND STAND BACK.
Enjoy for a few minutes a fantasia of lights
followed by a ROUSING finale.

Along the bottom a message ran in capital letters:

DO NOT IGNITE IN A CONFINED SPACE

'Pa-ra-ma-ri-bo!' said Otway again, eyeing the crushed shape of the headmaster's hat, smuggled to the AA hut under Sam's sweater.

Never in the old make-believe days when Biggles awarded him the

Distinguished Flying Cross had triumph tasted so good. But Biggles was yesterday; then Sam was someone else, someone younger. The real world was a good place after all.

Sam omitted to remind himself that that it was Jelly, not he, who had grabbed the Panama from a pile of hats as he was leaving the study (so there was even a chance that the deed would go undetected); but he had become skilled in at censoring inconvenient truths.

Two days later, as he ducked by the ogre's head after evening Line-Up he had the feeling of taking part in history. Parting the bushes at the entrance, he paused to take in the scene. He was not disappointed.

The battered P and O trunk lay open on the floor of the hut. On view inside were the plasticine head, a photograph of Illbury's scholarship class with Mr C-B seated in the middle, eyes likewise pierced by a pin, a bottle of lemonade and, in pride of place, the cone shape of the Galactic Rouser, its protruding taper awaiting ignition. On the ground at each corner of the trunk stood a lighted candle taken from the school chapel. But the strangest spectacle of all was Otway himself. On his head was Mr C-B's Panama hat stuffed with grass to prevent it covering his ears; in the band he had tucked what appeared to be a bloodstained feather and a postcard on which he had drawn a black swastika. His black button eyes flashed. He held the AA Book in one hand open at a page covered by diagrams with arrows, notes overflowing from the margins and every space occupied by capital letters, words underlined for emphasis and bright green exclamation marks.

As soon as the AA membership had settled into their places on the log inside the entrance, the ceremony began. Otway picked up the lemonade bottle and poured the contents to make a circle round the trunk, progressing in a dancing movement and chanting in a loud voice: 'Paramaribo!'

After two circuits the lemonade ran out. Otway paused to consult his notes. Still chanting under his breath, he picked up the photograph and holding it for the others to see he pierced the headmaster's eyes with the point of his safety pin. Then he put it back in the trunk and read out from his green book.

Paramaribo! I conjure thee O Godonay by the Great
Seal of Baal to bring the spirits of the Pentacle down on
Illbury, to smite down Mister C-B and all his Pumps!
Paramaribo!

He struck a match and lit the taper on the top of the Galactic
Rouser. There was a fizzing sound and a line of sparks shot from the
cone. Otway swept the headmaster's hat from his head, placed it over
the firework and bolted the trunk shut. Then calling: 'Paramaribo!' he
ran headlong from the hut.

Face down in the pathway under the tent of beeches, in the manner
taught at Bomb Drill, hands clasped over heads, thumbs in ears, the
Anarchists waited for Godonay to deliver his part of the bargain.

After a minute a wisp of black smoke issued reluctantly from the
AA hut. There was no bang. The half hour break was nearly over.
Cautiously Otway returned to the trunk and opened the lid. A black
cloud filled the air, and then cleared. Through a charred hole in the
top of the headmaster's hat they could see that the Galactic Rouser
had gone out.

'Not enough air,' said Jelly.

From the school came the sound of the warning bell for late chapel.

'Not enough fire,' said Otway. Seizing one of the lighted candles
he set it upright in the trunk and held the straw brim of the hat to the
flame. With a crackle the fire took hold; Sam could see its light dancing in Otway's black pupils.

The final bell sounded. Otway threw the hat into the trunk and
half-closed the lid.

They had to run. At the organ Mr C-B was too engrossed in a Bach
prelude requiring the use of both hands and feet to detect the Shirkers
as they slipped into their places in time to join in the opening verse of
Illbury's anthem.

> Faith of our Fathers! Holy Faith!
> Our fathers chained in prisons dark
> Were still in heart and conscience free:

The first sighting of the fire was from the air. An RAF pilot on the home run from a bombing raid on northern Germany reported spotting flames a few miles short of the Roman Hill runway. Roman Hill passed the details on to the local Fire Brigade, together with a map reference pinpointing Illbury Hall. The machinery of the security services was set in motion. The Fire Chief telephoned Illbury. Getting no reply during evening chapel, he despatched his full complement of three fire engines. Puzzled that there had been no report of an air raid he call the local ARP unit and the police, where the duty sergeant remembered the earlier hunt for an unexploded bomb. He in turn called the Sapper Bomb Disposal Squad where the same Captain Eales who had been in charge of the earlier search of the grounds took the call. Consulting his diary, Captain Eales dialled the Illbury number.

It was Mr Bloomer's day off. Returning from the pub, he heard the telephone ringing in the front hall as he reached the school steps. A minute later his hand was reaching out again, this time to pull the rope of the Invasion Bell.

For the second time the grounds of Illbury were taken over by uniformed men. The fire, brought under control by dawn, had destroyed a corner of the beech wood together with the boys' huts. A change of wind had saved the school itself.

At the special Line-Up that weekend attended by boys and masters alike, Otway's strategy of blanket denial – rehearsed many times and based on the principle that if you repeat a lie often enough you come to believe it – stood up well to public interrogation, despite an uncomfortable moment when Captain Eales held up the charred brim of a hat found caught in the top branch of a tree near what had once been was the AA hut. Identifying it as his own, Mr C-B appeared uneasy, almost as if he, too, was under suspicion. Sam had never seen the headmaster disconcerted before.

One of the parties to show the closest interest in the fire was Whitehall, in the shape of a man from the Air Ministry in civilian clothes who joined a group inspecting the cinders for evidence. Less tight-lipped than his military counterparts, he let it be known that his instructions were to establish whether the fire was part of an abortive air attack on the local RAF base at Roman Hill, indicating that having failed to intimidate the civilian population the Luftwaffe might now be switching the Blitz back to military targets.

Terrifying though the high-level attention was, the fire raisers themselves soon come to be grateful for the confusion generated by conflicting theories. The local police constable's more pedestrian explanation seemingly never reached official ears, but it reached Sam's, who overheard him saying: 'Reckon one of the little buggers was playing with matches and let off a banger.'

In chapel, Father Becket led a Novena of Thanksgiving for the change of wind in the night.

At Bomb Drill Mr Bloomer let it be known that he was co-operating with an official report for the Air Ministry.

Meanwhile the affair was to be treated as another security matter not to be mentioned in letters home.

12.

After the fire, the AA went underground. Its new meeting place was among the changing-room lockers where the smell of sweat and dried mud on rugby boots mingled with sour vapours coming through the swing door of the boys' lavatories next door. The Luftwaffe fleet had perished in the flames but the U-22 had been protected by its box, and was temporarily housed in a spare locker to which Otway had somehow got hold of the key. From the changing-room door a lookout was charged with signalling the approach of danger by the pull of a lavatory plug. This security measure was suspended to permit a full debate on the future of the organisation, and soon forgotten. The oversight was to prove Otway's first serious mistake.

Of the five AA members four favoured lying low. They had not reckoned with Otway's sense of theatre. The leading actor craved a larger audience and a bigger stage. Far from drawing in his horns Otway announced a programme of expansion.

The first phase was a drive for new membership. The normal

screening process had made short work of the internal candidates. Boys with a vested interest in the system – prefects, favourites of the headmaster, anyone thought to have eyes on the Honours Boards – were automatically disqualified. Of the others some were too young, others too wet or too unreliable. Only minnows were left. Otway had bigger fish in mind. He planned to cast his net wider, and deeper.

For teaching staff, wartime Illbury had to make do with older men and rejects from the call-up system. When Mr Allbright left, his place was taken by Mr Light who to the boys seemed a hundred years old. Mr Light took to sleeping in English class with his eyeballs showing white under half opened lids. The first time it happened, Sam thought the man was dead. One day a half bottle of whisky slid from his hand on to the classroom floor.

Mr Light was soon replaced by Mr Goodbody who delighted his classes with conjuring tricks. He had hands that deceived the eye. He could not only remove his thumb but produce the nine of diamonds from behind your ear and do ventriloquism. Boys mimicked his cry 'Watch the hands!' as they tried out his tricks on each other. The cry took on a new meaning when it was discovered that the same lightning hands were a hazard to better looking boys encountering their owner in corridors. Eagles and Hawks alike, his pupils accepted the unsolicited attentions as a small price to pay for magic. Eventually alerted, the authorities took a different view. Soon Mr Goodbody, like his predecessor, disappeared without trace.

Next a Mr Wyatt-Tooth was announced. Mr and Mrs C-B clearly considered him a catch. His accomplishments were heralded ahead of his arrival and quickly spun into legend. Having studied for some months in Paris, Mr Wyatt-Tooth would of course be bilingual. Mr Wyatt-Tooth had been evacuated by the Navy after the fall of France and later disqualified for military service by lung trouble; it followed that he had been gassed in an enemy attack and was a war hero. Mr Wyatt-Tooth had an Oxford degree in English. It was rumoured that he wrote poetry. There were hints of grand connections.

Mr C-B went to meet him at the station. Soon after he set off, a black limousine swept up the drive. Mrs C-B's Catechism class watched through the windows as a willowy figure floated up the front steps followed by a uniformed chauffeur carrying his bags.

Mrs C-B left the classroom. Sam heard her voice in the hall.

'We understood you were coming on the train…'

'My uncle Lord Axmouth sweetly had his chauffeur run me over…'

There was a pause: 'Let me show you to your room,' said Mrs Canterbury-Black in her drawing-room voice.

'Too good of you,' murmured Mr. Wyatt-Tooth.

For his first English class, Mr Wyatt-Tooth wore a lavender suit with mauve silk tie and dark glasses. He held a matching silk handkerchief to his mouth. He was accompanied by Mr C-B.

'I have you down to take French next.'

'French?'

'French. English and French. That's right isn't it?'

'If you say so, headmaster. Of course I hardly speak a word. Never had a head for languages. Still, I suppose I can always let them read the set books while I get on with my knitting.'

The headmaster hesitated, then turned on his heel and left the room. Still clutching his handkerchief to his mouth, Mr Wyatt-Tooth addressed the class: 'This chalk is really too much… Do any of you suffer from asthma?'

From the edge of his seat someone said: 'Kettle wheezes, sir.'

'I'm a martyr myself,' said Mr Wyatt-Tooth.

There was a stifled snigger.

'Sir, do you really do knitting sir?'

'No, but I might… Oh, and while I am about it,' Mr Wyatt-Tooth went on in unexpectedly robust voice, 'I should make something clear. I am here for the money. I have no desire to teach. I only wish to entertain. Entertain myself, that is. I intend to read poetry aloud to the class. If you don't want to listen, you needn't. But don't forget I am bigger than you are. If anyone makes a noise, or annoys me, I shall pinch his ear until he squeals. And if he says it's unfair, I shall twist his arm instead. I don't suppose any of you have heard of Robert Browning?'

Nobody had. 'Well, he wrote some of the best poetry in the English language. He also wrote' – he sighed – '"The Pied Piper of Hamelin", which is on the school syllabus for Recital.'

He opened his book and began to read aloud.

At first, they treated Mr Wyatt-Tooth with the guarded curiosity of a pack surrounding a strange but larger animal, unsure if it bit. There were tentative soundings. When Mr Wyatt-Tooth looked up to ask 'Are there any questions?' someone said: 'Sir, are you really a war hero?'

'Rather!' Mr Wyatt-Tooth replied cheerfully.

'Sir, did you come from France on an English navy warship?'

'For my sins. My uncle Lord Axmouth said one should always go on a foreign boat. There's none of that nonsense in an emergency about women and children first.'

'Sir, were you dive-bombed?'

'I never asked. There wasn't any point. You couldn't hear yourself speak.'

Much of the time the boys had no idea what Mr Wyatt-Tooth was talking about. By treating them as equals, without concession or condescension, he both flattered and baffled them. Gradually an uneasy rapport was established. Like Mr Allbright before him, he never sent a boy to the clock. Instead he devised his own punishments. A favourite was to make an offender write and read aloud a one-page essay describing his own face. He had little trouble keeping order.

Mr Wyatt-Tooth had one instant fan. After his first English class a slip of paper in Sam's locker announced an emergency AA meeting. At it Otway wrote WYATT-TOOTH downwards on a sheet of his diary and held it up to the mirror salvaged from the wreckage of the AA hut. He did the same with: AXMOUTH (LORD). 'A double mirror code word!'

A resolution was unanimously passed to invite Mr Wyatt-Tooth to become an honorary AA member and for Lord Axmouth to be Ex Gratia Honorary Life President in Absentia. Mr Wyatt-Tooth accepted the invitation on Lord Axmouth's behalf, and gave 'Hoot Hoot' as Lord Axmouth's password, claiming it to be his daily cry as he came down to breakfast. It, too, passed the mirror test.

Sam had never met anyone like Mr Wyatt-Tooth. As for Otway, the instant success of his recruiting drive only served to whet his appetite. He began to explore new avenues.

The early reverses suffered by the Allies in the war sat lightly on the shoulders of Illbury's pupils, it being a known fact that England was bound to win in the end. The news of the fall of France, the sinking of great battleships, the isolation of Britain reached them through a series of filters – in manicured BBC accents employing a vocabulary that allowed of enemy defeats but only allied tactical withdrawals; cinema newsreels poking fun at Germans; and a running commentary from Mr Bloomer to whom impartiality was the language of the Fifth Column, Quislings and collaborators.

In the sea of patriotic fervour the AA hut was a neutral port, Illbury's Anarchists taking a more pragmatic view of the enemy, with their point of departure being support for the activities of the Luftwaffe in the Hertfordshire area.

Otway's next opportunity to widen its scope came about by chance when he called at the masters' common room, a conservatory abutting the main school building and looking on to the front lawn. He was there to convey a formal invitation, carefully written in green ink, to persuade Mr Wyatt-Tooth to attend his own inauguration ceremony.

He found the new English master alone, stretched on the only sofa, silk handkerchief stuffed in his mouth, apparently choking with laughter. From the wireless set in the corner a braying voice was announcing to listeners that England's war effort was futile against the might of the Third Reich. Occasionally the owner of the voice interrupted himself to announce 'Chairmany calling, Chairmany calling...' Otway was waiting, standing on one foot, when he was sent flying by a stout figure making a lunge for the wireless. As he fell to the ground, Otway had a vision of a purple face and ginger moustache flashing by. From the floor he heard the words: 'As an Englishman and a patriot I will not permit that man's voice to desecrate this Common Room!'

The response from the sofa was a hoot of laughter. 'Oh, Mr Bloomer don't be such a SPOIL sport!' said Mr Wyatt-Tooth when he could speak. Mr Bloomer drew himself up. His eyes bulged with meaning as his head indicated Otway, climbing to his feet again: 'Mr Wyatt-Tooth! PAS DEVANT LES ENFANTS...!' This provoked a further paroxysm. 'You and Lord Haw Haw really should do a show together: it would be much funnier than the BBC's comedies.'

By nightfall the name HAW HAW (Lord) had passed the mirror test and was inscribed in Otway's green AA Book under AXMOUTH (Lord) on a page headed HONORARY LIFE MEMBERS (EX GRATIA).

So spellbound was the AA membership that nobody noticed the pair of watching eyes in the darkened corner of the changing room, until a dislodged rugby boot fell to the floor. In the shocked silence that followed Jelly was first to his feet. Charging in the direction of the sound, he came back a moment later dragging a kicking body after him. No one had thought of Stanley.

The trouble was that Stanley defied any security system. His age allowed him a freedom of movement denied older boys; he was small enough to pass unnoticed; and the certainty of terrible reprisals gave him immunity against physical assault. To cap it all he was a ruthless and experienced blackmailer.

'We've caught an enemy spy!' said Jelly. Profoundly impressed, the members fell silent. 'I'm not a spy,' said Stanley.

'What were you doing there?' asked Otway.

'I want to be in the AA.'

'What do you know about the AA?'

'If you don't let me join I'll tell…'

It was then that Otway made his second mistake. It is an axiom of counter-espionage that before disposing of a captured enemy agent you must first find out how much he knows. Otway jumped the gun.

'You tell,' he said, pulling a hideous face and rolling his eyes into the back of his head so that only the whites showed, 'and I will haunt you!' For several seconds Stanley stared back through his outsize spectacles in hostile silence. Then his lower lip began to tremble. He took a long, deep breath, and turned to run. His fat little legs had carried him to within reach of the kitchen door when he released the air from his lungs, and the first of his bloodcurdling howls rang down the corridor and echoed against the bare glazed tiles of the changing room walls.

The rest of the school took a little longer to make up their minds about the new English master. They hovered between incomprehension and amazement, hanging back to see the outcome of his increasingly open power struggle with Mr Bloomer. Then one day some boys invited Mr Wyatt-Tooth to play miniature cricket and he hit the ball over the house. After that all doubts were resolved.

It became the highest compliment to be addressed by Mr Wyatt-Tooth as a Hottentot. He became a cult figure. Understood or not, his jokes were unconditionally applauded. He devised what he called entertainments, to tease, in which it was impossible to know when he was being serious. Mr Wyatt-Tooth told his English class that a man's body secreted twenty separate fluids; the boys could account for four at the most. (Asked about women's bodies, Mr Wyatt-Tooth said: 'Heaven only knows what they get up to!') He taught the boys five-second chess, in which you lost your turn if you failed to move within five seconds. It became a school craze. Fights broke out over the timing. Otway brought a chess set to school with the black pieces carved in dark green malachite, and organised a Five Second Chess tournament with a sixpenny entrance fee, half for prize money, half to go to the AA Escape Fund.

In the Common Room Mr Wyatt-Tooth's fortunes took a different turn. At the start signs were favourable. There was talk of Lord Axmouth presenting the prizes on Parents' Day. Matron put her head on one side when Mr Wyatt-Tooth's name was mentioned. Mrs C-B continued to address him in her drawing-room voice. Only Mr Bloomer remained implacable. His suspicions, aroused by the Lord Haw Haw episode, were further inflamed by the liberties taken with chess, which Mr Bloomer like to play in the classical manner, setting out pieces to solve the problem in the *Herts Evening Gazette*. He declared five-second chess un-British, consequently unpatriotic. Mr Wyatt-Tooth countered, also in Sam's hearing, by declaring that the *Herts Evening Gazette* was downright common. Understood or not, all personal remarks were faithfully passed on to their intended destination.

Through the panes of the conservatory the boys became accustomed to the sight of Mr Bloomer and Mr Wyatt-Tooth, two hostile fish circling one another in a glass bowl, Mr Bloomer glaring at *The Times* held up by Mr Wyatt-Tooth as a shield against his bulging eyes. If Mr Bloomer produced his pipe, Mr Wyatt-Tooth stuffed a handkerchief to his mouth in a sudden bout of asthma. Mr Bloomer worked out a witticism which he was overheard sharing with Matron: 'When Mr Wyatt-Tooth told us his uncle Lord Axmouth had arranged to run him over in his car, I wish he had done the job properly.'

Mr Wyatt-Tooth was quick to respond. That same day the BBC informed the nation that Rudolph Hess, deputy to Adolf Hitler, had landed in Scotland apparently on Hitler's orders to try to make peace with England. Asked in class what he thought of Hitler, Mr Wyatt-Tooth deemed him too impossibly common; although nothing, but nothing, was more common than the Common Room at Illbury. A near knock-out ensued when Mr Bloomer announced that he had looked up Lord Axmouth in *Burke's Peerage* and found no mention of any Wyatt-Tooth relations. Lord Axmouth was not an uncle at all. 'Not uncle, cousin,' said Mr Wyatt-Tooth testily. 'On my mother's side. We all call him uncle.' After that Lord Axmouth became 'my kinsman Lord Axmouth'. But Mr Bloomer was clearly ahead on points when Mr Wyatt-Tooth exposed his flank to attack from another direction.

The day after Hess's defection Mr C-B made an announcement at the end of his Latin class. 'I have written a poem.' It was a joke, signalled by a guffaw. Turning to face the blackboard he wrote:

'So it's Hess?
'Yes'.
'That all?'
'Yes.'

'I've sent it to *Punch*.' There was a ripple of nervous laughter; then a loud clear treble shriek. It was Otway – Otway writhing, crying 'Oh yes!'; Otway holding his sides to contain his mirth. Peering into the fog of boys, Mr C-B acknowledged the applause with a grunt of self-approval and stalked away on his rubber heels over the tiled floor.

The headmaster's poem was still there when Mr Wyatt-Tooth walked into English class next day. The boys waited in crackling silence beside the baited trap.

'Sir, what does it mean?'
'Why do you ask me?'
'But, sir, you can write poetry.'

'Indeed. It runs in the family.'

Gazing at the blackboard, Mr Wyatt-Tooth told the class to get on with learning 'The Pied Piper'. He spent the next fifteen minutes scribbling on a sheet of paper. Hearing a movement, Sam looked up. Mr Wyatt-Tooth had left the master's chair and walked over to the blackboard. In one hand was a blackboard duster, in the other his silk handkerchief. Carefully he cleaned the board. Then he picked up a piece of chalk, and holding the handkerchief to his mouth he wrote:

> Illbury Herts
> Hurts
> Like Hell

He was smiling. 'Shorter. And more to the point, don't you think?' said Mr Wyatt-Tooth.

By next morning an unseen hand had cleaned the board. At about the same time Mrs C-B dropped her drawing-room voice in Mr Wyatt-Tooth's presence.

For some time after the Stanley episode, even Otway seemed subdued. For a while he seemed to lose interest in the AA. The months of the other war dragged on. Then one day Mr Bloomer held an extra Bomb Drill. He had written the words PEARL HARBOR and ADMIRAL YAMOMOTO on the blackboard behind him.

Mr Bloomer explained that on the other side of the world Admiral Yamamoto had sent the Japanese air force to stab England in the back by sinking the American fleet. But the Americans were not having that. They were joining up with Mr Churchill to win the war. Admiral Yamamoto had another think coming.

After Bomb Drill a more clandestine gathering took place. There was just time left before supper for Otway to hold up the name

> Y
> A
> M
> A

M
O
T
O

to the AA mirror and announce a brilliant addition that gave new life to an expansion programme that now included Mr Wyatt-Tooth, two lords and one enemy Admiral, not only Commander-in-Chief of the Combined Japanese Fleet but with a name that, being the longest, had the most powerful mirror image of all.

After two terms Mr Wyatt-Tooth put it about that he was weary of Illbury. At the same time he launched his final fatal entertainment. It started after Father Becket suggested he might like to take part in a procession in honour of Illbury's patron saint's day and Mr Wyatt-Tooth had revealed that he was not a believer.

'As my kinsman Lord Axmouth used to say,' Mr Wyatt-Tooth declared in English class, 'Thank God I'm an atheist.'

He waited for the new thought to be digested.

'Sir, if you're an atheist how can you – '

'A joke, Cork. An entertainment. To amuse me.'

'Yes, sir.'

For a week he kept it up. At the same time Mr Bloomer allowed it to be known that he had run into the English master in the local cinema in the company of a waitress from the Cadena Coffee Shop. Far from being embarrassed, Mr Wyatt-Tooth had offered him a tip on a horse on which he had just punted a month's salary. Mr Bloomer had declined the offer, and the horse had come in at fifteen to one.

With funds in his pocket Mr Wyatt-Tooth appeared to become light-headed. He told his class that God was invented by man to keep women and children in order; that sin made the world go round; and that the world itself did not look to him like the product a single creator – more like the work of a committee; as to Heaven, it would be sheer Hell if it was filled with old crocks from the last war: 'Imagine the Common Room, only for all eternity…'

Finally he went too far. He said the Consecration was a conjuring trick. Asked if he believed in Jesus he replied:

'Well, but look where HE ended up!'

A few days later Mr Wyatt-Tooth disappeared.

For the theme of his sermon that Sunday Father Becket chose Blasphemy.

'Satan speaks in many voices,' Father Becket intoned in sonorous baritone. 'The scriptures tell us that Blasphemy is the work of the Anti-Christ, Satan in disguise. Facing him fifty pairs of eyes stared unfocussed into space.

'A Father who came back recently from South America told a story of his evil deeds.

'In the seventeenth century a Jesuit missionary founded a Christian school in a remote hill village of South America. The mission flourished and made many converts before swollen rains swept away the path leading to it. For more than three hundred years it was cut off from the world. Then a year or so ago another missionary landed in a helicopter near the village.

'The little building set up by the founding fathers was still being used as a place of worship. There was even a fresco on its walls of the Last Supper, in which the figures, carefully cleaned and touched up, were still clearly recognisable. But something had gone terribly wrong. Over the years ignorant hands had become the tools of the Anti-Christ and done his blasphemous work. In place of the figure of Christ, the central position was now occupied by Judas Iscariot. Not only that but Judas himself had become a focal point for the pagan rites of the village and was venerated as a god.

'Of course the mission father knew what to do and quickly set matters to rights. He conducted a service to exorcise the evil spirit and whitewashed over the sacrilege; soon everything was back to normal.'

To keep himself awake Sam stole a glance at his neighbours. Beside him Kettle's mouth hung ajar. He looked across the aisle to where Otway sat among the Hawks. To his surprise, far from looking bored, the boy leaned eagerly forward, hanging on the preacher's words, black eyes as full of Vigilance as Father Becket could ever have wished.

There was no mention of Mr Wyatt-Tooth, but Father Becket's final words made his message clear. 'The story of the mission may seem to you a remote event in a faraway place. But I am telling you boys, that even this school has not been free from the stealth of the Anti-Christ. Blasphemous and sacrilegious words have been uttered. You must put them out of your minds and remember instead the third commandment: "Thou shalt not take the name of the Lord thy God in vain."'

He ended on a lighter note. Looking up with a smile he said: 'The latest news we have from the mssion is that the fathers are teaching the local boys to play cricket.'

A thin smile towards the pew where the headmaster sat with his wife appeared to indicate that he was quietly pleased with his sermon.

Otway certainly was. His enthusiasm came close to causing the first mutiny in the Anarchists' ranks. When he put up the names of Judas Iscariot and the Anti-Christ as candidates for AA membership, Mott declared himself firmly against for fear of being struck dead. Even Jelly seemed doubtful; Kettle, as usual, held his peace. Sam himself did not much like Judas, and when he tried to picture the Anti-Christ, the image that appeared was of Mr C-B. A trial of strength was averted, however, when, written vertically, both the candidates' names failed the mirror test.

13.

'Shocking about the headmaster of Wellington,' Aunt Olive said from behind *The Times*. 'His poor wife.' She spread the newspaper across the breakfast table. 'He was killed. By an air raid. There's a picture.'

It showed a house with its roof partly blown off and upstairs windows blackened. Men wearing helmets and ARP armbands worked on a pile of rubble where the front door had been. Another picture showed a man with a moustache – milder looking than Mr C-B.

Sam was suddenly very still. A curious feeling began to steal over him. He looked at the caption:

ENEMY BOMB KILLS HEADMASTER

Aunt Olive read out: 'Enemy action today damaged several buildings at Wellington College killing Mr Robert Longden, the headmaster. Mr Longden had emerged from his house after the night raid to survey the damage to the famous Home Counties school.'

Sam held his breath while Aunt Olive turned the page. 'As he stood on his front doorstep the porch collapsed over his head and struck him dead. He was buried under the rubble.'

Sam stared at the headline. It stared back at him accusingly. Had there been a dreadful misunderstanding? Perhaps prayers went astray, like letters. Had his prayer for an air raid been Insufficiently Addressed and killed the wrong headmaster?

Worse than a death on his conscience, the thought came to him that he would have to confess under pain of eternal damnation to Father Becket. Next term his class was due to make their first confession in preparation for First Communion. Father Becket was in league with Mr C-B. They were taught in Catechism about the seal of confession, but the bond between Church and School was more real in Sam's mind than the bond of silence. Father Becket would tell, on one of those walks round the school bounds during Prep, Father Becket in his priest's black hat, Mr C-B in a new Panama. Or worse, Father Becket would make Sam tell Mr C-B himself, as a penance. The thought was more frightening than Hell.

By lunchtime Sam had persuaded himself that he was a killer on the run. He contemplated giving himself up to the police to avoid going back to school. but like Father Becket they would probably hand him over to the enemy. Otway would know what to do; but Otway was not there. In the old days Sam would have confided in Daisy, but school life had loosened the ties between brother and sister, and in her present mood she was best left alone. The more he turned it over the worse it got. If he did not take First Communion, he would have to give an explanation. If he went to Communion without confessing to a mortal sin, Sacrilege would be added to Murder, meriting double damnation, perhaps even Excommunication. Sam held out until mid-afternoon. Then he asked Daisy to come to the tree house.

'Do the nuns say what happens if you kill someone?'

Daisy was her usual brisk self once more. 'You go to Hell forever.'

It was just like the old days.

'Does killing the wrong person by mistake count?'

She thought for a moment. 'You burn in Purgatory. I'm not sure how long.'

When Sam told her the whole story, she had the answer to that, too. 'Confess to Father O'Rourke, silly.'

He thought of the elderly priest with the gravelly Irish voice who came over to the camp on Sundays to say Mass and sometimes smelled of gin. 'But we haven't done Confession. We don't do Contrition till next term.'

'Confessing isn't a sin. At least I don't think so. Anyway you don't have to tell them at Illbury that you've been to confession. I wouldn't.'

'At your school you don't get beaten if you get caught.'

'You get put on Silence. But I don't care.'

There lay the trouble. Sam did care. He was afraid, afraid of damnation, even more afraid of Mr C-B. He did not know which way to turn. He was like his prayer, a letter lost in the post.

'Father Becket might find out.'

After a decade's study of her brother, Daisy had reached the conclusion that Aunt Olive was right: men were the weaker vessels. Their mother had explained to her that Sam was 'sensitive'. Daisy made plain her own view: she considered him feeble. She chose one of Aunt Olive's expressions: 'Stuff and nonsense,' she said. It was as if, in the natural order of things, she had become the older sibling.

Sam reached the Catholic parish church on his bicycle at tea-time. In the cavernous Victorian building, larger than its present congregation warranted, Father O'Rourke's name was written over a carved confessional cubicle in a side aisle. A pair of heels projected from the curtain drawn across it. There was a prolonged hoarse whispering sound, then the priest's muffled voice. Sam knelt in a nearby pew and waited. There was still time to change his mind.

A wooden kneeler scraping against stone echoed like a rifle shot through the empty church. The curtain was drawn back and the owner of the whisper came out and knelt a pew at the back of the church. A half-door across the confessional was thrown open and

Father O'Rourke's arm emerged to switch on a red light above his head. Seeing Sam, he beckoned him in. There was no going back.

He knew the first bit. 'Bless me Father for I have sinned.'

There was a muttering of Latin, then silence.

'Well, my child? How long since your last confession?'

He hadn't thought of that. 'It's the first time, Father.'

'And what sins have you committed?' The voice was kind enough. Sam pictured the man he had seen drinking pink gin.

'I have broken the Commandments, Father.'

'And which Commandments have you broken?'

'The fifth Commandment, Father.'

There was a pause.

'Do you know what the fifth Commandment is?'

'Thou Shalt not Kill,' said Sam.

'And have you killed someone?' There was no reproof in the voice, only mild curiosity. Sam took a deep breath.

'I prayed for an air raid at my school and it killed the headmaster of Wellington.'

'I see you are a man of action. And what is your school?'

Sam hesitated. If he did not tell, perhaps Fr O'Rourke would refuse absolution. He made up his mind: 'Illbury Hall.'

'That's a very well-known school. And why did you pray for an air raid, my child?'

'I hate it there.'

'Sometimes we all hate school.' Sam tried to imagine Father O'Rourke as a schoolboy, and wondered if he had hated school as much as he did. Most of all he wondered what the penance was for murder. 'But it's not very charitable to want an air raid. Innocent people might be killed.'

'Yes, Father.'

He was not entirely sure that Father O'Rourke had got the point. He could hear the priest breathing. He wondered if there was the smell of gin, but he could only make out dust.

'You have a tender conscience, my child. There are times when we all feel hate. But we must pray for our enemies, not for air raids, and learn to forgive them. Pray for Charity.

'Remember, God is all-powerful. God will give you what you ask Him. Now, have you committed any other sins?'

He had not thought about confessing anything except the murder. Perhaps it was the Irish brogue that decided him: or perhaps the softness of the worn black leather covering the kneeler, unlike the bare polished planks at school that dig into his kneecaps. He was surprised how easily the words come out: 'Also we burned down the school wood. The wind changed so the school was saved.'

He could hear the priest's large body heaving in the confined space. 'You committed arson, my child?'

Sam ran through the Seven Deadly Sins in his head, but he could not place arson.

'It was by mistake, Father.'

'Well, you can't commit a sin by mistake, can you?' The notion had not occurred to Sam. 'An accident with matches was it?'

'Sort of, Father.' It seemed best to keep quiet about the spell and Godonay for the moment.

'Then maybe it was a sin of disobedience.' The voice came through the grille again. 'Though the police may still think it's arson, of course. Does anyone know you did it?'

'No, Father. Will I have to tell the police?'

'Well now my child, is the fire out?'

'Oh yes, Father.'

'And everybody safe?'

'Yes, Father.'

'Well, what do you want to go bothering the police for? Over an accident with matches. With everyone so busy with fighting the war… Now, is there anything else that you have to confess?'

There was more stirring and sighing on the other side of the grille, the heavy sounds of a judge about to pass sentence: 'For your penance say Three Hail Marys and make an Act of Contrition.'

Sam hesitated. 'We haven't done contrition at school, Father.'

'This the first time you have been to confession? Well, it's enough if you say "I'm sorry for my sins." As well as your penance.'

Through the grille Sam could see the outline of a hand held up in absolution. There were more Latin words. Then: 'And say an extra

Hail Mary for me.'

Sam knelt in the ugly nave and, holding his breath from habit, said his penance prayer in one go. It was the first time since going to Illbury that he had felt himself to be in the presence once more of a God of Love. Unlike Father Becket, Father O'Rourke was on his side. Yet in spite of himself, somewhere inside, Sam had a sense of anticlimax, as if the penance was not important enough for his sin.

As he was leaving the church, he felt an arm round his shoulder.

'You are Geraldine Cork's son?'

'Yes, Father.'

'A terrible thing to lose your mother. God rest her soul.'

'Yes, Father.'

'And your father taken prisoner, too.'

'Yes, Father.'

'Sometimes life seems unfair. God's ways are mysterious. Sometimes He seems not to give us a chance.'

'Yes, Father.'

'But, remember: there's always a second chance. With God, I mean. Although it's not always what you pray for. Remember Christ built His church on a man who denied him three times.'

Light as the air, Sam pedalled home with the priest's parting words singing in his ears: 'Courage, my child! Courage!' To his surprise he discovered that his fear had vanished. By the time he was half way he had forgotten about eternal damnation.

Turning his mind instead to the problems of this world, he thought about his new supporter. Father O'Rourke had a warmth that belonged to the holidays. Sam reckoned he must also have God's ear; but he doubted if he was any match for Father Becket, especially in term time. In term time there was a sinister shift in the balance of Divine Power. The trouble was there was no knowing for sure which side God Himself was on. And another thing: He was not entirely reliable. God was supposed to be all-powerful, but when Sam asked Him to bomb Illbury He had missed and hit the wrong school.

Thoughtfully Sam steered his bicycle into the sandy lane lined with pines and red-hot pokers, another pilgrim pondering the inscrutable workings of Providence.

Old Parrot, the regular local taxi driver, was waiting as usual for the school train in the station yard. The Great War veteran with his clipped moustache and military bearing was part of the ritual of going back to school. His inability to read or write set him apart in Sam's mind, as if illiteracy conferred special powers of insight. Parrot had a technique for holding the attention of his passengers by releasing fragments of cryptic information at skilfully judged intervals, like clues in a treasure hunt. His speciality was bad news.

'You'll have to double up – there's another battleship gone.'

Untroubled by non sequiturs, the boys piled into the fleet of old Humber taxis hired to ferry them the few miles to school. Parrot pressed the starter button and the machine shuddered into life.

Sam had already worked out that doubling up saved petrol and so was part of the War Effort. This still did not explain the battleship. Nor why Mr and Mrs C-B had not come to the station in the usual way to help out with the school's two big Austins. There was no point in asking. Parrot could not be rushed.

They had reached a flat stretch of Hertfordshire shot through with overhead wires before Parrot spoke again: 'U-boat torpedo, the wireless said. Off Gibraltar. Just like that. Set the ship alight and the powder magazine went up. A thousand went down I shouldn't wonder. Maybe more.' He pondered for a moment. 'Yes. There's likely more.'

Parrot dropped a final clue as they reached the Illbury drive, the last turning before a new outer ring of barbed wire surrounding Roman Hill as part of its conversion into an American air base. 'Only got the telegrams out this morning. Didn't give us time to get an extra driver.'

The Canterbury-Blacks were not on the front steps to meet them. With the others Sam rushed to the notice board. In Mr Bloomer's handwriting was an announcement that Mr C-B would not be taking classes on Monday evening. It was like a reprieve.

Everywhere the feeling of drama communicated itself. There was a subdued air about Matron as she checked the overnight bags against a school list. As the boys sat down on the long wooden benches for supper, Mr Bloomer cleared his throat to announce that on the way home from the Far East the battleship *HMS St George* had been sunk by a

U-boat. Among the dead was Sub Lieutenant T. Canterbury-Black.

Sam tried to picture the stocky young man who did not smile; but he could not give a clear face to the memory, only gold letters on a notice board. He remembered the poem about a Gatling gun that jammed (perhaps it had jammed again?) But the thought that eclipsed all the others was about how this would affect the C-Bs. Would Illbury cease to exist? The idea set up a fleeting guilty thrill.

Line-Up next morning was supervised by Mr Bloomer. Then at Mass, Mr C-B appeared in a dark brown tweed suit with a crepe black bandage on his arm. Mrs C-B, red eyed, was by his side. She had exchanged her dark blue chiffon robes for black. Stanley wore a smaller black crepe armband. The school staff seemed strangely diminished, like actors without lines.

A state of mourning was proclaimed to honour Illbury's first war casualty. A candle-lit altar was decorated as a shrine in the school chapel and boys invited to take part in a rotating three-day vigil.

After a week, Mr C-B resumed Monday evening class. After two, Mrs C-B returned to the kitchen. A new prize was announced: the Thompson Canterbury-Black Memorial Cup for the Boy of the Year.

After three weeks life was back to normal.

14.

Sam lay propped on his elbows with his back to a cloudless sky. As a security measure he had wrapped the loose cover of a book from the Good Reading shelves round the thick spine of *The Adventures of Bulldog Drummond.*

> With the howl of an enraged beast Drummond hurled
> himself at the red-headed Russian Yulowski, and when
> seconds later a dozen black-hooded figures swarmed
> in through the door for an instant they paused in sheer
> horror. Pinned to the wall with his own bayonet...

He had already reread the passage several times; each time it got better. He turned the page, idly observing the blackness of the shadow made by his hand on the print, but too engrossed to note that instead of disappearing when he withdrew it the shadow grew larger and blacker... or that the practice piano in B Classroom had fallen silent.

Suddenly Drummond and the villainous Yulowski ceased to exist. Giant fingers smelling of fresh soap took the book from his grasp. Sam looked up to see red eyes peering at the page he had been reading.

Mr C-B turned the book over to expose the title on the back of the paper cover: *Lives of the Catholic Martyrs*. There was a grunt of acknowledgement, non-committal: 'I have something to discuss with you, Cork. Let's go for a little walk.'

He turned and padded silently across the lawn bearing the book, a panther making off with its kill. In vain Sam tried to think of spells, then to imagine what Otway would do in his place. He took a deep breath to call on his courage, but all he succeeded in summoning up was the sour taste in his mouth of panic.

There was a single shaft of hope. Mr C-B was not wearing his reading spectacles, without which he could not read small print. At the very least, discovery was postponed. Sam's strategy was every schoolboy's: play for time and hope for the best.

They came to the clearing in the beech wood uncomfortably close to where the boys' huts had been before the fire. The man paused, motioning Sam to walk beside him.

'How much have you been told,' he asked, his voice dropping, 'about the Facts of Life?'

Here was strange territory, and with no obvious link to the object now tucked under his arm with a finger still marking Sam's place.

'Don't know, sir.'

'Do you know what I am talking about when I say Facts of Life?"

'Yes, sir.' He thought again, anything to gain time: 'No, sir!'

'It is time you knew about certain things.' An unfamiliar conspiratorial note had crept into the headmaster's voice, making it roll like quiet thunder. Sam had become aware that he was being told something considered important, dangerous even, like a secret formula passed between agents. There were technical sounding words – 'coupling' and 'impregnation' – like the ones his older cousin used when he was explaining the internal combustion engine to Aunt Olive. Then there were the unidentified 'male partner' and 'female partner', which made him think of his dead mother's Fred Astaire Dance Manual, with dotted lines and footprints for the steps. More disturbing were the 'mounting' and the baffling 'organ' which Daisy had told him about after her first term at the convent. He contemplated the piccolo between his thighs; clearly there must be more to it than met the eye. But what?

'Are you following what I am saying?'

'Yes, sir.'

And it was true, up to a point. The Facts as set out made clear how the deed was done, though not why. After all the mystery, it did not sound to Sam like the sort of thing anyone normal would actually want to do; more like a grown-up version of gym, which he did not enjoy much anyway, with a new set of rules to be learned. He felt vaguely disappointed in the Act of Love. Clearly there was something missing. Afterwards he thought, why Love? But he didn't dare say anything that might arouse the wrath of the man holding his illegal book as hostage.

Mr C-B's voice rumbled on: 'When you get to your next school be on your guard against older boys.'

'Yes, sir.'

'Do you know what I mean by abuse?'

'Sir?'

'Older boys may try to sit on your bed and talk smut. They may even try touching. You must tell them to get off pretty quick.'

'Yes, sir.'

'Tell me if there's anything you don't understand.'

Sam tried hard to think of a question, anything to keep off the subject of the book. Reaching out he said: 'Like Mr Goodbody, sir?'

'What about Mr Goodbody?'

'He used to press, sir.'

'Press?'

'Yes, sir. Especially Mott.'

'Tell me exactly what happened.'

The voice had dropped again to a conspiratorial level. Sam was taken aback by the headmaster's interest.

'Mott wriggled, sir.'

'Were any other boys involved? Did Mr Goodbody ever make an approach to you?'

Unsure what an approach was, Sam was flummoxed.

'He sometimes stopped us in the corridor.'

'And?'

'Sir?'

'Apart from pressing, I mean.'

'Nothing, sir.'

'No touching?'

'Touching, sir?'

'Rubbing?'

'No sir!'

There was a silence. The headmaster came to a halt, and turned to face Sam. 'What I would like to know,' he said slowly, 'is why you didn't report all this to me at the time.'

Somewhere, Sam was not sure where, the conversation seemed to have taken a wrong turning.

'Don't know sir.'

'It is your duty to bring such matters to my attention! As it is, it was left to my own six year old son to report it; together with certain other matters, in huts…'

Sam waited, horrified. Thinking to make for safer ground, he had headed into a minefield. They had reached the area of the beech wood levelled by the fire, out of bounds and cordoned off until only recently. They came to a stop near a circle of blackened stumps open to the sky. It was unrecognisable save for the ogre's head, charred but still staring open-mouthed, from where he had first spotted Stanley in the under-growth. Who knew what 'other matters' had been reported?

A new thought seemed to strike Mr C-B. He chuckled: 'It's a funny thing. As you may remember, one of the objects found here after the fire was the remains of a straw hat. My straw hat… How it came to be there is a mystery.' Sam was very still. 'At least it was a mystery until quite recently. You see, Stanley tells me that a few days before the fire he saw a boy heading towards the hut, carrying something under his jersey the shape of a hat. A boy' – Sam could feel red coals burning his cheeks – 'who looked remarkably like you!… I wonder if you can enlighten me?'

The price of telling the truth was too high even to contemplate. Besides he was irreversibly committed to the AA policy of blanket denial. The difficult part was not whether to lie (a lie was only a small sin) but which lie to tell and how to bring the lie off. Mr C-B had a way of wringing the truth out of boys.

'Well?'

Sam's whole body had begun to shake. With his cheeks signalling red for lie, he struggled to register surprised innocence: 'No sir!'

The man turned, resumed the slow walk, head bowed in thought: 'Of course, Stanley couldn't be sure at a distance…'

It sounded all right; but thunder had a way of circling overhead and returning to the same place. The man had stopped again, this time near on the spot where the AA hut once stood. 'I have heard interesting things about happenings in the AA hut. Tell me about them.'

'The AA hut got burned down in the fire, sir.'

'Don't quibble with me, boy! Answer my question! I want to know more about this so-called AA's activities.'

Sam was fast running out of ways of gaining time. He tried to think. Above all he must not say anything that would let the cat out of the bag about the fire. The trouble was, there were all at once so many other cats in other bags as well. What had Stanley heard? What had Stanley seen? Above all, what had Stanley said?

The man was standing, feet apart, holding the Bulldog Drummond book open, pretending to study it, the way he studied his stopwatch in class. Any minute now he would see what he was reading. The voice went on: 'To start with, why AA? What does AA stand for?'

Sam forced himself to remember his Security Procedure. Reciting from memory the words Otway had taught him, he stammered out: 'AA is a school club, sir. A is for the A team, the best. Double AA is even better…' What had sounded clever at the time now sounded lame and unconvincing.

'And who are the other members of this so-called club?'

It was like being a prisoner of war: you were only obliged to tell your name, rank and number. He had only to stop at: 'Jellicoe, sir.

And Mott. And Otway…' Instead he lost his head. In a fatal attempt to add respectability to the list, he added: '…and Lord Axmouth is Honorary President.'

The headmaster pounced. 'Lord who?'

'Lord Axmouth, sir. Mr Wyatt-Tooth's kinsman.'

'What has Mr Wyatt-Tooth got to do with this?' Mr C-B had a way of taking not just the bait offered but the whole arm with it as well.

'Mr Wyatt-Tooth was an honorary AA member, sir.'

He knew it was a mistake even before spoke; but it was as if his will was no longer his own.

'Are you aware, boy,' said the headmaster, 'what a blasphemer is?'

'Boy' was a bad sign, not as bad as 'sir', but not as good as 'Cork'.

'Yes, sir…'

He had forgotten about blasphemy. Until now he had only been concerned with the fire. But blasphemy could lead to Godonay: Godonay would lead to the fire. He had locked and barred the front of the house but left the back door open.

'Mr Wyatt-Tooth made a mockery of the name of God! I had to dismiss him. What blasphemies has the AA club been up to?'

Sam remembered something. This time the indignation in his voice was genuine as he plunged on. 'None sir! Judas Iscariot did not pass the mirror test.'

'Mirror test? Judas Iscariot? Explain yourself, boy.'

Sam's head began to swim.

'The Anti-Christ didn't pass either, sir… '

'The what, boy?'

'The Anti-Christ, sir. Both failed, so they couldn't be in the AA.'

There was a moment's quiet. 'Is all this Mr Wyatt-Tooth's work?'

'Oh no, sir! It wasn't his idea… Mr Wyatt-Tooth had gone.'

'Then,' said the headmaster softly, 'whose idea was it?'

It was the end-game. There were only a few moves left, no way out.

'Speak up, boy! I'm waiting!' The bully was loose. 'Was it yours?'

'No, sir.'

'I'm waiting, boy! I want to know, and I want to know now!'

Afterwards, Sam thought a thousand times, all he had to do was to do nothing. Stay silent. Nobody could make you speak if you kept your mouth shut. Little did he know that the choice he made now would change his life forever.

Was this the final part of the breaking-down process, when his fear would turn him, like a double agent, so that he was ready to conspire with his enemy, even to bring about his own downfall? He was a single twist in the spiral of guilt short of the unholy place where the victim's secret desire to please his torturer is awakened, and pain and pleasure meet. But just then he was only aware of being ready to do anything to earn relief from the nausea of his panic. He was ready to welcome the respite, however short-lived and whatever the consequences, of a full confession: even the relief that an act of betrayal would buy.

He looked at the man who could knock out Joe Louis, and whose mouth now twitched at the corner. He remembered his blood oath to the AA. A voice in his head said that perhaps it would not count as treachery so long as he did not mention the fire; another in his heart said that this was a lie. The red eyes turned from him to the book and back again, fastening on him. Sam was cornered. Either way was checkmate. His nerve snapped.

Miserably he said: 'It was Otway's, sir.'

The man grunted. Tucking the book under the other arm, he resumed the slow pacing. He had got what he wanted. Now he wanted more: he wanted everything.

'I wonder what else happens in AA gatherings?

'We played chess, sir. Five second chess. Mr Wyatt-Tooth taught us.'

The man did not take the bait. 'And what else?'

'Nothing, sir.'

'Don't lie to me boy!' The thunder rolled louder. 'I can tell when you are hiding something!'

Once or twice he stalled again. But the fight had gone out of him. 'There was counting, sir.'

'Counting?'

'Yes, sir. The marks. After a whacking.'

'What else? Speak up, boy!'

'You got a gobstopper for six, sir.'

Finally he had said enough. He hung his head in silence. In silence, too, they walked back to the school where Mr C-B handed him back the book, his thirty pieces of Judas silver.

That night as he lay in his bed he hated the man who had taken his honour and made him betray his friend. He hated him for being three times his size and frightening him so that he could not think. But most of all he hated himself for his deed of shame. He had fallen into enemy hands, and instead of being white clean through he had shown his yellow streak. Judas betrayed out of greed, others for a belief. He had betrayed out of fear, the most craven motive of all. From now and for all time he would bear the mark of Cain.

A loneliness he thought he had left behind engulfed him once more.

At first he thought it was a mistake. The week's class lists had been posted on the notice board as usual in alphabetical order, but Otway's name was missing from its among the O's. In its way it was a relief not even to have to see the name of the boy he had betrayed. But it was puzzling. Mr C-B did not usually make mistakes.

In chapel Sam moved his head to take in Otway's pew across the aisle among the Hawks, slightly behind him towards the corner of his line of vision. Sharply he turned back. Otway was not there.

Afterwards he went back to the notice board. On Mrs C-B's Milk and Biscuits roster a thin pencil line ran through Otway's name.

It was Jelly, blunt and breathless, who brought matters out into the open. Even he seemed impressed.

'Otway's been expelled! For blasphemy.' Staring at Sam, he added: 'And I know who sneaked…'

Sam looked away. It had not taken long.

Head lowered he slunk to his locker to collect his exercise book. There was a note inside:

> Paramaribo! I am free! I place the AA Expeditionary
> Fleet under your command. Paramaribo!
> Horatius Ariel Otway
> PS Watch the Cricket pitch for the start of the Great AA
> Counter Offensive!
> PPSS PARA-MARA-MARIBO!

Attached to the note was a key. Sam recognised it at once. It belonged to the spare locker in the Changing Room where the U-22 was housed.

Mott was his neighbour in that term's joint Recital class. Now it was Mott's turn: tilting open the lid of his desk so that he could not been seen talking, he hissed a vow across the aisle separating them that he would take it on himself to annihilate the culprit. He added, in a stage whisper: 'And this time it will be a pleasure to pick on someone smaller than myself.'

Now Sam understood. The other AA members all assumed that the betrayer was Stanley.

But the solitary knowledge of his treachery left him no peace. Sam paced the school corridors, restaging a hundred times in his mind the interrogation by Mr C-B, with himself stoutly refusing to divulge all information beyond name, rank and number. But nothing would silence the voice of conscience. He was a coward. It rang in his head like a leper's bell.

There was no place for the unclean to hide.

15.

Sam had forgotten about the postscript in Otway's farewell note. Even when Mr Bloomer reported an unidentified stain spreading on the cricket ground he did not make the connection.

It started with a brownish strip in the closely mown grass stretching across the middle of Illbury's First Eleven cricket pitch. On the second day another appeared, at a right angle to the first. Brown turned to black. Mr C-B was informed. At first, nobody thought of Otway. An assistant master suggested Colorado beetle, a new threat taken up by a national press seeking relief from endless war reportage. An official came from the Ministry of Agriculture. Mr Bloomer told the boys he was a boffin. The boffin diagnosed petrol burns. Two cans were found to be missing from the pump-house containing the school's electricity generator. Fuel being rationed it was put it down to theft, probably by black marketeers, the latest menace attributed by the sports master to enemy agents bent on smashing England. The police were informed.

There was talk of a saboteur, though still not of Otway. Invoking the AA oath of secrecy, Sam decided to show Mott Otway's note. Sam had not allowed for Mott's own sense of melodrama, nor perhaps for the risk Mott ran of being punished twice for each misdemeanour. Mott not only swore secrecy; he declared himself ready to take an oath in court that the conversation with Sam had never taken place. In addition to being freshly banned, the AA was a secret society plotting against the state and attracting excommunication. He delivered his parting words in a hiss: 'We must not be seen talking together… Say nothing! Destroy the evidence! All of it…'

Looking back, Sam would understand why he had never quite trusted Mott. Like Otway, Mott was against the system. But there was a difference. Otway was out to undermine it: Mott was out to manipulate it. Otway was an Anarchist. Mott was a politician.

It was the time of year when older boys sat the entrance exam for their public school. Concerned that their diffident nephew might fail, Kettle's uncle and aunt decided to remove him from Illbury and have him intensively coached at home. Mott won a scholarship and was odds-on favourite to become the first winner of the new Boy of the Year cup. Having joined the establishment, he could no longer be counted on for revolutionary activity. Without Otway, the AA was breaking up, but Sam was out to salvage the threadbare remains of his loyalty to his fellow AA members. His chief fear now was that Mott, who knew where the U-boat was kept, might become a security risk. He was only too willing to conceal the evidence, if only from Mott.

That evening in the break before prayers he walked deep into the beechwood with the U-boat wrapped in cloth under his arm, into the area that was now out of bounds, to where the ogre's face leered at a blackened underworld. Sam put his hand inside the gaping mouth where the AA Hut lookout once crouched, to clear a space for the submarine. Under a covering of damp leaves his fingers felt the contact of something hard and cold. Half filling the hollow was an almost empty can; he had guessed its contents even before recognising the smell of petrol. Placing the *U-22* in its wrapping beside it, he packed the leaves back into place. Then he ran back to the school.

Meanwhile, the stain continued to grow. Two of the lines formed a cross. The First Eleven cricket pitch was roped off. More right angles appeared. A giant geometrical figure began to emerge.

The telephone at Illbury came to life. Fifty pairs of ears and eyes followed developments, trading rumour and report, piecing the day's events together. Sam learned that they began with a call from the *Herts Evening Gazette* to check a report coming from an American air base somewhere in southern England. A reporter asked to speak to the sports master. He was told that it was his day off but that he would probably be at the Red Lion in town later that evening.

The deputy Chief Constable of Hertfordshire was seen arriving in a police car with a driver. Emerging from his consultations the headmaster announced an information black-out – and another topic to be struck off the list for letters home.

Next day Mr Bloomer was sighted at the tank trap half way up the school drive waiting for the delivery boy to bring the lunchtime edition of the *Herts Evening Gazette*. Throughout Good Reading he was observed sitting motionless in his chair in the glass conservatory studying the newspaper. At Junior Cricket he was in unusually jaunty mood. His respect for the headmaster's information blackout held out until evening class, when a small group of boys were permitted a glimpse of the *Gazette*.

An aerial photograph of Illbury Hall filled the width of the front page. It showed the roof-tops of a medium sized country house surrounded by parkland, a wood, and sports grounds in which, scorched into the grass in lines of startling clarity, was a large swastika.

Beneath the headline GESTAPO HEADQUARTERS? was a subheading HOME COUNTIES SWASTIKA HOAX.

Sam read: 'American bomber pilots returning from a bombing raid over Germany were startled to observe a giant swastika on the ground as they came in to land somewhere in the Home Counties. Initial investigation located the mysterious swastika in the grounds of a well-known preparatory school.'

To comply with wartime security regulations the school was not identified. But Mr Bloomer was. Cheek by jowl with a picture of

Lieutenant General Ernest Doolittle, in command of United States Army Air Forces in Southern England, was a photograph of the sports master in his flat-cap with a pint of beer in his hand.

The caption ran: '*Gazette* Reader in Hush-Hush Inquiry'. Mr Bloomer's words were quoted in bold print: 'In the interests of security I can go no further than state that a deplorable outrage has been perpetrated and is under urgent investigation by the appropriate authorities.'

The rest of the page was devoted to an interview with Airman First Class I. Wayne Wasserman from Big Spring, West Texas: 'At first I thought someone had lost the war back in England while we were out there bombing the hell out of the Germans. Then I remembered your British sense of humour.' Asked by the *Gazette* reporter if he felt outraged Mr Wassermann replied: 'Heck no! If you're coming in to land and low on gas it comes in useful to have a landmark. The boys soon got used to it: you make a left over the swastika – you aren't likely to get the wrong swastika. I guess there aren't too many around in England these days – no offence meant, but it's a bit like trying to find a cold beer.'

In response to public ridicule the Illbury authorities adopted a less light-hearted approach. At Line-Up, the wheels of justice began to turn. Laboriously the finger of suspicion veered towards Otway. In absence of the chief suspect, the other members of the AA were summoned for interrogation. Mott's taste for histrionics was nearly his undoing. Borrowing the words of a wife strangler in *The Hand of the Law*, he declared repeatedly: 'I deny everything! I deny everything!'

Sam's own denials were too late and too little to undo the damage he had already done. Otway was gone forever and nothing could bring him back. With a final brilliant burst the comet had run its course.

In the week of Kettle's departure a letter arrived from Aunt Olive to say that Mr Canterbury-Black had asked her to come for a talk about Sam's future.

She looked the same as she always did as she shook Mr C-B's hand on the front steps. She was wearing rubber galoshes over laced brown shoes against the possibility of rain, and a silvery scarf framed her finely lined face, with its grey-blue unblinking eyes and docile smile.

Turning Ebb out of the drawing-room with his foot, Mr C-B motioned Sam to wait in his study. In the glass-fronted Pound Cupboard the box marked 'Galactic Rousers', half full now, still stood in a layer in dust. Somewhere out of sight among the catapults, penknives and other confiscated items were his mother's diary and little Turkish mirror. Sam tiptoed to the connecting door into the drawing-room and pressed his ear to the keyhole, remembering another occasion long ago when he listened at a door while his future was being discussed. This time he could hear the voices clearly.

'His father was at Belmont, with the Jesuits. He always wanted Sam to follow in his footsteps.' Aunt Olive's voice was the gentle patter of light rain on autumn leaves.

'Belmont has a fine record.'

'The curious thing is that he wasn't happy at Belmont. He never talked about it, you know. I don't think the Jesuits did him much good.'

'It's an excellent school. Many of our boys go on there. Have you another school in mind?'

'Sam seems rather keen on Wellington. It was in the news recently, when the headmaster was tragically killed in an air raid.'

'Wellington? It's not even a Catholic school. I really could not recommend a non-Catholic school. Already I'm afraid your nephew is an inconsistent and hardly a robust character. There's no knowing what might become of him without proper guidance.'

'Oh dear! If you are right, then those Jesuits will fill his head all too easily with their hocus pocus.'

'I don't believe,' the headmaster said, raising his voice slightly, 'that his father would take that view. I really do think, Miss Cork, you should let us be the judge of what is best for your nephew's education. Belmont has a fine record. And the father's wishes are binding.'

A silence fell, broken by Mr C-B's voice. 'There's another matter I want to raise with you. I have had cause of late to be seriously concerned about your nephew. There has been an unfortunate incident in the school. A case of blasphemous behaviour. And I'm afraid your nephew was been involved. I had to take the appropriate action, including expelling the ringleader. The other parents...'

'I expect it was just another of Sam's pranks,' Aunt Olive broke in, lightly. 'They do get up to the funniest things when they're that age.'

Through the woodwork the listener could detect the delicate tinkle of her laughter, like a tiny glass bell.

'I'm afraid that's not all: your nephew tells lies.'

The listener at the study door shifted uncomfortably.

'Yes, I know that.' Aunt Olive sounded as if she was chiding him.

'Some time ago he wrote a diary. A pack of lies. I had to confiscate it.' Aunt Olive said nothing. 'It was an act of deliberate disobedience. I had to punish him.'

There was another pause, then Aunt Olive's voice. It seemed to be growing gentler. 'Why do you think he wrote the diary?' Musing now, 'Perhaps it's because he is not happy?'

'I'm not concerned with why he wrote the diary. I'm concerned with why he tells lies!' The fire was back in the headmaster's tone.

'Oh that's quite simple!' said Aunt Olive. 'He tells lies because he's frightened of you.'

'On the contrary, Miss Cork: if he's frightened, it's because he tells lies! And he has found out that at Illbury we don't tolerate liars!'

'Oh Mr Canterbury-Black!' said Aunt Olive, 'I do believe you are a bit of a bully!'

Unable to trust his ears, Sam put an his eye to the keyhole instead; more than anything in the world at that moment he longed to see the man's face, but all he could make out of the seated figures was the back of a sofa. When his ear was back in position again the voice was raised, but now there was a note of bluster. The steady raindrops had done their work: the fire had begun to smoke.

'... it may not be easy to understand from a woman's point of view, but I believe I would have Major Cork's full support in defending the need for discipline.'

'Oh yes, certainly,' Aunt Olive agreed meekly. 'My brother always believed in trusting to the professionals.'

'At Illbury, as well as scholarship, we build character. We instil a sense of duty and service, the old school values. Sometimes it is necessary to be firm. At Illbury,' there was a returning confidence in the voice, 'our curriculum is the curriculum of life.'

'What about love?'

'Love?'

'It doesn't sound as if there's much love in your curriculum.'

'Really Miss Cork. I don't think Major Cork had in mind this sort of approach to his son's welfare...'

'No. I don't suppose he did...'

'More a woman's approach, if I may say so...'

'Oh, his mother's view was quite different. His mother wanted him to train to be a businessman and make money. His uncle was a businessman, you know. Cotton I think it was.'

'At Illbury we prepare for the professions, Miss Cork. We don't encourage our pupils to go into trade.'

Another silence. 'Well, I will have to be catching my train. But first I'd like a few moments with Sam. I'm glad we have had this little talk. Good-bye, Mr Canterbury-Black.'

Peering again through the spy hole, Sam could see the man on his feet, shaking hands with his aunt.

'I'll get your nephew. He's waiting in my study.'

'Thank you,' said Aunt Olive. 'And while you are there, perhaps you could also bring his property.'

'Property?'

'Yes. His diary.'

'Miss Cork, your nephew knows the diary was confiscated with good reason...'

'Oh if he can't have it at school, I'll keep it safe for him at home. It was his mother's you know...'

The coals glowed, then died down again. Almost meekly Mr C-B turned to leave, then charged towards the study door. Sam sprang back as it flew open.

'You can go in now,' the headmaster snapped.

Standing in the drawing-room, Sam's attention was divided between his aunt, whom he now saw bathed in a new light, and the partly open study door. Through it he watched Mr C-B take a little key from the tray on his desk and unlock the pound cabinet, which creaked on its ageing hinges. Inserting an arm, the headmaster pulled out the red book, marched back into the drawing-room and handed it without a word to Aunt Olive, waiting patiently on the sofa that smelled of dogs. Turning on his heel, he left the room.

The time had come to say good-bye. As Parrot, the taxi driver who had once taken his mother to the station, held open the door of the waiting Humber, a drum beat inside Sam's head. He watched with pride as Aunt Olive stepped into the old machine, unaware that she was mounting the pavilion steps at Lords after knocking the world's most dangerous bodyline bowler for six.

When she was gone, he felt a pang. It was not for Aunt Olive but for memory of the last time he had been in the Illbury drawing-room, when he begged his mother in vain to take him away. Aunt Olive had never tried to take her place; but he could not help wondering if his mother would have served him as well that afternoon. He banished the treasonous thought before it had time to take hold.

Not until Aunt Olive had gone did he think of the Turkish looking-glass. He had not had the presence of mind at the time to mention it to her. The issue was to come up sooner than he expected.

A month into the summer term a special service was held in Chapel to inaugurate the Thompson Canterbury-Black Memorial Cup, bearing the inscription 'For All Round Excellence', to be presented on Parents' Day. During the singing of the school anthem, Sam became aware of a pair of eyes watching him. A quick glance took in the line of prefects behind him, a second one the assistant masters' pew beyond it. His eye came to rest on the Canterbury-Black family pew. Stanley was staring straight back at him with an expression he could not immediately interpret, of triumph tinged with fear. As their eyes met, the child glanced quickly up to his mother beside him; at the same time, a small fat fist closed round something shiny that he had been playing with, but not before Sam had time to recognise it. Evidently a distribution of confiscated property had taken place, and Stanley's share of the booty was the little Turkish looking-glass, Sam's lifeline to his mother.

Sam turned back, his pulses racing. Then an ice-cold feeling began to take its hold. At first he could not identify it. It was something beyond anger that he did not know was there: something implacable, all-powerful, that drove out his fear.

The dark box in his mind had opened once again, this time to yield up its poisoned harvest. Gradually, like a dam bursting but in slow motion, its venom spread through his veins.

> Oh how our hearts beat high with joy
> Whene'er we hear that glorious word…
> Faith of our Fathers Holy Faith!

As the Illbury hymn drew to a close, the venom reached his heart. It was Sam's first taste of naked hate. With it came a thirst for vengeance.

Suddenly he knew what he was going to do.

In the milk and biscuits break he emptied the books from his locker to pull out the big cardboard box that had been lying neglected under them. On its lid *HMS St George* was firing a salvo into a sunlit horizon. Inside a series of packages lay torn open as he had left them, beside an unopened instruction booklet on how to assemble an Imperial Class battleship. He read the booklet carefully during French class. There were three weeks to go until Parents' Day, technical terms to be mastered, much to be done.

On the first day he matched the balsa wood guns to the diagrams, counting the mountings, settling where they fitted into the hull. In a pocket of the box he found a pot of glue smelling of ether that would attach the masts and funnels. There were tubes of paint and different sized brushes. A crew of tiny uniformed wooden sailors waited in a slot in the lid to be painted blue and white before being fastened to the deck, their fate forever linked to that of their craft; in a smaller slot of his own an officer was saluting, palm down, navy style. Within a week the assembly reached the point where the rigging, in a separate envelope and made of stiffened cotton netting, and the taffrail, a stretch of tin to be cut, were trimmed and ready to be slotted on to the superstructure. Then the paintwork began: the first coat transformed his handiwork, which began to resemble the picture on the lid.

It also attracted the attention of other boys. Among them was Mott. Mott came to watch as Sam was painting the nameplate with the letters *HMS ST GEORGE* on the side of the hull. It was delicate work, involving applying exactly the correct quantity of paint over a transparent cellophane stencil with the letters cut out.

After a few minutes the other boy spoke: 'If you show me how to paint I could help.'

'Sorry. Too busy.'

'What's the rush?'

'It has to be ready by Parents' Day.'

'For the Thompson Canterbury-Black Cup presentation?'

Sam hesitated for a fraction of a second. 'Sort of.'

Mott was not to be fobbed off easily. Though he had a scholar-ship under his belt, he was already weak in sports, and he could hope to earn points for handicraft through association with Sam's handi-work and so clinch his qualifications for all round excellence and the Thompson Canterbury-Black Cup. And where there was an edge to be gained Mott was not one to let it pass.

'Let me know if you change your mind.'

Other boys showed varying degrees of curiosity. But Sam made clear he did not want assistance. This was private business.

The first coat of paint was a silvery white. He had to wait a day for it to dry before putting on its matt battleship grey topcoat.

During the wait he had one more mission to undertake.

As luck would have it, on the second night the school generator broke down. Through the dormitory window his ear picked up a flut-ter in the heart beat in the copse; stopping, starting again, faltering once more; stopping for good.

New sounds came from the window. Footsteps on gravel. Sam crept over to look out. In the gap in the rhododendrons where the entrance to the forbidden area lay, light from a torch cast a huge shadow of a figure bending against the bushes. From a doorway below a woman's voice said something indistinct; he could hear the word 'black-out'. The light was switched off. From the rhododendrons a bass voice came through the still summer night: 'I can't see where Mr Bloomer has put the generator fuel. Can you bring the spare can from the study?'

The bluish figure of Mrs C-B emerged on the gravel two floors below. A metal can glinted in her hand against an almost full moon. 'I'll hold the torch.'

The diversion was Sam's opportunity. To his surprise his heart beat normally. Pausing to remind himself that Bulldog Drummond could move and see in the dark with the uncanny silence of a cat (in spite of his thirteen stone of solid muscle), Sam crept along the creaking floorboards. Mindful of his father's injunction about Time Spent on Reconnaissance, he had left his slippers behind and wore only pyjamas, to support his alibi of sleepwalking. Unlike Bulldog Drummond he could see nothing. Moreover he felt very small.

The foot of the stairs was separated from Mr C-B's study by the unlit length of the Long Hall: there would be nowhere to hide before he reached the wooden screen at the far end. But the blackout was in his favour, and bare feet would make no sound on the tiled floor. He ran the open stretch past the clock, the Honours Board and where Mr Bloomer's sandbag emplacement, abandoned since German air raids had almost ceased, stood half dismantled. At the big screen he paused. From there he tiptoed to the door of the headmaster's study.

There was still no sound from the pump-house. The front door was wide open. More important still, Mrs C-B had left the study door ajar.

It was like a giant's lair. Crystals of moonlight streaming through the open sash window give a phosphorescent aura to the enormous desk. A thousand sparks danced on the outsized cut-glass inkwell with a ledge for pens; beside it stood a tray for pencils, a blotting pad and a tidy row of India rubbers, elastic bands and paper clips. Mr C-B was a methodical man. There, beside a calendar with a sliding window marking the right date was the small key which Sam had seen Mr C-B use to open the Pound Cupboard for Aunt Olive. His eye travelled from the desk to the desk drawer in which he knew Mr C-B kept his strap. For a moment Sam felt his courage ebb through his fingertips. Listening to his heartbeat, he picked up the key.

He surveyed the room, eyes pausing at a whitish dome glowing in the moonlight on top of a glass door. The dome resolved itself into a pyramid of hats from which the nerveless Jelly had lifted the Panama. Drawing nearer he identified the Pound Cupboard. Through its panes he could make out in ghostly outline the cardboard box with a notice saying DANGER FIREWORKS.

Deliberately he put the key into the lock and turned. The creak of the opening door was twice as loud as he remembered.

leading to the top-most platform, providing an ideal temporary berth. Then he ran to the wood to collect the U-boat.

His work was completed well before the match ended, as it regularly did since Thompson Canterbury-Black's marathon innings, in a stage-managed draw. Fathers were not supposed to win. They declared before the general's turn at the wicket. As a result, the spectators never got to see whether General Doolittle would use his baseball bat to play.

Sam's one fear was rain. The prize-giving ceremony followed on time, but under an increasingly threatening sky. Sam prayed hard that speeches would be brief enough to give him the time he needed before the rain came. Hearing Father Becket's voice, he feared there had been a change of plan. Father Becket on the Mandarin Class could last a good twenty minutes.

Instead he heard the priest's mellow tones calling on the assembled company to rise and stand for a minute's silence in honour of a gallant old boy who had given his life defending his country at sea; after which he would call on General Doolittle to present the Memorial Cup honouring the name of Thompson Canterbury-Black.

There was the sound of sliding chairs, then a hush as everyone, masters, parents and boys, stood to bow their heads. There was a round of applause as Mott junior's name was called and he stepped up to the podium. To be on the safe side, in case of a pause in the proceedings, Sam waited for the regular prize-giving to begin.

Like Mr Wyatt-Tooth, the general had no difficulty with the age gap, with the difference that Mr Wyatt-Tooth spoke to the boys as if they were his age while the general spoke to them as if he were theirs. He liked jokes and surprises. He began with a joke. 'I was planning to talk to you today about a matter of urgent international importance,' he declared. 'Baseball!' Brandishing his bat, he went on: 'But when I started my research I got a shock. It seems there's nothing I can tell you about baseball that you don't already know. I thought we Americans had invented our own national game; then I found out you had, right here in England. It started out as rounders: all we did was speed it up a little and call it baseball. You slowed it down and called it cricket.'

There was a ripple of happy applause from the fathers. 'But there's one thing I do know about. It's what we do at Roman Hill. We call it

Strategic Support. It's what the fighting men up at the front count on to help them win the war. Now you're fighting men here, as I've seen today. So instead of talk I have brought along some Strategic Support, courtesy of the United States Air Force.'

He made a sign to the aide-de-camp who began distributing packets from a crate marked Wrigley's Spearmint. There was a cheer, this time from the boys – all the more enthusiastic because chewing gum was banned at Illbury.

Like Mr Wyatt-Tooth, the general was a hit. Sam's prayer was that he would also be brief. The general did not let him down. The hoped for words came with mock-fierce military brevity: 'Your business is winning prizes. Mine is giving them out. Let's get started.'

Side by side at the podium Mr C-B announced the prizes and the general called out the winners.

Sam looked up. The rain clouds were lightening. So far everything was going according to plan. He signalled to Aunt Olive, who detached herself from the general's ADC. What could be more natural than a boy taking his elderly aunt to the bathroom? He led Aunt Olive to the bench beside swimming pool where, a year before, Otway's mother and sister had sat. What with both lessons and sports prizes, Sam estimated that there was a good half hour's respite. Distant clapping for the prize-winners was just audible.

Taking a final check of the objects hidden under the diving board, he picked up the box of matches beside him. All his faculties were concentrated now on the most delicate task of all. Taking the balsa wood battleship in both hands, he thrust it firmly into the swimming pool.

He was watching for the signal that would tell him that everything was working. The launch itself was a success: he managed to light the Galactic Rouser's multi-stage fuse without setting fire to the rest of the ship; he gave the craft exactly the right amount of impetus to propel it to the middle of the pool, where it slowed gracefully to a stop and waited, bows turning gently in the water to display the miniature fifteen-inch gun emplacements, twin lines of portholes, officers and crew glued to the deck in their immaculate hand-painted uniforms. From the masthead the White Ensign stood out proudly on stiffened paper.

Still Sam held his breath. Then from one of the funnels between the twin masts of *HMS St George* a thin line of sparks flew skyward.

With perfect timing, Sam launched the U-boat.

At the same moment the one event for which he had made no contingency plan occurred. An Air Raid warning siren sounded.

Perfected by three years of war, Illbury's Air Raid Precautions went into immediate effect. Mr Bloomer took charge: using his megaphone he invited the assembled company to retreat in orderly fashion to the sanctuary of the Long Hall, in the school. To reach it they would have to proceed past the swimming pool.

This they did.

As the first of the spectators reached the pool, the All Clear sounded to indicate a false alarm. The advance guard paused. Looked around.

Sam scarcely heard the gasp of wonder as some of the visitors recognised the insignia of *HMS St George*. With a hiss like rending silk, a jewelled shower shot into the air from the twin funnels. Pausing as if supported by invisible hands, it performed a series of multicoloured arabesques ending in delicate exploding puffs of white smoke; then, escorted by a miniature constellation of gold and silver stars, the embers descended gracefully towards the water. The firework's first stage, advertised as a 'fantasia of lights', had lived up to its promise.

From somewhere the voice of General Doolittle called out: 'Great ship!' No one else spoke.

Not all the embers reached their intended destination, but enough sparks fell on to the *St George* to ignite the generator fuel impregnating its porous decks. The spectators watched in silence as a sheet of flame engulfed the length of the vessel.

For reasons of security Sam had been unable to conduct field trials to ensure the correct angle of the U-boat's rudder. He had jammed it to cause the tin craft to travel in a circle wide enough to encompass the battleship, but he had no means of gauging the radius. In the event, powered by its clockwork motor, it veered closer to the edge of the pool than he would have wished.

But he had the advantage of surprise. No outstretched arms impeded its passage as the U-boat passed by on its lap of honour: the watchers remained as firmly fastened to the ground as the officers and crew of *HMS St George* to the deck of their doomed battleship. They stared in fascination at the outsized swastikas gleaming on either side of the U-boat's bows and grotesque banner that floated from its periscope bearing on one side the initials AA and on the other a word that nobody could make out: PARAMARIBO!

This time the Galactic Rouser did not let him down. Burning steadily inside its watertight compartment, the fuse reached the final stage of its journey. With an explosion worthy of Guy Fawkes night, the smouldering hull of the *St George* flew into the air and, descending in blazing fragments, turned the swimming pool into its funeral pyre.

Suddenly Sam didn't care anymore. His play had worked exactly as he planned it. His eyes turn to face the spectators. He felt no fear. He was ready.

Mrs C-B was the first to move. With a cry she turned her back on the miniature inferno, gesticulating and muttering to Father Becket. Mr C-B seemed suddenly to come alive. Shouting, 'What do you think you are doing, boy!' he started forward.

Sam was waiting for him. Standing his ground, he raised his fist in the air and cried at the top of his voice: 'Paramaribo!'

The headmaster peered through his spectacles. As suddenly as he had started, he stopped again, brought up to find himself staring into the eyes of an eleven year-old boy boy with murder in his heart.

Sam remembered the rest later: at the time he did not take in the spectacle of Mr Bloomer trying to capture the passing U-boat with a net used for cleaning the pool, failing, almost toppling into the water; the expression on the face of Mott, father and son, trumped in their moment of glory; the parents turning to ask each other what was happening; General Doolittle's undefeated smile; and finally the gentle voice in his ear, saying: 'I think we had better be going now, Sam,' as Aunt Olive led him, still shaking like a terrier, to the taxi where Parrot waited at the wheel with a look of lugubrious satisfaction on his face.

SECOND CHANCE

Sam sat numbed in his seat as the desert bus left the staging post, shaken by the surge of raw feeling generated by memory. Two decades on he still had a debt to pay and now, with Horatius Otway under arrest, perhaps even a chance, however remote, to find a way to pay it.

At the gates the driver turned beside a concrete statue, many times life size, of the man who had recently shot his way to power. The colossal figure stood with arms outstretched in paternal greeting, but the crude features conveyed menace rather than protection, a visionary with blood on his hands. The Chinese passengers who had just joined the bus crowded round the windows to stare and point, and nod their solidarity. Among the Mao uniforms, Sam spotted the girl he had seen arriving as Horatius Otway had departed in handcuffs earlier in the day. A wisp of blonde hair had escaped from the thatch piled under her hat. From the sand-stained face a long nose pointed fastidiously at the passengers around her: the slightly slanted eyes were withdrawn and hostile. She looked like an exotic wild animal caught in a trap.

From nowhere a sandstorm got up. Gusts of wind plucked at the surface sand; soon it was lashing at the windows. The bus slowed to walking pace. The landscape whited out, a Japanese print in which isolated objects, a tree, a cart, a Bedouin encampment, a watching face hung for a moment, detached from their background, then vanished forever. The dividing line between past and present melted away and other faces, from another dimension, joined the parade: boys in a school photograph rigid in their Sunday suits, competing to look grown-up, all unsmiling, but for one (already as a boy Otway had the confident twinkle of a man with an ace up his sleeve.) Next to them, Matron in her joyless starches, with her dried holly leaf of a mouth; then there were gaps, which Sam gradually filled in – assistant masters whom he could still name, even at this distance in time. Another giant figure floated past, but in place of the Leader was a man with huge hands and red eyes that glared short-sightedly through horn-rimmed spectacles, seated in the centre of the photograph.

But Sam's main thoughts were elsewhere, with the man somewhere on the desert road in front... Yes, he had a debt to pay.

17.

The wife of Her Majesty's ambassador surveyed the hotel dining room over the rim of her glass, using her drink as a shield to conceal the disdainful curl of her lip. Clutching with her free hand at the powder pink wisp of shawl round her shoulders, she gave a little shiver.

Eager to outshine their Swiss predecessors, the new revolutionary management of the former Royal Grand Hotel had turned up the air-conditioning to the full, so that while the city outside lay prostrate in the embers of a desert August sun the hotel guests politely froze at their tables. Sealed within sound-proofed plate-glass walls, they passed the time waiting for dinner to be served watching the hotel's old Chevrolet taxis grinding by in eerie silence, their door-handles bound with string to prevent them incinerating their passengers' fingers.

The Royal Grand, until a month ago showpiece of the king's modernisation programme, had since been renamed The New Arab Hotel, although the change had not reached the glass in Lady Quicke's hand which still bore the dead monarch's arms.

The spectacle before her was a poor parody of democracy: at a nearby table identical to the British ambassador's the newly arrived Communist Chinese chargé d'affaires and his wife were anchored impassively in box-shaped Mao uniforms; they alone seemed impervious to the cold. As far away on the other side of the room as geography permitted, the outgoing Nationalist Chinese ambassador sat with a clutch of attachés in western tropical suits. Taiwan's credentials had been revoked when the new regime recognised Communist China, and the staff had been ordered to leave the country at once, a measure rendered academic by the simultaneous closure of the frontiers. Instead, like the British ambassador and his personal staff, they too had been moved into the hotel when a mob had sacked the British embassy and its residence. The official explanation to both parties was the need to protect them from the wrath of the people; the commonly accepted one was that surveillance was easier to conduct in a carefully bugged hotel.

The other diners were the flotsam and jetsam of revolution: frightened European residents seeking sanctuary, waiting to find a way out; entrepreneurs who had found their way in to bid for contracts from the country's new masters; technical and political advisers. Protruding here and there under the table cloths, Lady Quicke's eye picked out the grey plastic shoes worn by East European trade delegates. And then of course there was the press... She gave an angry shudder. Sir Hubert and she had no part in this grotesque Camino Real.

How different from the Queen's Birthday reception a few weeks before... Then guests had been led by the Crown Prince and the King, a shy young man who had made his getaway early to play polo with the British officers in his entourage. The party had been held in the embassy's grand salon opening onto a shaded garden, as imposing if not larger than the one in the palace itself and a reminder of where, until a few short weeks ago, true power lay.

Near the door a group of foreign correspondents scrambled to their feet as a man in a crumpled military uniform joined their table. His face looked familiar. 'The new Minister of National Guidance,' Sir Hubert said in his wife's ear. 'You'll have seen his photograph in the papers. Typical left-wing London School of Economics product.'

Lady Quicke studied the drooping black moustache, somehow at odds with the uniform. She leaned forward. 'Why, it's the king's vet!' she murmured. 'He looked after my animals... He's called Siddiq Shanshal... I used to know him quite well. At least I thought I did.'

'That could come in useful, my dear,' said the ambassador.

For a moment Lady Quicke felt sick. She closed her eyes at the memory of twin pet gazelles that had lived in the embassy compound, driven frantic and chased to their death into the flames by a laughing crowd. She took a sip from her gin and tonic, angrily set it down again and turned to her husband: 'The only thing that's warm in this room is the drink. These people...'

Lady Quicke blamed all her present woes on 'these people' – but privately she reminded herself that she had been fighting a losing campaign for ice since she had left her native America to marry into an English family. Ice had only been the start: her main mission had been her husband's career. Lady Quicke looked at the man beside her, twenty years her senior, now on his third scotch, his pale eyes swimming in yellowed pools. Just then she minded more about the gazelles than the sudden reversal in her husband's fortunes.

It had been a copybook coup, brief, brutal and effective. An army corps, led by a well rehearsed cabal of officers and whipped into a frenzy by Cairo's Voice of the Arabs broadcasts, had moved into the capital under cover of darkness with tanks, seized the radio station and airport, and declared all frontiers closed. After waiting to see which way the tide would turn, the local garrison joined in on the winning side and in a demonstration of revolutionary zeal set off to assassinate the young king and his family. It had all been over by dawn when the British military attaché hurried to the embassy residence to escort the ambassador and his wife to the safety of the Royal Grand. By then the crowds, summoned from their beds by radio and loudhailers had gathered in the streets chanting slogans; two splinter groups, their ringleaders armed with petrol cans, had headed for the bus station and the British embassy.

Instead of adjusting to the changing tide like the astute political surf-rider his wife had once known, Sir Hubert had taken refuge in the bottle. The suddenness of events, mentioned only as a remote threat in despatches home (and then only on the insistence of his intelligence officer), had left him winded. His misreading had dealt a mortal blow to his pride, as well as his reputation. Sir Hubert was of the old school, a paternalist who counted himself progressive for embracing and imposing the notion of gradual self-rule on British terms; he saw outright nationalism as the work of international communism, designed to upset the steady march of a grateful nation from colonial status to a mutually profitable trading partnership. He had enjoyed his role of counsellor to the young monarch. He was near to retiring age, perhaps even the presidency of an Oxbridge college. Now he contemplated the remains of a career that had ended in ashes together with the gazelles, the outsize Rolls Royce and its vice-regal pennant. This would his last post. He had muffed it.

Two figures rose from the press table and headed in his direction. Sir Hubert could not identify them. He had made it a rule to communicate with correspondents only through his press attaché – another old-fashioned attitude that came with a price: when news of the revolution reached London, one tabloid newspaper called him Sir Hubert Slowe.

'Sir Hubert, I wonder if I may have a word?'

It was Lady Quicke who recognised Noori, the Pakistani editor of the local English language newspaper who had so persistently canvassed her support for his membership of the Alwiya Club, British in all but name, of which the ambassador was honorary co-President. Noori was quite a pest. With him was a young Englishman she did not recall having seen before.

'Your Excellency, this is Mr Cork, from the head office of the Universal News Agency, for which I acted here as the local stringer correspondent until the revolution…'

'You should know by now that I don't give interviews in public places…' The ambassador spoke without looking up. His voice was an ice pick.

The testiness was not lost on Sam. He was agreeably surprised to hear the firmness in his own reply.

'I don't want an interview, sir. It's about a colleague who has gone missing… A British national.'

'The consul is responsible for British nationals. Look here, my wife and I were enjoying a little privacy…'

'His name is Otway. Horatius Otway…'

'What about Horatius Otway?' The voice was Lady Quicke's.

There was no change of expression in the pale yellow eyes as slowly they slid to his wife's face. Sir Hubert gave no sign of noticing the pink spots that had suddenly appeared on her cheekbones.

'You'd better sit down… though it's quite pointless to try to get a drink out of those people…'

Sam made the account of his bus ride as brief as possible, making no mention of links with the past. All the while the yellow eyes rested on his face. 'How can you be sure of the identity of this person?'

'We were at school together.'

Lady Quicke turned to her husband. 'Didn't Earnshawe say today he was at school with Otway?'

Sam frowned. 'I don't remember an Earnshawe.'

'Not school. University. My wife is American. Mr Earnshawe is one of our Second Secretaries.' Sir Hubert looked at his watch. 'No sense doing anything tonight. Tomorrow morning the consulate opens at nine. Meanwhile, this conversation is off the record of course.'

The yellow gaze slid back to his whisky. The audience was over. Sam rose, pausing to say:

'I think Otway may be in danger.'

'No doubt,' said the ambassador dryly. 'No doubt about it at all.' Sam thought there was almost a note of satisfaction in his voice. As he turned to go back to his table, Sam heard the ambassador mutter under his breath but with vehemence: 'Confound that Otway!'

Dinner, imported tinned food heated up by local chefs, was the same for everyone. By the time it arrived, the light had begun to fade as the sun set on another former fragment of the British Empire.

18.

Sam was catapulted into consciousness by the telephone bell at his hotel bedside.

'Are you sleeping well?'

'Who is this?'

'I am Noori.'

'What time is it?'

'A quarter to six.'

'What's happened?'

'Preparations for visiting Her Majesty's consul.'

'It's a bit early Noori. The appointment is for nine o'clock.'

'British punctuality. I await your wishes. I am on the ball.'

'I meant very early.'

'We must map out the day to come.' The voice remained sprightly.

'I will await you.'

'Where?'

'In your hotel.'

'When?' An uncomfortable thought struck him. 'Where are you?'

'Downstairs. In the lobby.' Sam could feel self-congratulations throbbing on the line. Ten minutes later as he stepped into the hotel's indoor breakfast patio to be greeted by the bowing Pakistani, he heard himself saying: 'I'm afraid I have kept you waiting. You are very punctual.' Noori beamed and bowed again. Sam looked at the bare concrete walls enclosing the empty space. 'Is there anywhere else we could go for coffee?'

Noori seemed perplexed. 'This is the number one breakfast spot in town.'

He led the way to a table, where a waiter in hotel uniform and slippers served Nescafé. There were no other customers. Placing his hand on his heart by way of declining anything for himself, Noori waited for the man to shuffle away, then leaned forward urgently 'There is a matter of capital importance to be discussed, involving principally Mr Horatius Otway; with whom you have a personal bond, the bond of school; with whom I, too, have a personal bond, the bond of friendship. Mr Horatius has many times taken my daughter Farida to paddle in the Alwiya Club pool. He has invited me to use his Christian name. So. We both have a personal interest' – the spaniel eyes fastened on to Sam's face – 'but in addition to personal interest, there is the matter of' – he paused again to look round the empty room: Sam imagined the man rehearsing his pauses at home in the mirror – 'professional interest. This is the matter of capital importance.'

'What sort of professional interest?'

Noori looked almost relieved as he plunged on. 'Acting as my personal representative, Mr Horatius was engaged in journalistic activities on behalf of the agency, commissioned by myself. He was in short my assistant stringer. His work enabled me to gain access to the hub of events. As an English national, Mr Horatius had automatic membership of the Alwiya Club. He had contacts with everyone there. When the club voted to allow in a quota of non-British local members after the revolution, my own application was shelved despite my status as full member of the British Commonwealth, entitling me to priority consideration. It is only thanks to Mr Horatius that I am on the ball. I have since been seeking an amendment of the club's regulations to redress the injustice.'

'So you want to become a member of the Alwiya Club, for working purposes. I am sure that can be arranged.'

For the first time since they met the Pakistani looked happy. Sam switched the conversation back to Horatius Otway.

'Is there any reason to think his arrest is connected with his work for the agency?'

'There is no reason given for arrests. The reason does not matter. Here what matters is to be arrested.'

'Had any of his despatches upset the new regime?'

'There was the one about pygmies.'

'Pygmies? Pygmies are in Africa.'

'Yes. But they had asked for human interest stories. Mr Horatius suggested pygmies.'

'What happened to the pygmy story?'

'It went all over the world. Very popular. They asked for more.'

'And there were complaints?'

'Mainly from the British embassy. They said it was irresponsible.'

'What else did Mr Horatius write about?'

'He was working on background to oil.'

'Did that go round the world as well?'

'No. So far as I know he never sent anything.'

'What happened leading up to the arrest?'

'It seems a telephone call came when he was at home. Mr Horatius set off at once by desert taxi. I know this because the driver, Karim, who is also his gardener, is back. He says the police picked them up near the border and let him go. I at once informed Mr Horatius' sister who is staying with him. Also London Head Office, through the embassy as cables are not permitted, but I have so far had no reply.'

'What else does he do here, for a living I mean?'

'He is an important expert on art. He deals in ancient local objects to do with early writing. Also old masters from Europe.'

'Old masters, in a Moslem country?'

'He has many in his house. Also seals with writing many thousand years old. Would you like to see them?'

'I'd like very much to see his house.'

'I have already arranged your visit. We can go at once. I have the car outside.'

Noori rose abruptly, evidently his way of showing he was on the ball. Abandoning his unfinished coffee, Sam followed him. In the blinding morning light outside the heat, like an unseen colossus, was gathering its strength for the coming day's onslaught. Noori's little car was waiting in an unshaded car park, the string round the door handles already hot to the touch. Sitting upright in the back seat was an olive-eyed girl.

'This is Farida, my daughter. She is seven years old.' Hearing her father's words the child stepped out of the car, curtsied solemnly in her clean red frock and climbed back into her place.

'Has she been waiting all this time in the heat?'

'It is no matter.'

'She could have come into the hotel.'

'She does not mind.' Sam turned to smile at the girl who nodded to him demurely and continued staring in front of her. He's right, he thought. She really doesn't.

They turned off the main shopping street where the souk was already in full swing, into a wilderness of adobe houses gathered within the sinewy arm of the dike visible on the horizon, built in the days of the mandate to protect the city from the river in the rainy season. Just then flooding seemed the least imminent of threats. As they left the centre of town behind, the trees became sparser, like parched stragglers of a retreating army destined to succumb to thirst. To either side of the little car unmarked mud streets expired in dry rubble, picked over by gangs of barefoot children.

'Poor people, Mr Cork. Not a good area.' Sam hesitated, then decided to let the equation pass unchallenged. He thought of asking the Pakistani to address him by his first name, and then dismissed that thought as well for fear that, like poverty, undue familiarity might not be considered respectable either. He decided on another tack.

'Do you plan to stay on here?'

'Since the revolution I have been planning to move to England.'

'Have you ever been to England?'

'I myself have not. But my wife's brother lives in Bognor Regis. We might join him there. Have you been in Bognor Regis?'

'Once, as a child. It's by the seaside. I expect Farida would like it. King George the Fifth went there. I don't think he liked it much, though. His last words are supposed to have been "Bugger Bognor".'

There was a silence. Then: 'Was he executed?' asked Noori.

'That was King Charles the First.'

Another silence.

'What plans do you have if you go to England?'

'I plan to work in the London Head Office of the agency. But to secure my transfer I must first be officially reinstated by the new regime and promoted to full correspondent status. This will also assist the membership of the Alwiya Club, pending the move.'

Sam hesitated, his head beginning to swim. He searched for inspiration. 'I think it's an excellent plan. Of course, there can't be a lot of Moslems in Bognor. There might be difficulties with local customs.'

'Do they have Customs in Bognor?'

'Religious customs.'

Noori's face cleared. 'This is no problem. Mr Horatius says the reason we are friends is that he is a bad Christian and I am a bad Moslem. The trouble comes with the good ones. They make the revolutions.'

'Perhaps he has a point.'

'Mr Horatius has very many points.'

The arrival of the car in the European residential quarter halted the discussion. It was like an oasis. The houses were suddenly larger. The road surface improved and the temperature dropped noticeably. Trees lined the streets again. They swung into the drive of quite a large house. It was square, built to resemble a miniature fortress, with iron bars at the small high windows and a flat roof with castellated battlements from which flew a green flag with a four-leaf clover motif that brought to mind a secret society rather than a club or a nation. Centrally placed in the outside wall, with shrubs to either side, was a teak door. It was ajar.

'Come inside please,' said Noori.

A flash of reflected sunlight caught Sam's eye. It came from the windscreen of a car half hidden in the drive under a sun shelter of thatched shrubbery resting on upright poles. It was the largest make of Daimler.

'The former car of the British ambassador,' Noori explained. 'obtained by Mr Horatius as payment for an old master painting when the embassy got the Rolls Royce.'

Sam gazed at the enormous machine. Most agency correspondents had small office cars; stringers like Noori used their own for agency work and charged mileage: others had bicycles. The only Daimler in the agency was one used by the chairman to attend board meetings.

'Was Otway – Mr Horatius – on a special agency payroll?'

Noori's eyes avoided his. 'I was not able to persuade London of the importance of paying for a man on the spot in the Alwiya Club. Mr Horatius worked gratis.' He dusted his palms together. 'He is a very good friend.'

'I wonder why he didn't take the Daimler with him.'

'He was travelling incognito. The car is very well known. Nobody would notice a desert taxi.'

'So how,' Sam wondered aloud, 'did they pick him up before he reached the frontier?'

The front door of the house opened on to a generous courtyard to which all the rooms had access. Its walls were several feet thick. The floor was paved in stone, and narrow roofing ran all the way round its edges to provide shade from the sun at any time of day. There were rugs on the floor, basketwork sofas, chairs with cushions made from threshed cotton covered with Indian silk scarves; on a side table a pair of silver candlesticks sparkled in the sunlight cheek by jowl with a green and gold Sèvres coffee service. On another were laid out various Mesapotamian seals and cuneiform tablets, similar to ones in the capital's museum. Beside a wall clock with a pendulum a still-life oil painting of cherries in a mediaeval setting hung in a carved gilt frame labelled Spanish School.

'Business must be pretty good,' Sam observed, looking round, a question in his voice.

'Business is no good since the revolution. Very quiet.'

'Well, the art market must be holding up quite well.'

A door at the back of the building opened to let the evening shamal breeze in to cool the house. It was open now. Through it, Sam could see the river and beyond it the desert. Running down to the water's edge was a garden with rose trees. Standing by one of the trees with a hosepipe in her hand was a figure he recognised. It was the girl from the bus.

He had an opportunity to study her for the first time as she walked towards them to turn off the hosepipe tap. She moved hesitantly, almost as if she was unused to her own body, unaware of her own natural grace. Her hair was tied up with a bootlace at the back, revealing small, exquisite ears. He noticed that Farida ran over to stand near her.

Noori spoke first: 'Please excuse us. The door was open.'

'I left it open for you.' An imperceptible lingering over the vowels lent a haunting lilt to her delivery. 'Besides it's bad to water once the sun is out. Karim was supposed to come early to do it.'

She seemed unaware, too, of the strangeness of her voice. Unceremoniously she gathered up the hosepipe and dragged it across the esparto grass into the shade.

As she straightened up to cast a closed, suspicious look in his direction Sam became aware that he was in the presence of a startlingly beautiful young woman.

'This is the friend of Mr Horatius I told you about who has seen Mr Horatius. This is Miss Laura, Mr Horatius' sister.' Farida looked up at her with a smile.

'Half-sister,' she corrected him. At that moment, more than anything else in the world Sam longed for her to smile, too.

She frowned.

'You must have been with Horatius on the bus, before the staging post.' She made it sound like an accusation. 'I saw you. He was taken off there.'

'I didn't recognise him at first. I haven't seen him since school.' Somehow it seemed like a lame excuse. 'I'm afraid I don't know where they took him.' He decided not to mention the handcuffs.

The girl said nothing. Noori asked: 'Did your brother say anything to you before his departure?'

'I was out. He just left a note about an urgent consignment, I presumed to do with a painting or exporting a cuneiform tablet or a cylinder seal of the kind he deals in. That was three days ago. Then the embassy rang to say they had a tip-off from a confidential source that he had been stopped near the border and would probably be brought back on the desert bus. And saying not to talk about... Well, just not to talk. To anyone.'

There was no point in pressing. Noori broke the silence.

'I would like to show Mr Horatius' friend some of his collection.' Sam followed the girl's glance towards one of the closed doors in the courtyard.

'It's locked up. Horatius doesn't like people poking around when he's not there.'

It was as if he had been caught prying. Perhaps to salvage the prestige of his guest, Noori went on: 'Mr Cork has made an appointment to see the British consul.'

'He's useless. He says there's nothing he can do. He hasn't even found out where they are holding him. Timothy Kettle has been trying since he got here this morning. Do you know him?'

Something in Sam's memory stirred. 'Now I come to think of it, the name does sound familiar. Yes, Horatius and I were at prep school with a Kettle.'

'Horatius was helping him with some sort of assignment. He didn't tell me what.'

'If we find anything out...' Sam said. 'Or maybe if you do... Perhaps it's all a misunderstanding.'

The girl looked at him with scorn. 'Horatius would not run away unless there was a good reason.' Absently, she added: 'He always trusted too many people.'

Sam was still searching through the card index system in his memory as they turned to leave. He heard her murmuring, half to herself: 'I wonder why Karim hasn't come...'

But it was the other K, for Kettle, he was looking for, not the missing gardener.

19.

Behind its charred facade the British embassy had risen to the challenge. Two sentries provided by the Revolutionary Council guarded the entrance to the chancery (in passing Sam wondered whether they had also taken part in the sacking) where the consulate had been housed since the revolution. The receptionist, revealed as they emerged from a slalom of sandbags leading to a makeshift lobby, was a brisk middle-aged Englishwoman with a fresh permanent wave and a blue tint to her silvering hair.

'Mr Cork? The second secretary will be seeing you this morning instead of the consul.' She consulted an old fashioned alarm clock that ticked loudly on the trestle table acting as her desk. She appeared to be thoroughly at home with the emergency arrangements; perhaps they reminded her of the Blitz. She glanced over Sam's shoulder to where Noori hung back: 'Mr Earnshawe is expecting you alone. If your friend will wait here...'

On the Pakistani's features a feeling of slight did momentary battle with his innate respect for authority; then putting his head on one side in a gesture of resignation, he subsided into one of the ambassador's rescued Chippendale dining-room chairs that formed a makeshift waiting area.

The second secretary's temporary office, in an undamaged wing, was tidy and spartan: a copy of an Annigoni portrait of the Queen hung on a wall. Suspended from the ceiling the blades of a metal fan rotated slowly like giant ladles stirring warm soup. A wooden clamp holding a month's supply of the air mail edition of *The Times*, printed on lightweight India paper, lay on a coffee table between two Ministry of Works brown leather chairs and a sofa. The bulk of an incongruously English partner's desk seemed to fill rest of the room. From behind it a bronzed muscular figure in shirt sleeves rose to greet him:

'Earnshawe,' the man said. 'I suggest you take your coat off. The fan in here isn't up to the job. I hate air conditioning.'

Sam found himself looking into a coarse face with intelligent, watchful eyes. Powerfully built, Earnshawe looked both efficient and impatient, a bit like a detective in a thriller. Sam had the impression that not being up to the job would be high on his list of aversions. The man sat in one of the leather chairs, brusquely waving Sam to the sofa.

'Where did you come across Otway?' Evidently he was not given to wasting time.

'We were at school together.'

Earnshawe grunted. 'So I hear. I meant after his arrest.'

For the second time that morning Sam recounted the story, this time including the detail of the handcuffs. 'That's all I know. Except Noori... Perhaps I should explain. Noori used Otway as an occasional stringer for the agency. I found out when I got here. It seems he has excellent contacts...'

'What I can't understand,' Earnshawe said slowly, 'is why anyone would hire Otway under any circumstances to do anything.'

Sam thought: the right answer was that Otway was one of the most exceptional human beings he had ever met. Instead the weasel words came out: 'I haven't seen him since prep school.' Sam found himself on the defensive before he could stop himself. Why did he feel the need to excuse himself? 'Noori hired him...'

'Noori should have known better. I had the misfortune of coming across Otway myself at university. Once, that is. He had been expelled from his public school for dressing up as a priest and hearing other boys' confessions. His idea of a joke. He claimed membership of a string of bogus university societies to pad out his curriculum vitae so as to impress prospective employers. He had a visiting card calling himself President of The Voltaire Society, which never actually met. The man is devoid of moral sense. He was known for it. Did you hear about the pygmies?'

'Well, something, yes. That is, Noori reminded me. Noori...'

'We had complaints from the Revolutionary Council. You should understand that in third world countries they assume we control our press like they control theirs. They hold us responsible for the way you people behave. Her Majesty's government has already got enough on its plate dealing with the new rulers here without journalists trying to make monkeys out of them.'

'Or pygmies.'

Earnshawe did not smile. 'Otway seems to think life is one long practical joke. Now he's in real hot water, hotter than he knows. And deeper. He was asking for it.'

'What do you think is going to happen to him?'

'What happens to him is a headache for the consul. It's what he's been being dabbling in that concerns me. What do you know about his other activities?'

'I understand he's an art dealer. Cuneiform tablets, old masters...'

Earnshawe snorted. 'You mean he sells fakes to the British community. Including the ambassador's wife.'

'Fakes?'

'Just another of his so-called activities. Apart from being dishonest, that's merely embarrassing. No. I am referring to more serious involvement.'

'Well I've only just got here... Maybe you should talk to Noori. He's outside.'

The man didn't react. Sam gave up: he was no good with bullies. All he could think of was to repeat: 'Perhaps Noori can help.' Earnshawe took no notice. The shrewd eyes scanned his face for a full half-minute, as if he was debating whether to take Sam further into his confidence. Seeming to think better of it, he rose to his feet.

'My advice to you and your agency is to have nothing to do with Otway. Keep well away.'

As he left, Sam thought, that wasn't advice; it was an order. He was mortified that he had allowed himself to be intimidated: after all the man wasn't a policeman – or a schoolmaster. What was Earnshawe after? Sam had been unable to think clearly. It was not until he was in the car with Noori that he remembered something else.

'What can you tell me about the oil research project you mentioned? Earnshawe was trying to get at something in there.'

'Mr Earnshawe and Mr Horatius are not good friends. Not at all.'

'That I gathered. There was something about selling fakes.'

'Mr Earnshawe made an accusation impugning Mr Horatius' honour about a painting. So Mr Horatius was forced to tell the truth about Mr Earnshawe.'

'Noori, what is all this about?'

'It is top secret information I am giving you.'

'If it helps Otway, Mr Horatius, perhaps you better trust me with it.'

'All information is at your disposal as senior member of the Universal News Agency. This goes without saying.'

'Thank you, Noori. Well?'

'It is better we talk at the club and I will tell you. On safe ground.'

Sam remembered the girl in the back seat. 'You mean, while Farida has her paddle?'

Noori nodded enthusiastically. Irony had no place in his repertoire.

Trees shrouded the formal entrance to a long low building set back in esparto grass that stretched to the banks of the river.

'The Alwiya Club,' announced Noori. 'I have applied for your automatic membership to be processed. Visiting cards can be printed at the newspaper. I have the format here for you to inspect.' He put his hand to a clip attached to the dashboard and, head on one side, handed a card to Sam. It read:

K. S. Noori Esquire
Editor, *The Desert Times*
Fully Qualified Stringer Correspondent,
Universal News Agency
Club: Alwiya (membership applied for)

The card was engraved. As he ran his finger over the print Sam felt the spaniel eyes fastened to his face.

They changed into swimming trunks and settled in chairs beside the pool. At the shallow end Farida sat with her toes dipped decorously in the water, taking no notice of the British children screaming and splashing; she was the most self-contained child Sam had ever known.

'Well?' he began again.

'Well. You see Mr Horatius made available a priceless European painting of the 17th century to Lady Quicke for her drawing-room; in part exchange she arranged for him to have the Daimler of the embassy which was being upgraded for the Rolls Royce that was subsequently destroyed in the fire. Then Mr Earnshawe spread the rumour that it was not a true old master, because it had a bowl of tomatoes in it, and he says tomatoes did not come to Europe until the 19th century. All this was a great libel to defame Mr Horatius.'

'Where is this painting now? It would be interesting to see it.'

'The old master was tragically destroyed in the fire. But it is all a red herring. The real truth is that Mr Horatius knew that Mr Earnshawe was not what he seemed. He is not a true diplomat. Did you see the London *Times* newspaper in his office?'

'Yes. The air mail edition.'

'Mr Horatius says that proves he is a spy. Proper members of the Foreign Office on the diplomatic list get the ordinary London edition sent in the diplomatic bag.'

'If he was a spy, surely he would have thought of that?'

Noori threw up his hands. 'That is the root of the trouble! Mr Horatius said he was not just a spy. He said he was a third class spy. Mr Earnshawe did not like that at all.'

'I don't suppose he did.'

'He also said Mr Earnshawe was not so very clever. To get into the Foreign Office proper you had to have at least a second class university degree. He looked up Mr Earnshawe in the records: he only got a third class degree. Which he said meant that Mr Earnshawe was really a spy. A third class spy, he said.'

'You mean he's the embassy's resident MI6 man?'

'Mr Horatius did not say. After this they are' – the dark eyes flashed – 'at daggers drawn!'

'Well, I do see that putting it around that he was a spy could complicate the work of collecting intelligence.'

'And letting it be known that Mr Horatius was selling fakes was bad for the art business. Very bad.'

'And what about the oil project?'

'He didn't tell me. I only know Mr Horatius saw many people. He spent time at the Ministry of Defence – in the old days. He had friends there. And even one now high up in the Revolutionary Council.'

Otway seemed to have friends everywhere. But then Otway always had, even at school.

A shadow fell across Sam's face. A small man with fine grey eyes and beetling eyebrows to match was gazing intently down at them.

Despite the heat he wore a two-tone biscuit coloured cardigan over an open khaki shirt. On his head was a flat-cap. Sam's first impression was of a retired major who had strayed off a Surrey golf course, but there was something not quite convincing about the military appearance: perhaps it was the wink as he announced himself: 'They told me I'd find you here. You must be the UP men. James Tuffet, *Empire News.* They call me Jackie.'

Noori rose to his feet, put his hand over his heart and executed a bow in his swimming trunks. 'And this is Mr Cork from our London head office.'

'I just got in off the London press charter. Anyone fancy a noggin?'

Noori's hand returned to his heart. 'Thank you but we are about to attend the noon briefing at the New Arab Hotel. I can offer you a lift.'

'I don't believe in briefings myself. All you get out of briefings is what they want you to know. I leave that to you agency folk. It's the angles my paper goes for.' Without taking his eyes off them, the little man jerked his head in the direction of the bar in the shade beside the pool. 'Tell you what. I'll be over there when you get back. Drinks on me. Fair's fair. You fill me in; I fill you up.'

The little man winked again, then still staring at them, slowly shook his head. 'I don't know how you can stand the heat out here.' With which, he hopped away like a cock-sparrow towards the shade of the poolside bar.

The press charter bringing Tuffet had arrived unannounced. It was an outcome of a new policy of mending fences with the outside world announced by the nation's new masters, but being both inexperienced and naturally secretive they had made no provisions for the sudden flood of pressmen. When Sam and Noori reached the hotel, they found the Minister of Guidance personally telephoning to other hotels to cope with the overflow. Noori explained that, although nominally responsible for the foreign press, as a civilian the minister was little more than a messenger boy for the Ministry of Defence where the Leader held office and all decisions were taken; and probably himself had only been told at the last minute. Sam caught the former vet at the hotel reception desk between telephone calls, and took him to one side to ask news of Noori's accreditation.

'So you are in a hurry to leave our country?'

'My agency has ordered me home as soon as I have a permanent replacement.'

'You can tell them the Ministry has accepted the application for Noori. Now all that remains for the Ministry of Defence to endorse it.'

'Is that just a formality?'

'Yes, a formality,' said the minister, adding after a slight pause: 'I hope… Now, if you will excuse me?'

'Perhaps we can talk again later, after the press conference?'

That day's noon briefing was held in the hotel's hastily reopened ballroom where the world's press sat on gilded wooden chairs that looked like leftovers from a London coming-out dance.

Already in appearance the minister seemed to be more victim than master of events. His drooping moustache gave him a naturally crest-fallen air; caught in crossfire between the regime he represented and a largely hostile press corps, the former vet reminded Sam of a new teacher struggling to keep order in class. Before taking up veterinary surgery, Siddiq Shanshal had acquired his socialist credentials at the London School of Economics. To create an atmosphere for informal intellectual debate about the aims of the revolution, he had abandoned the ill-fitting uniform of the night before in favour of a crumpled djel-labah and black walking shoes. In vain. His lecture on the oppressive legacy of imperialism and the virtues of socialism for developing coun-tries fell on stony ground. The hard-bitten pressmen only wanted to hear about the recent purges.

The *Times* correspondent said: 'Purges are not the way we do justice in the west.'

The minister replied: 'Ist ist Ist…'

His audience looked nonplussed.

'The words of your Mr Kipling, a good journalist and imperialist propagandist, like you. And West is West. And never the twins shall meet.'

'Twain,' said the *Times* man.

'There you are,' said the minister. 'You do things your way. We do things our way.'

As if conferring a privilege, the minister announced a relaxation of security precautions: curfew and travel restrictions would be eased for foreign correspondents to allow them to see for themselves the new nation's achievements. Cable lines would be restored for press use for the first time since the revolution a month before, in time to report a mammoth parade in support of the Leader. With a doomed attempt at jauntiness, the minister announced a treat: a visit to a new technical college donated by East Germany, organised on socialist principles.

By way of response the *Daily Telegraph* correspondent asked when the show trials would begin. The Minister of Guidance then committed what every schoolboy would have recognised as a fatal error: he lost his temper. Picking up his papers he stalked to the door, turning to shriek: 'Why do you only talk of purges and trials? Why is news only bad news? You have no interest in what we are trying to build! No wonder your empire is in decay!'

As he left, Sam told Noori in an aside that he did not think this was the moment to press the minister about his accreditation. The Pakistani put his head on one side in the gesture that Sam was coming to know; and left to put next day's edition of *The Desert Times* to bed.

Tuffet was waiting at the poolside bar. He was perched on a stool glaring at the barman. 'I've been here since breakfast trying to teach this man how to make a dry martini.'

There were two drinks on the counter. Tuffet handed one to Sam, took a sip from his own, and shook his head with a sigh: 'All Martini and no gin. I hate these foreign places. Cheers.'

Sam told him about the debacle at the briefing, ending with: 'I'm afraid I may not be much use to you. Actually this is my first foreign assignment.'

Tuffet nodded sympathetically: 'You're lucky. I stick to the home beat too, when I can. I'm supposed to be the chief crime reporter, but they were short-handed so they picked on me. I've been away all bloody summer.' He took off his cap, revealing a near bald pate, and placed it beside his drink on the counter. 'Still, there's nothing to it. They're all the same, these foreign countries.' He looked keenly at Sam. 'All you need is a system.'

After studying the younger man for a few more moments, Tuffet leaned forward confidentially: 'Take my advice. Stick to the bar where the other correspondents drink and all will be revealed to you. They all know each other. Even if they hate each other's guts, they daren't let anyone out of their sight for fear of being scooped. After a couple of drinks they'll all be boasting about the exclusives they have sent to their papers. All you have to do is keep your ears open. Never fails.'

'Is that your system?'

'Part of it, yes.'

Smiling contentedly, he pulled a crumpled press cutting from a pocket in his cardigan and spread it on the counter.

Under the by-line 'James Tuffet, Algiers' Sam read: 'I stood on the roof of the Hotel Aletti as rebels attacked the Kasbah...'

'That's it. Hasn't let me down yet. It's a sort of signature tune. Take this dump. First thing when I did after booking in was to type out: "I stood on the roof of the New Arab Hotel as..." Later today, I'll fill in the rest. That is, when I know what the rest is.' He gave another wink. 'If it's anything big, it's bound to happen near to the hotel. And if there isn't anything big,' Tuffet tapped the side of his nose with his index finger, 'that's where the angle comes in.'

He took another sip of his cocktail. 'Of course you have to know what they want. I go for the British angle. My newspaper still believes wogs begin at Calais. What they like is the empire. They think foreigners can't organise anything.'

He drained his martini and put the glass down in disgust. 'See what I mean. Can't even make a decent drink. I wonder what the barman drinks at home.'

'He's a Moslem. They don't drink at all.'

'My point exactly.'

He gave Sam a friendly dig in the ribs. 'Of course you've got to watch some of these correspondents. Mind who you make a deal with. *The Times* is all right, usually. But watch out for that Danvers Nelson from *The Sunday Tribune*. He's my direct opposition, though he does television as well. He's here. He'll try to pick your brains. You don't want to tell him anything.' A look of pain passed across Tuffet's countenance. 'He'll distort it. Shocking what he makes up. And then he believes his own lies.' He clicked his tongue, gave an upward jerk of the chin and raised his eyes to the canopy over his head. 'I must be off.'

Donning his cap he gave Sam a farewell wink, and set out into the scorching afternoon in search of an angle.

Sam lay among the other bathers on the hot coarse esparto grass surrounding the pool, so unlike the cool English lawns of his childhood. The combination of heat and Tuffet's martinis had planted what felt like a tomahawk between his eyes.

'S-Samuel Cork?'

He had already spotted the Englishman out of the corner of his eye, ill at ease lying under the ferocious sun, edging in his direction. Even without the slight stammer, the pale hair and deathly white of his body, reddening now in unhealthy patches, singled him out from the other sunbathers.

'It is Cork, isn't it?'

'Yes. I'm Sam Cork,' he said. 'How do you do? Have we met?'

'Remember me? – Illbury…'

Sam turned to look more closely at the man, beside him now, awkwardly stretched in the blinding sun. Idly he noted that its light showed through the shell of his slightly protruding ears. If the ears were a starting point, the slight stammer was confirmation of his identity.

'You're Kettle!'

'Yes… Timothy Kettle.'

There was something else to remember, linked to the stammer, but Sam could not immediately put his finger in it. To gain time, while he completed his search, he went on: 'The sun's stronger than you think. You'd better be careful…'

The eyes showed gratitude. 'I know. I can't stand the heat…'

'But you've been out here since this morning. I noticed you before.'

'I n-needed to talk to you. But on your own. I had to be sure…' The eyes turned round apprehensively to the other bathers. 'Not here. In private. Really p-private.'

'If I didn't know better, I'd call it a coincidence! You're the second Illbury boy I've seen in two days. I saw another only yesterday: Otway…' He scarcely noticed the lapse into his prep schoolboy's habit of surnames. 'A double coincidence…'

'Actually it's not really a coincidence at all. Horatius Otway's the reason I am here... He came out here to do a job for me. Laura told me you were here, also about you seeing Horatius in the bus.'

'She told me you were here, too. But no more than that.'

'I can explain. Let's change, then t-talk indoors.'

Sam followed Kettle into the shade of the club. It was curious how everyone to do with Otway was veiled in secrecy. He felt as if he was being drawn into some sort of conspiracy. It seemed extraordinary; but then with Otway everything always had been extraordinary. There was no reason for things to be different now.

With Noori he had not been inside the club premises. He waited in the entrance hall while Kettle finished changing. A portrait of the Leader, hastily appointed honorary president in place of the dead king, stared messianically from one of side of an arched doorway, while the Queen smiled benignly on the other, head tilted at a slightly different angle, as if politely freezing him out. When Kettle arrived, Sam followed him into an empty room serving as a library, with worn green leather chairs like a London club.

Once they were alone, he said: 'You know Otway's been arrested?'

'Y-Yes. Laura told me. I was on the press charter. It was the first flight in.'

'Are you with a newspaper?'

'No. Nothing like that. I'm an insurance ass...ss...'

The sudden spasm distorting Kettle's face acted as a prompt. While Sam was debating whether to say 'assessor' for him, he was reminded of the other affliction that had bedevilled Kettle's school days. Looking at the grown man he could not help wondering if it still troubled him.

'I work at Lloyds in insurance,' Kettle enunciated. 'Horatius was helping me, unofficially. Laura told me I would find you here.' Kettle turned his slightly helpless eyes on Sam. 'I hope you won't mind my saying this but what I am telling you is confidential. Please don't mention it outside. It's not s-safe. I haven't even told Earnshawe I'm here.'

'Why Earnshawe?'

'At the embassy. I had a message in London saying Horatius had been arrested and that I should keep away. But I had to come. I managed to talk my way in with the press. It was the best I could do. I'll explain. But first can you promise you will not use anything I tell you as newspaper copy? Horatius Otway's life could depend on it.'

Sam was trying to concentrate, but the sub-plot of the past kept threatening to take centre stage in his head. It was not a man trained to be a claims expert that Sam saw sitting before him; it was a beleaguered schoolboy who attracted the derision of other boys for his stammer and bed-wetting, the cruelty of the rest of the litter towards the runt. The memory brought with it a pinprick of guilt: his own role had not been beyond reproach.

What he said was: 'Of course you have my word.'

Timothy Kettle rose and closed the door.

Even at the moment of suspense as he waited to hear what Kettle had to tell him, he was dredging up another memory: as a schoolboy Otway had appointed himself to be Kettle's defender, which at the time Sam had found puzzling. Perhaps this fragment from the past was a clue to the main plot. Cursing Tuffet and his martinis, he tried to clear his head.

Timothy Kettle's story came from a world outside Sam's experience. Two years before the revolution, during the Suez war of 1956, a major pipeline carrying the nation's oil to the Mediterranean had been blown up. The British-owned oil company had lodged a record-breaking claim with Lloyds, its insurers. One syndicate that had underwritten part of the insurance was owned by the Kettle family and Timothy Kettle, who had gone into the family firm, had the task of investigating it. Many millions of pounds were riding on the outcome, and with them a sizeable portion of the Kettle family fortune.

The terms of the policy stipulated that it only offered protection against attack by external terrorists. In the event of sabotage by an internal revolutionary group, there was no protection.

'A sort of third party only policy,' Kettle explained.

But the culprits had never been identified. It was not a question of no suspects but of too many – almost every party with an interest in the Middle East might have had a motive.

The explosion happened on the Syrian border; and as Syria's relations with the old regime were deteriorating fast, on-the-spot investigations were not easy. The pipeline was never repaired.

At first it was assumed that it was just another casualty of the war, covered by the policy. But rumours got about; and Kettle's company began to have strong suspicions that the deed was in fact internal sabotage – the work of nationalists out to destabilise the old regime which depended on oil revenues. So they launched an investigation.

'Apparently,' said Timothy Kettle, 'you don't just blow up a pipeline with a homemade bomb. It is a major operation calling for professional skills and equipment. So it should have left traces somewhere. The monarchies in the area, together with Turkey, were members of the Baghdad Pact, a mutual defence treaty in which the British held the dominant role – the last throes of Pax Britannica. It was thought that the Pact files might throw some light on the affair.'

Before the revolution the embassy, eager to play down any suggestion of internal dissent, had been uncooperative. Nobody wanted to risk upsetting the apple cart to please a group of London insurance companies. Whitehall refused access to Pact files; the Foreign Office, out to upset nobody, refused all information. That left local sources. The old regime here, locked in Byzantine politics, was beyond reach.

Acting through specialised agencies, Kettle had set investigators to work. He had even put local nationals working in the Defence Ministry on his payroll to look up archived records that might be revealing.

He had also hired Horatius Otway.

'Of course,' Sam breathed. 'The oil project…'

'As it happened,' Timothy Kettle went on, 'Horatius turned out to be the most productive source of information of all.'

It seemed that Kettle had provided the finance to set Otway up locally as an art dealer, by way of a cover. Otway also occasionally worked as a string correspondent for *The Desert Times* to provide a pretext for his inquiries. All this had come with the promise of a really big reward if he could track down the information Kettle needed. Otway had got down to work, even learning good enough Arabic to deal in artefacts. Apparently he was beginning to get results: he reported having got hold of a classified document indicating military activity on the Syrian border at the relevant time involving a 'certain' group of officers. There was more, but Otway did not want to discuss it further on the telephone and would get a photocopy to Kettle as soon as he could.

'Then came the revolution and a black-out on all communications. Everything changed. In the old days a blind eye was turned when foreign contractors offered bribes to government officials. Now it is treated as treason. People have been put on trial and even executed. What was then just undercover investigation is now called espionage. If they discover what Horatius has been up to, anything might happen to him. And now that he's been arrested…'

The helpless eyes turned to Sam. 'Laura thinks the embassy is useless. And Colonel Shehab has told her to leave everything to him.'

'Colonel Shehab, the Interior Minister?'

'Yes. He was Horatius' top contact at the Defence Ministry in the old days, in charge of archives. Even then he was a high flyer, but without any known allegiances except to money. He asked big sums for his cooperation, but it was worth it to us. The three of us used to play chess, but we never quite knew where he stood. It wasn't particularly important at the time. What mattered was Horatius' access to the archives, although I don't know exactly what else he turned up, as he was arrested before he could tell me. Apparently Shehab signed a letter just before the revolution about which Horatius was very excited but, as I said, he didn't want to talk on the telephone.

'With the revolution Shehab was transferred from his defence post to be Interior Minister and put in charge of the police. Now suddenly everything depends on him, and he hasn't returned my calls. I suppose he would like to bury the past. And I don't know how much power he really has. He's only in charge of the civil and special police, but not the military branch.

'What about the British embassy?'

'Laura says they are useless. They want to be on terms with the new regime; and here was a huge potential anti-British propaganda coup being handed to it on a plate – a British imperialist spy prying into the nation's secrets.

'They tried to make Horatius agree to leave as quickly and quietly as possible, threatening to disown him publicly if he was caught. They advised me to stay away, too. But a source got a message to me that he had been arrested and I came out on the press flight, which got in earlier today.'

There was a long pause. Sam heard himself saying: 'Where do I come into this? Is there anything you want me to do to help?'

The helpless eyes turned on him again, Kettle said: 'You see, we don't even know where he is being held, and as a journalist you can travel without attracting s-suspicion.'

Idly Sam noted the return of the stammer, Kettle's stress signal.

20.

Outside the offices of *The Desert Times* barefoot street children were playing a game with ropes. It was the blank afternoon hour when the air turned to molten lead, and they had the world to themselves. Through slatted shutters in the empty newsroom Sam watched with growing curiosity as a boy lying trussed up on his back was pulled by two others through the hot dust to whoops of triumph. Another with withered legs, squatting on a barrel top that doubled as begging platform, followed behind, propelling himself along by his hands with astonishing dexterity. It was impossible to guess his age – he probably did not know it himself. Slowly the meaning of the game dawned on Sam. After setting fire to the British embassy, the revolutionary mob had lynched the ageing prime minister and dragged his naked body through the streets. The boys were doing what healthy children do: copying the grown-ups.

Sam, too, had been left to himself. *The Desert Times* went to press at noon after the Minister of Guidance's briefing, and Noori and his tiny staff had vanished. Sam had never felt more alone. The prospect of Otway being put on trial as a spy ticked away like a time bomb inside his head. Horatius Ariel Otway... Ariel, a free spirit from the invisible world, caught in a trap for earthlings...

Ten days had passed since his talk with Timothy Kettle. Quite what he expected of Sam was unclear. Kettle himself hovered in the background, restlessly disappearing and reappearing like an accusing ghost, seeming to expect him to do something. His parting words haunted Sam. 'As a correspondent you can travel about the country without raising suspicion. Once we know where he is being held...'

His voice had trailed off, the way Sam remembered in school Recital, into an inscrutable void.

If what Kettle expected of him was unclear, what Sam expected of himself was not much clearer. Even setting aside his fears, he had no idea where to start. He was like a detective with no clues. The embassy had already clarified its position: it would distance itself from any scandal damaging to Her Majesty's interests. Sam had repeatedly applied for an interview with Colonel Shehab and repeatedly, if politely, been told to be patient. Meanwhile he could not confide his secret about Otway's activities to anyone else, least of all Noori, who would risk arrest if found to be withholding information about an enemy of the state. At all costs it must be kept from the other correspondents: as a news item it would double as a death warrant for Otway. Nor, even had he wanted, could Sam consult head office with censors monitoring all communications.

Then there was Laura... But Laura had vanished on a hunt of her own, taking Timothy Kettle with her and leaving the shutters closed across the windows of the little fort. Sam was on his own.

For an office he had to make do with a desk in the news room, Noori having given up the editor's front room to the censor, a schoolmaster by training who had visited Moscow on a student grant and returned fired with revolutionary fervour that translated into a local brand of neo-Marxist Arab nationalism, earning him the trust of the new military regime.

The only link with the outside world was the incoming agency teleprinter, bringing Universal's world service to which *The Desert Times* subscribed for its foreign news, now silent in its corner. The censors had cut the line to London along with the telephone. The incoming line worked intermittently, seemingly by whim of the officials controlling it. Just then the machine came to life. Turning from the scene outside Sam glanced at the incoming tape; and found a message addressed to himself from head office.

Cork care Desert Times stop need matcher soonest
Empire News splash with Tuffet by-line on terrified
British families held at gunpoint in capital's main hotel

exclusive account smuggled out to evade Draconian censorship stop your instructions to return London soonest once Noori accreditation confirmed.

So the little man in his flat cap had his angle. Even so, it was strange: the only knowledge that Sam had of gunmen anywhere near the hotel were the two special policemen in grey uniform who lounged in the lobby and reluctantly got to their feet when a member of the regime appeared. Then he remembered the loquacious hotel barber with his grotesquely exaggerated tales of terrorised civilians...

Savagely he tore the message off the machine and put it in his pocket. It was all very well for the visiting foreign correspondents. If Universal sent a distorted story round the world, there would be enquiries, high level complaints, consequences for the resident correspondent and the agency's contractual arrangements. Tuffet was in the hit-and-run business, with a private charter to make his getaway. If he was challenged, he would not be besieged by guilt. His conscience lay not with the truth but with his paper's circulation figures.

In search of a 'matcher' Sam turned to the latest copy of *The Desert Times* lying fresh on the censor's desk.

Since the censor spoke only a few words of English, he took almost no part in either the editing or the censoring process, but Noori the pragmatist was not one for half measures. Leaving no stone unturned to keep in with the new regime (and thereby removing any impediments to his accreditation to Universal News), he had invited the former schoolteacher to advise on a new post-revolutionary layout. Beneath the masthead topped out with the flag of the new republic in place of the Union Jack the inch-high headline announced a speech, filling the front page, by the Minister of Guidance congratulating China on entering its second decade of socialism. The visit of a local trade delegation to Leningrad led the foreign page. There was an article on the Abominable Snowman, a report that Alitalia was to acquire its first jet airliner; news from Britain featured an election speech by Mr Gaitskell (promising controlled expansion under a Labour government) and another by Mr Macmillan (promising no interference under a Conservative one). The rest of the page was filled by an advertisement for *Son of Paleface* with Bob Hope, currently showing at the open air Sinbad Cinema. Horror tales from British families returning from the former kingdom had been prudently omitted: *The Desert Times* was as clean as a whistle. There was nothing remotely resembling a 'matcher' to be gleaned from it. The Alwiya club's poolside readership might react with derision, but as the paper had no competition there would be no loss of circulation. And no official complaints. It augured well for Noori's reinstatement as stringer correspondent for the agency. It made life easier for everyone.

Sam decided to return to the hotel.

As he put the paper down, an item caught his eye in the STOP PRESS column next to the Rupert Bear comic strip with the heading: TREASON AND CORRUPTION: 'The trials of enemies of the state will be held in public starting in the next few weeks and shown on the newly established national television network. Sentence has already been passed on some of the guilty parties.'

The story, wrung from the Minister of Guidance at his morning conference was an old one which Sam had already filed to London. But the day of reckoning was getting ever closer. A sickening dread settled in his stomach.

As he climbed into the waiting hotel taxi, another shriek, this time of protest, came from the playing children. Apparently it was someone else's turn to play corpse.

A voice interrupted his thoughts. 'You are Mister Cork.' The staccato delivery made it sound more like a statement than a question. Looking up Sam saw a pair of eyes watching him in the driving mirror. 'I have been away. With Mr Danvers Nelson. From the television. There is a message.'

Sam frowned. The famous television reporter had last been seen heading for the desert. 'A message from Danvers Nelson? He doesn't even know me.'

'A message from my brother. From Ramada.'

'What has this to do with me?'

'The message. Is for you.' The man pushed a scrap of cardboard over his shoulder. It had been torn from the cover of a packet of cigarettes. Sam turned it over. Hurriedly pencilled in block letters was the word PARAMARIBO!

That was all. For a moment he could not think. The exclamation mark alone opened the door on a corridor of memories. 'How did your brother get this? Have you seen Mr Otway?' The man put his finger to his lips. 'My brother is in the army at the garrison at Ramada. You must not tell about this. It will be very bad.'

'Does Mr Danvers Nelson know about this?'

'Mr Nelson he knows nothing. You must not tell…'

'What else can you remember? Did you see Mr Otway? Where is he now? It is very important.'

The man shrugged: not indifference, just fatalism. 'My brother did not say. All he said was your name. To give it to you. At the hotel.'

When they got there, Sam climbed out of the car and went round to the driver's window. 'Can you contact your brother?'

'It is very dangerous. That is all I know. Please…'

Ignoring the extra money in Sam's outstretched fingers, the man drove off.

Sam had to wait until that evening to see the MI6 man. Calling from his hotel room, he recognised the matronly voice of the embassy receptionist with the permanent wave. Mr Earnshawe was busy until six, but would see him then. Mr Cork would have to be sure to be punctual. Mr Earnshawe was a busy man.

The next item in the daily routine was a tea-time gathering at the pool in the British Club where correspondents formed temporary alliances to barter information and pick each other's brains. The afternoon heat, with leaden siesta following an expense account lunch, divided evening from morning as effectively as a second night.

Then came the daily briefing for British correspondents at the embassy. This was conducted by a meticulously courteous press officer who relished understatement (the old school, Sam noted, unlike Earnshawe). He insisted that he could not comment on the record, but undertook instead to 'do my best to help' by 'putting things into context'. The British press corps was only too happy for him to do their analysing for them. Towards the new regime he adopted the air of long suffering parent towards a distressingly errant offspring. At the same time he appeared to derive a quiet satisfaction from drawing attention to a growing split between its civilian and military elements, 'the velvet glove of milk-and-water socialism and the iron fist of real power'. He spoke in simple phrases ripe for the plucking, waiting to be turned into newspaper copy. Sam soon came to recognise that his guiding hand was subtle, shrewd and lethally effective. The signal he was sending that day in thinly disguised code was that the Ministry of Guidance had not long to survive and the Ministry of Defence, where the Leader had his headquarters, was taking over all the levers of power.

Every now and then a correspondent got away from the pack and the others, fearful of being scooped, checked his destination with the hotel taxi drivers. Danvers Nelson was one of these. Sam knew of the celebrated television reporter and regularly read 'Nelson's Column' with the Sunday tabloids, but had never met the man in person.

Like Tuffet, Nelson was also in the hit and run business. He had been spotted at the Ministry of Guidance on the first morning with his television crew: the veteran reporter had expressed interest, without batting an eyelid, in reassuring British viewers (as well as readers of Nelson's Column) how well the new regime was treating the British community. Promised full co-operation, he was last seen in a hotel taxi with a ministry guide heading into the desert.

After the embassy briefing, Sam waited impatiently on one of the ambassador's Chippendale chairs to see Earnshawe, leaving the other reporters to the rest of their routine. This consisted of a retreat to their hotel rooms to write their day's news story; then a meeting at the bar for last minute trading of titbits, and so to the censor and finally the cable office where the staff were only too happy to accept bribes to transmit each correspondent's copy ahead of his rivals.

The second secretary was punctual and, as predicted, in a hurry. This time he did not trouble to invite Sam to sit down. But he listened with close attention and without disparagement when Sam explained to him the significance of the private code word between Horatius and himself dating back to school days.

'From Ramada,' said Earnshawe thoughtfully. 'That means he is being held by military not civilian police.'

'Is that good or bad?' asked Sam.

'It means we know where to address our inquiries,' responded the other dryly. 'As you are aware the civilian politicians are being edged out of power. Several senior Baathist officials have already disappeared, some we have reason to believe have been executed for treason, in other words plotting to form alliances with other Arab states like the United Arab Republic of Egypt and Syria.'

'Would it help to go public? Let it be known to the media that the British government is demanding to know the fate of a British subject?'

Earnshawe snorted. 'If you want to seal Otway's fate once and for all. We don't know how much if anything they already know about his clandestine activities. He may have just been picked up by chance trying to leave the country illegally. On the other hand he may have been caught at his old tricks, embarrassing to everyone involved, not excluding HMG. A protest at this stage would be an invitation to the military to find a reason to put him on trial. It could well be fatal to force their hand. The best course is to wait and watch. These people are capable of anything: they are naïve, brutal and entirely unpredictable. You really must leave this to the professionals.'

Thoughtfully he went on, almost as if addressing himself: 'The key figure may be Colonel Shehab, according to Kettle Otway's one time informant when he was working at the Defence Ministry. He is the senior surviving civilian in the regime. It might not be in his interest to have Otway in court. It also suggests that Shehab may not have as much influence as he would like.' He broke off.

Hoping for a trade-off by way of some useful information in return, Sam recounted his conversation with Timothy Kettle, only omitting to mention where it had taken place. The other man heard Sam out with mounting impatience. It was clear to Sam he was not telling Earnshawe anything he did not already know.

'My advice to Kettle remains what it has always been: to stay put in London and keep his mouth shut. We'll keep him informed if we have further news of Otway.'

As Sam rose to leave, a thought seemed to strike Earnshawe: 'How did you contact Kettle with the telephone lines cut?' As Sam hesitated Earnshawe held his eye: 'Where is Timothy Kettle now?'

When Sam told him, the MI6 man looked as if he would explode.

'You realise he will be called as a material witness if they find out his connection with Otway? Who else has the bloody fool been blabbing to? Instead of swanning around the country courting arrest like a bunch of amateurs why can't your friends leave it to the professionals who know what they're doing?'

The repeated mention of professionals reminded Sam of his father's words overheard through the drawing-room door during a long forgotten argument with his mother. At the same time it was the first indication that Earnshawe might have something up his sleeve; if so, he was not sharing it with Sam. It was not the miracle he hoped for, but it at least it was a crumb of comfort.

'It's time your friends Kettle and Co. understood they are not at school any more. I need hardly remind you that this a dangerous place run by a Marxist zealot surrounded by gangsters. They don't play by the rules.'

The parting exchange left Sam feeling once more, even at this remove, that he was taking orders: 'And for God's sake, man, have the good sense to keep all this to yourself.'

Man – the language of the Victorian school bully. It was partly of Otway that he was thinking as he returned to the waiting taxi, but mainly he was asking himself why he had never learned to defend himself against the Earnshawes of this world.

He needed to clear his mind. At least he now had the clue of Horatius Otway's whereabouts. To put off the moment of rejoining the gaggle of visiting foreign correspondents, he stopped his taxi short of the hotel and decided to walk the rest of the way, despite the searing heat. Looking up he saw a pile of rubble.

The first thing he saw in the rubble was a grin. Then the figure of a small boy in rags, perhaps four years old, emerged and sprinted towards him; seizing his hand with both his own he lifted his feet off the ground. Sam crooked his arm to lift him and swung the feather-weight frame the air. The boy gave a shriek of pleasure. After two more swings he released himself and sprinted away again, shouting with triumph, towards the rubble from which he had come. A second later he was gone forever.

But not from Sam's mind. The seemingly trivial reminder of the immediate, simple, but vital priorities of childhood, so different from those of his adult self, stayed with him. He could not help wishing that his problems were as easily settled without the risk of the fearsome reprisals evoked by Earnshawe's words.

21.

Sam was still hoping for a miracle that would somehow lead to the rescue of Horatius Otway without having to expose himself to suicidal risk when *The Empire News* with Tuffet's article in it reached official eyes in the capital.

Glancing at the censor's desk while the former schoolmaster was in the newsroom, Sam saw the front page of the paper laid out on it. He had time to read the opening paragraph.

> I stood on the roof of the Arab Hotel as the New Republic's Air Force of six ageing fighters flew over-head. They passed once, then again, to create an illusion of numbers – like the Ruritanian army in a low budget theatrical production...

There was an invitation to readers to turn to inside pages for 'bloodcurdling eyewitness accounts of treatment of victims of the brutal regime'. One cited was the hotel barber.

'Ruritanian' was underlined in the censor's red ink. Lying beside the newspaper was a print-out of the earlier message from head office to himself where the words 'Draconian censorship' also bore a red mark. He wondered to himself how Noori, acting as the censor's interpreter, would translate them.

Even more, Sam wondered how the regime would respond. He did not have long to wait.

By that afternoon entry visas had been suspended. Unauthorised travel by correspondents more than ten miles outside the capital was forbidden. The morning press conference was transferred to the Minister of Defence where the correspondents were summoned to a midday briefing.

Armed soldiers frisked them as they stepped out of their taxis to enter the compound, surrounded by a wall of sandbags. In a spartan barrack room with sentries at each corner three men sat in silence at a table facing their audience. All were in uniform. Sam noted the fixed staring eyes of the one in the middle; it was the first time he had seen the Leader in person. On his right sat a stout man in glasses whom Sam recognised from photographs in *The Desert Times* as Colonel Mahdawi, the President of the People's Court (and effectively public prosecutor, rolled into one). On his left was Colonel Shehab, the Interior Minister, in the grey uniform of colonel of the special police. This, then, was Horatius Otway's former contact and chief informant. He had come along way since being charge of Ministry of Defence archives.

The trio formed the Revolutionary Council, which acted as ultimate authority in place of the murdered king and his prime minister. These were the men with the real power. The room crackled with awareness of their presence.

The Leader read out a prepared statement in Arabic in a high-pitched monotone, interrupting his chant for an interpreter to relay his words in English. Whatever dramatic effects it might have had were lost in the clichés of translation:

'All Arabs are brothers! The new Islamic Republic is dedicated to the good of all its citizens, to the cause of justice and mercy... Having thrown off the yoke of imperialism we extend a fraternal welcome to all our brothers in Islam... and the socialist world.

'In the coming weeks we will be announcing measures to bring forward our Modernisation Programme...'

For a man with a reputation for ruthless brutality, it was a curiously unimpressive performance. Except, thought Sam, for those zealot's eyes. Here was a man with no doubts, one of the hallmarks of tyranny.

The address was received in silence, the local reporters overawed, the international press corps wondering when to ask questions. Their dilemma was resolved when the Leader rose to his feet. An order rang out, a door opened and the trio processed from the room. A moment later the man in grey special police uniform was back.

Colonel Shehab, too, had an announcement to make. He did so

in near-perfect English, speaking quietly and looking straight into the eyes of the correspondents facing him.

'There has been a rearrangement of government responsibilities. The Minister of Guidance has too many commitments elsewhere to continue to take personal responsibility for the foreign press. In future the daily press conference will be held here by myself, as Interior Minister, at the Ministry of Defence.

'This measure follows inaccurate and damaging press reports concerning our revolutionary government and even our Leader himself... In view of these unfortunate lapses a new military censor has been appointed to ensure that a true picture of the new republic is disseminated to the world...'

He invited questions. So, Sam thought, Tuffet's article has really come home to roost. He felt rattled. The more seasoned *Times* correspondent was not put off his stride. Putting his hand up, he asked yet again for a date when the public trials would start.

The colonel remained unruffled. There was even in his eyes a twinkle that might have been humour, or was it just mockery? There was no question about who was in control in *this* classroom.

'They will start as soon as the machinery of justice is in place. The People's Court will ensure that all will get a fair trial.'

'What about the people you have already executed for treason?'

'We have only executed the guilty ones.'

'How do you know they are guilty if they haven't been tried?'

The colonel smiled comfortably and spread his hands: 'All of them confessed...'

A television film camera began to roll noisily in the back of the room. A BBC reporter asked: 'What is the point of announcing trials if you pre-empt them with summary justice?'

'What is the point of holding a trial of people who have already pleaded guilty?'

At the British embassy, the press officer gave his opinion in his world weary voice that the tightening of security following Tuffet's article – in his view no more or less inaccurate than other press stories the Foreign Office had to put up with day in day out – was a smokescreen to conceal a quiet internal coup by the inner group of Free

Officers who had masterminded the revolution and were determined to hold on to power against the politicians, in particular those of the Baath party who wanted to form a union with other Arab countries.

Their first move had been to make the Interior Ministry, and with it the internal police, answerable directly to the Ministry of Defence, under the Leader's overall fiefdom. The iron was beginning to show through the threadbare velvet. The press officer spoke with the air of someone with good sources. His assessment sounded convincing. It did not augur well for Horatius Otway.

Glancing at the Leader's written statement, the spokesman murmured: 'Ah yes, all Arabs are brothers – just like Cain and Abel.'

That, too, he hastened to add, was off the record. Of course, the correspondents said deferentially; and wrote down his words to be presented in due course to their readers as their own. In what sounded like a carefully rehearsed aside he suggested that it might be 'rewarding' to keep an eye on Colonel Shehab, 'yesterday not averse to the fleshpots of the west, today the voice of the regime. Colonel Shehab has already travelled a long way. It would be interesting to know what final destination he has in mind.'

Now the days rolled by with the unseen menace of a Greek drama, the action taking place elsewhere, reported by messengers to the characters on stage; the messengers being foreign correspondents who had found their way in and, unable to leave town, spent their time scavenging for news of the forthcoming treason trials and rumours of unrest; the stage moving from the Ministry of Defence where the deputy minister made claims for the advance of the revolutionary programme, to the British Embassy where the press officer quietly undermined them. Meanwhile the ambassador, waiting on a decision from London on its long-term policy towards the new regime, remained unavailable for interview.

After a week's waiting, Sam had an urge for the comfort of Aunt Olive's platitudes – it was Aunt Olive who had said to him when in an anguished rush he had told her about his betrayal of Otway as a schoolboy: 'Well, you did your best: and that's all any of us can do – our best'. Time had taught him that behind the platitudes was a will of iron. It was equally Aunt Olive who had taken it on herself to remove him from Illbury, and made it her business to overrule her brother in his prisoner of war camp. The difference between them was that, having done her best, Aunt Olive would go back to being her serene self. Sam's nature was to feel inadequate: doing his best was never enough. Just then all he longed for was an escape from the claustrophobia of the desert dustbowl. But there was no escape and nothing to do but wait in a limbo of uncertainty.

The wait came unexpectedly to an end with the arrival of an official car at the main entrance of the hotel. The driver, in smart police uniform, asked to speak with him.

'Colonel Shehab presents his compliments and requests that you accompany me to pay him a visit.'

They drove in silence to the Defence Ministry where Sam found the colonel waiting for him in an air-conditioned office wearing what Sam's eye recognized as a Savile Row suit, a handmade white silk shirt and impeccably knotted tie. A triangle, also white, and poking from his handkerchief pocket neatly offset that standard credential of Arab manhood, a well trimmed black moustache. His turnout was perfect, but for the want of that casual imperfection that would have made it look more authentic; perhaps in the colonel's line of business imperfections were a dangerous luxury. He proffered a steely smile and a handshake to match.

'Have a seat, Mr Cork.'

He sat opposite Sam in an upright chair, crossing his legs to display feet elegantly shod in polished black brogues. Lobb, thought Sam. Looking up he could not clearly make out the man's features against the window behind him. He recalled how in fiction interrogators sat with their back to the light. Perhaps not just in fiction?

'Your agency is seeking accreditation with our country's new government for a Pakistani national.'

'Noori has been here a long time working for us. The Minister of Guidance said it was a matter of confirmation. A formality...'

'It is difficult... It is better you find a correspondent born here in this country.'

'The trouble is it is also difficult to find anyone who speaks English and is trained in journalism.' Sam refrained from pointing out another difficulty, that there was certainly no other candidate who would not be a creature of the regime.

'You try…' The colonel spread his hands in a now familiar gesture. 'You try… A national would be more, let us say, acceptable to our new government.'

There was a silence. More to gain time than to satisfy his curiosity Sam looked around the room. His eye lighted on a chess set laid out as if for a game on a table in one corner. In particular he noted that the black pieces were not black, but dark green. He looked more closely to check a detail caught in his memory. The elaborately carved knights carried miniature lances. He had seen the set before; it was the one Otway had at school to play five-second chess, or an exact facsimile.

He felt the colonel's gaze on him, amused, reading his thoughts.

'I think you are a friend of Horatius Otway.'

Too surprised to think, Sam looked at the man blankly. Just then it was genuinely vexing not to be able to see his expression clearly.

'Also Tim-othy Kettle, recently here in the capital.' He pronounced Kettle's Christian name as if, like Sam before him, he, too, found it strange that he had one.

'We were all three at school together. But we met up here by coincidence.'

Without moving, Colonel Shehab said: 'Horatius Otway has been arrested.'

'Yes…'

'I would like to be able to help him. He and Timothy Kettle were my partners.'

Sam's brain was racing now.

'Your business partners?'

The colonel smiled easily. 'My chess partners. Horatius Otway presented me with this set. We played together. Before our revolution.'

Sam could feel rather than see the man's eyes on his face. 'I think you are in a position to help Horatius Otway.'

Sam said. 'Well, obviously, anything I can do. Anything at all… But how? Why me?'

'I will tell you.'

At that moment a manservant came in bearing a brass tray with cups of tea. When he had gone, the colonel resumed.

'Before the revolution – our revolution – our friend Horatius Otway was here trying to help his old school friend Kettle over some insurance claims against Kettle's firm to do with the oil pipeline to the Mediterranean that was blown up by unknown saboteurs at the time of the Suez war. As I am sure you are aware, it was insured against sabotage by enemies of our country, but not against internal saboteurs. Horatius Otway was looking for evidence that local dissident groups were responsible, in which case Kettle's firm would avoid paying out large – very large – sums of money. He consulted me, but I could not do much to help as most of the material was classified. In the course of his researches he began to play games, silly games, some of them involving forged documents. They are also dangerous games. With the revolution they came to be regarded as a more serious matter. They came to the notice of military intelligence. Military police do not have a reputation for being, let us say, subtle in their methods.

'I endeavoured to help him by advising him to leave the country and forget about the insurance claims. Unfortunately our friend was caught trying to escape illegally and arrested by the army. He is now waiting the decision of the public prosecutor. About that I can do nothing. It is a matter between military intelligence and the People's Court.

'But I have made certain inquiries. Most of the evidence against Otway consists of documents concerning the sabotage of the oil pipeline, some of them in part forgeries. But it has recently come to my attention that they include one document supposedly authenticating the findings in the other documents, using the names of senior people in government circles, including even my own.' The minister shrugged, as if to convey that the idea of his own involvement was too absurd to be taken seriously. 'Of course it is a silly forgery, but it would be unfortunate if a court believed it to be authentic. Unfortunate for the people he has named and unfortunate for Horatius Otway, who could be exposed to a charge of military espionage.'

Fearful of revealing the tremor that had begun to affect his hand, Sam left his teacup untouched on the table beside him.

'I don't quite see how I come into this.'

'I think you are an intelligent man. I have reason to believe this document has not yet reached London, but some of its contents were recently leaked by a clerk in the Defence Ministry at the time. If Timothy Kettle uses it in London to dispute the claim, Otway's part will come out. This will be very bad. For Horatius Otway, you understand. You should explain this to him.'

'And maybe even worse for you,' thought Sam. Aloud, he said: 'Haven't you already told him?'

'The last time I spoke to him the question of the document had not come up. And Timothy Kettle made no mention of any document.'

'I can't imagine Kettle doing anything to endanger Horatius.'

'He might not quite understand the implications. It is best to be sure. Quite sure,' said the colonel. 'Quite sure the document is destroyed and never referred to again. Naturally I do not want to interfere personally until this question is cleared up. As I said, it is a military matter. I can, however, perhaps arrange for you to talk to our friend, in your role of foreign correspondent conducting an interview, before it is too late.'

Sam was struggling to keep up. There was a lot he could not follow. 'But why me? Why can you not say this to him yourself?'

'Because the information has only just come to light, and it is best to handle these matters, shall we say – diplomatically. It is too late to approach Kettle. The hotel register shows that he left three days ago.'

'I think he is still in the country…' The words came out before Sam had time to think.

'I was not told of this,' said the colonel softly. 'Why was I not told of this?' he muttered again, to himself. He turned to pick up a telephone on his desk. A staccato question in Arabic followed by what Sam took to be invective poured into the machine. There was a new edge to the man's voice, the policeman's uniform showing under the Savile Row suit. He turned back to face Sam.

'Who told you Kettle was still here?'

It sounded like an accusation. Once more that sub-plot called the past came back to life. All he needed to say was that he overheard some journalists talking at the bar, but he knew it wasn't so, and his mind refused to improvise: he knew precisely that it was Noori who had told him that Kettle and Laura had gone off together to try to track down the whereabouts of Horatius; equally that he must not say so or Noori might somehow be implicated and lose his last chance of re-accreditation.

He said: 'I can't remember.' It sounded reasonable. Then to make it more convincing he added: 'I really can't remember.' But it came out wrong, with a hesitant edge.

The colonel did not move.

'Where is Kettle now?'

'I don't know.'

It was the truth. The trouble was that in the past the truth had frequently proved fatal. He needed to gain time until he could think clearly. Horatius would have thought of a way out. But he was not Horatius. All he could do was stall, play for time. Silence would be progress of sorts, a tiny tactical victory, inches gained in the long drawn out trench war against his past.

'And you are quite sure you don't remember who told you Kettle was here.'

'No, I don't recall.'

There was another pause. This time the colonel ended it.

'Well if he's here we'll find him.'

The colonel was himself again, in control. He resumed a veneer of affability as he rose to his feet.

'So,' he said. 'You will let me know the moment you hear anything of Timothy Kettle's whereabouts.'

'I understand,' said Sam.

But he still didn't.

'And maybe I can help you in other ways, as a friend of Horatius. With the problem of accreditation. Also perhaps news. Your agency likes scoops, I think you call it that?'

'Yes. Very much.'

'Tomorrow we shall be announcing at the press conference the intention of nationalising all our oil resources, including the British company that runs most of them. If you say that in your despatch tonight you will have a scoop I think?'

'And can I quote you as the source?'

'Naturally… I will arrange for the censor not to give you any difficulties.'

At the door they shook hands again. Sam paused, trying to assemble some of the unasked questions he had not had time to formulate. He asked the first to come into focus in his head.

'When will it be possible to see Horatius?'

'Soon… I hope. I will be in touch… Very soon.'

The steel smile gave nothing away. Even so Sam's head was clear enough to recognize that what he was being offered was not a favour, but a deal. The colonel needed to protect himself. If Sam did what he wanted, he would ensure Noori's appointment, perhaps even Horatius' release. Meanwhile, as a foretaste of more in store, a scoop or two would be thrown in to boot. But there was still a piece missing in the puzzle: why did Shehab want to use him, Sam, to talk Horatius into doing his bidding, rather than doing it himself? In their talk he had been evasive on the subject.

That evening while Sam waited in *The Desert Times* newsroom, the teleprinter in the corner stuttered into life. He felt a buzz of pleasure to read his own words coming back from London, checked and edited by the subs desk, leading the world news of the day and carrying his own name as by-line. Perhaps they would make worldwide headlines. Such a thing never happened in Obits.

Shehab had been as good as his word. The censor had given him no trouble. He had even allowed Sam to send a service message that Noori was safe and awaiting accreditation. He did not mention that this was now imminent: the nearest he could get to taking action to defend Otway was to stay as close to Shehab as possible. But he alerted Noori to watch for the green light.

The Pakistani put his head to one side. 'It is vital also for London to understand that it is not possible to operate as a fully accredited agency correspondent without the credentials of membership of the British club.'

Sam was all too conscious of the deeper motive: even as they spoke, she sat waiting patiently for her afternoon swim in Noori's car outside. He looked into the pleading eyes – 'I'll have a word with the club secretary – the moment the accreditation is confirmed.'

At the hotel bar that evening he recognised the famous features of the veteran correspondent Danvers Nelson, older and fleshier than the face known to millions at the top of 'Nelson's Column'. And redder, he thought, than his image on black-and-white television suggested. Watching this modern Falstaff as he held court, gesturing with his hands, indiscriminately addressing as 'Dear boy' the group that instinctively gathered round him, Sam felt an instant aversion. In return to listening to his adventures, and how he had given his guide the slip, his fellow correspondents got to buy him champagne and call him Tom, the name known to his intimates that he had borne until his newspaper had thought up Danvers.

Someone asked if he would be at Shehab's next press conference.

'Alas, dear boy, tomorrow's morning visit to the Defence Ministry is a pleasure I shall have to forego. An accommodating pilot has kindly offered his services...'

Like Tuffet, he would not be there to face the music.

No one took any notice of Sam: news of his scoop had not yet reached the bar of the New Arab Hotel. He ordered a whisky and installed himself in a dark corner at the far of the room and went over the day's developments.

His first image was of the chess set with the black pieces carved in green, the only personal item in Colonel's Shehab's office. Clearly he had intended Sam to notice it as a talisman of his friendship. But something was wrong. Like his Savile Row suit, the minister's concern for Horatius sat ill with the cold watchful eyes that had fastened on him as he left the room with his scoop and the half promise to help with Noori's accreditation. Sam was conscious that Shehab was playing a deeper game than he had revealed, with himself and Timothy Kettle as expendable pawns. Horatius clearly had a higher value, but exactly what, and exactly what longer-term strategy was Shehab following? Sam did not have enough information to think the necessary number of moves ahead. Not knowing redoubled his unease.

By chance it was the ever-conscientious Noori who unwittingly supplied the missing piece of information. He came over to bring it to Sam from the bar where he had made himself a part of the Danvers

Nelson fan club to pick up crumbs. Among these was a report that relations between the court president and Shehab, the two heirs apparent in the Revolutionary Council, had reached an all-time low ebb, with Mahdawi letting drop hints of information damaging to his rival.

Ready as ever to parade his command of English idioms, Noori said: 'It is a fight with no holes barred.'

'Holds.'

Noori nodded enthusiastically.

'Yes. To the death.'

Noori did not know the source of the reports, but Sam thought he detected the hand of the embassy press officer. Noori drifted back to the bar.

It fitted. The Leader was single-mindedly dedicated to his mission of forming a socialist Arab state, regardless of the power struggle taking place around him. The politicians, seeing the advantages of closer links with other Arab states, were losing ground: already their Baath party flag was disappearing from public buildings.

Of the Leader's two acolytes, Shehab, the civilian and a politician by nature, was in the weaker position. Sam concluded that Colonel Mahdawi was on the scent of evidence damaging to Shebab, doubtless to do with his involvement in Horatius' oil project; and the military element would close ranks behind Mahdawi. This would explain why Shehab did not want to be seen to be tackling Horatius directly. Instead he would use Sam. But exactly what was Sam going to be asked to do? And what was this document? Was it really a forgery (a Horatius Otway speciality) or had Shehab indeed once been incautious enough to let his name, even his signature, be used so as to earn his doubtless generous fee? Either way spelt serious trouble for Horatius.

And for Sam. He pulled out Otway's note: 'Paramaribo!' The single word was a summons, stark and unequivocal, and it was addressed to him. There was no way out.

Was this an assignment from the gods, his second chance, an opportunity to redeem himself? After he, Sam, had failed the test so dismally that first time were there any grounds to suppose that he had grown the necessary courage in the interim? Was such a change possible? There were some signs of it in Timothy Kettle: Sam had noticed his new assertiveness since the days long ago when he had been the butt of schoolboy contempt. But what of himself?

Then he remembered that Parents' Day at Illbury two decades before when he had finally shown a flash of steel. True, it had come too late to change the outcome; and true, he had had Aunt Olive as an ally and protector. But he had discovered in himself a new determination he had been unaware of possessing. It had been an act of revenge, executed with fearlessness, powered by rage. And it had tasted sweet.

Perhaps after all he was not quite the wimp he had imagined himself to be ever since his betrayal of Horatius Otway.

22.

A scene change took place at the bar of the New Arab Hotel as Danvers Nelson and his party moved noisily into dinner, taking their mood of euphoria with them. They left behind a darkened stage.

Solitude had schooled Sam in the low level erotic charge of bars at the moment when a nicely judged dose of alcohol freed the imagination to weave fantasies out of the human props around him. He was wondering what would follow Falstaff's exit when his travelling eye spotted a figure he had not noticed before. Where the smooth leather and teak of the bar counter curved away into the far corner of the room a girl sat hunched in her own shadow, her small boned shoulders gathered up like a bird against a storm. Her back was three-quarters turned to him. For a moment the light splashed her face as she looked up to order a refill of vodka. It was several seconds before he recognised Laura.

It was the movement as much as the features that singled her out, awkward and graceful at the same time, a delicate enigma from a world where Falstaff's bluster had no place. The scene change was complete.

He became aware of an increase in his heartbeat as two thoughts flashed simultaneously into his head: he had a message that would win Laura's attention; but at some time he would have to tell her he was under orders to return to London, abandoning her brother to his fate.

He was silently grateful for the alcohol as he walked toward her. 'I've got news. Of Horatius.'

Her forehead narrowed into a frown. He felt like an intruder, claiming entry into her private lair. At any moment she would scratch his eyes out. The slightly slanted frowning eyes never left his while he told her about the note from Horatius.

'Did you get the name of the driver?'

'I think he's called Sayid.'

'Sayid... He-e's all right.' Though by now familiar with the lilt in her voice, it still took Sam by surprise. It was part of her private language, exclusive to herself, inaccessible to the uninitiated. 'I'd better go and look for him.' She started to get to her feet.

'There's something else. I was called in today to see Colonel Shehab. He was asking about Horatius.'

She sat down again. 'He can't be trusted.' She spoke with finality. 'Horatius said so. He used to be Horatius' friend.' She added, as if she was accusing Sam: 'He's a kil-ler.'

'He said he could help Horatius. He seemed to think I could help him recover a document he was planning to give, or already had given, to Timothy Kettle. He assumed Timothy had gone back to London. Some sort of forgery, he said it was. He said it was important. For Horatius. But I think it was just as important for Colonel Shehab. At least it's a lead. I thought you might know something.'

She appeared not to be listening. 'Horatius always trusted too many people.' After a pause she went on: 'So that was it. I thought it was the paintings.'

Sam could only wait. Along with the voice went her convoluted private thought process. 'Later on the day you came to the house a man tipped us off that the police wanted to search it. I recognised him as one of Horatius' former government contacts. I thought it was to do with the paintings, so I took them down and left them with a friend. When I came back today I found them there – the police, I mean – but not just ordinary police, the security police who work for Colonel Shehab. They didn't ask me about paintings, or the antique writing tablets. They were after documents. I realised it was more serious then, and I knew Horatius had left an envelope with documents behind one of the paintings because I sewed it in for him. They said they were coming back. I still don't know what they were after. Horatius always said it was best that I didn't know too much so I couldn't get tricked into talking. Even Timothy only hinted that the more serious matter had to do with work Horatius was doing with him.'

'There's nothing more we can do tonight. But I think I can tell you a bit more about the more serious matter. Look, the hotel bar is perhaps not the best place to talk. You can assume someone is listening in. Let's go and eat something and I'll tell you all I know. The food's bad in the dining room, but it's the only place I know.'

Suddenly she looked drained, the suspicion in her eyes turned to fear, as if of a trap, the way she had looked when he had first seen her in the desert bus. Sam ordered the barman to fill their glasses, conscious that it would be one more drink than he wanted. What he needed above all was a clear head: equally it was one drink she needed.

'I know a place. Horatius uses it. In the river bank. In fact it is run by a cousin of Sayid's. And there won't be any press.'

She seemed oblivious of the insult.

Firelight etched hollows in her cheekbones and set tiny shadows the shape of seashells swinging under her ears where the bare neck ended and delicate line of her jaw began. They were sitting on wooden crates on a jigsaw of dry mud that formed the exposed part of the river bed in summer. Eating local river salmon baked in the boatmen's braziers, he told her all he knew about the oil project. She must have already guessed at most of it. At first it was as if she was only half listening. Then, quite slowly, she smiled.

'So that was what Horatius meant.'

'About what?'

'About going for the grand slam. He was always talking about making a grand slam. When he decided to come out here he said it again.' She was not really even talking to him, but to herself. 'I told him Kettle didn't look like a man with a grand slam up his sleeve. Horatius just laughed. He always laughed.'

She too was smiling, a little ruefully. It was as if Sam had just put his cards on the table and laid down a grand slam against her.

'And will you be on the next press plane out?' She sounded almost casual.

Afterwards he thought, the answer was easy. The price of taking the risk of staying on was high. The price of not taking it was a thousand times higher. 'No. No, I won't.' He omitted to mention the factor of waiting for Noori's accreditation. 'I am waiting for Shehab to get me access to Horatius.'

'I can come with you. If you can get me a pass.'

'I don't know what he has in mind, but I doubt it will be like that.'

Quite suddenly her mood seemed to change.

'The Europeans don't dare risk it here.' It was the first time he had heard her laugh, a lazy, amused chuckle that made his heart leap. It was like a prize, an inch gained in his war of attrition. 'Horatius claims his stomach was galvanised by a decade of English public school hygiene; he eats the skin as well.'

Solid nourishment began to dissipate the effects of alcohol, and Sam's unease began to return. As though he needed to establish his credentials, he started eating the crisp skin. She said nothing. He took her silence as a rebuff. An inch lost.

'Did Horatius tell you we were friends at school?'

'I don't think Horatius thought much of school.'

Another rebuff. Another inch. Another silence. He cursed himself for not knowing how to break it. Then she surprised him by volunteering: 'Horatius and I had the same mother. Different fathers.'

'What is your family name?'

'Anastasia Katerina Laurentina Fitzwilliam.'

He was on the point of explaining 'I meant surname...' when he stopped himself. Something in his memory surfaced to break the vicious spiral. He was looking across to where boatmen squatted on their haunches beside the fire at the river's edge. A picture floated into his mind, dancing in the flames.

It was Parents' Day at Illbury. He was launching Kettle's model submarine with the freshly painted swastika in the swimming pool. He became aware that he was being watched by a beautiful woman and a girl with dark eyes, long nose and a hat which seemed too old for her years. She had followed him. He had asked her name. He remembered her reply. Then as now she had made it sound like a single word.

Laura was talking again. This time he broke in: 'Didn't you come to Illbury once? You wore a straw hat. And you said your name the same way as just now.'

'My mother made me wear that hat. I ha-ated it.'

She ignored the rest of his question. He resigned himself to another conversational cul-de-sac. Then she went on: 'I hated my name. She made me say it too. I felt stupid. I changed it to plain English Laura. Laura was enough. Quite enough.' He thought she had come to another stop, when the strange voice continued: 'The trouble with my family is they don't know about enough – enough being enough, that is. It runs in the blood. Our mother is part Ukrainian.' She said it with finality, as if that explained everything. 'At least my father was Scottish. But it's on both sides as far as Horatius is concerned. Irish and Slav, a bit of Jewish thrown in.'

The common factor in their separate trains of thought was that they all led back to Horatius.

'He was always on about the grand slam,' the curious voice droned on. 'It's why we did not leave when the revolution was imminent. He said he stood to make a kil-ling if he stayed. He was confident he would.' She paused to frown at the darkened central channel of the river where the water flowed faster on its stately thousand-mile journey to the ocean. 'Horatius always had confidence.'

Sam said: 'Timothy should have told him to leave.'

'I don't think he could talk Horatius out of it.'

'And by staying now himself he's a danger to Horatius. As a possible witness… And even if his company had to pay out he could still afford to cut his losses.'

'Oh, Timothy's presence was never just about money. It was a question of loyalty. He always had loyalty towards Horatius.'

She stopped again to stare at the river. 'Of course I don't have it.'

'I should have thought you had loyalty in abundance.'

'Co-onfidence… I don't have self co-onfidence. Not like Horatius.'

Sam was taken aback. It had never crossed his mind that this exotic and, to him, intimidating creature should not be sure of herself.

He was never certain afterwards exactly when it happened. Had it already started much earlier as he watched her climb down from the bar stool at the hotel to come to dinner with him? Was it when she asked him to come back to the little fort to look for clues as to what the police were searching for? Or was it at that moment when she permitted herself that first, faint smile as she acknowledged her own vulnerability?

Whichever it was, as they set off in the little boat piloted by the silent standing figure of Sayid's cousin, he was suddenly sure he had found what he had been searching for for as long as he could remember. An oceanic certainty enveloped him, taking him back to a morning when he had stood near a creosote fence outside the family bungalow and felt the presence of his mother sleeping behind the drawn blinds of the window a few feet away, and he had been filled with love for the whole world. That had been the dress rehearsal: this was the real event.

The rush of water past the prow of the boat as carved its way upstream towards the fort's landing-stage made his head swim. He was swept along by a feeling at once elusive, desperate and sublime, whose cosmic importance was beyond question. A fierce joy made his heart sing; he wanted to cry out to the river gods. He held the key to the universe within his grasp.

He took a deep breath of evening air, but awareness of Laura's proximity only served to intoxicate him more. It did not occur to him that just then she might not be thinking of him at all, but only of Horatius.

The whisky had done its work.

Sayid's cousin cut his engine as they reached the landing-stage. Sam was touched by the man's good manners as, promising to find Sayid and send him round, he bowed and held out both hands for payment, before slipping silently downstream into the night.

The door opening on to the river at the back of the courtyard of the little adobe fort had been left ajar so as to catch the first gusts of the *shamal* breeze that would bring relief from the high summer sun. But there was no relief. Inside the air was motionless.

The courtyard showed signs of a search abandoned halfway through. Some of the rugs had been turned over, to reveal bare paved floor. The cushions of a basketwork sofa had been piled on top of one another; where Laura had removed the oil painting of cherries there was a bare wall; some prints remained. Several tables carrying trinkets were untouched. Others, where Horatius kept samples of early writing on cuneiform tablets and Mesopotamian cylinder seals, were bare where Laura had removed them for safe-keeping from prying eyes.

The silver candlesticks and china coffee service were in their places. A wedge of folded paper had been tucked under one of the carved wooden legs supporting the tray where the paving was uneven. On a whim Sam pulled it out: it was a press card signed by Noori, with a photograph of Otway certifying that he was a representative of Universal News. Clearly Noori had been using his initiative to get access to the Alwiya Club: had it been authorized, Sam would have been told by head office.

'Horatius must have forgotten it,' Laura said. 'Anyway the real search has been happening in here.' He followed her to the door in the courtyard that had been locked on his last visit. 'He keeps his pictures in here: I removed most of them.'

It was open now. Sam eyed desk the blank walls and easels with no canvasses. The drawers and pigeonholes of a mahogany desk had been emptied on to the floor. Papers lay where they had been thrown. The searchers had even found the little secret compartment for photographs, love letters and wills. It was empty.

'He used that for stationery, I remember.'

Inside the little compartment a corner of white paper had slipped down a crack. Sam pulled at it. His hand came out with two unused sheets of writing paper bearing the royal crest, and headed: *Ministry of Defence*. He looked at Laura. She answered his unspoken question with a shrug.

'He collects headed writing paper. It is a sort of challenge – the harder to get the better: he gives himself marks for inaccessible items: once he wrote from school on Buckingham Palace paper. It was always one of his hobbies.'

'Have you any idea what has been taken?'

'He kept what he called his office in a briefcase. I can't find it anywhere. He must have taken it with him. Otherwise it's just this mess.'

Sam felt helpless. There did not seem to be any more he could do.

He looked across to where Laura stood; white-faced, aloof, a text he could not decipher. Smelling defeat, he imagined walking home. He would not mind the curfew; it was the voice inside him condemning his faint heart. To hide his indecision he was about to say:

'In the morning I will make the arrangements with London, and maybe we can go to Ramada together when the moment is ripe...' when she interrupted his thoughts:

'We could go on the roof.'

A wooden ladder in the hallway led them up to an open trapdoor; on the flat roof above, like a stage set inside a dragon's mouth waiting for the play, a rooftop eyrie lay open to the sky; the dragon's teeth of the battlements silhouetted against a pale night sky served as floats; more rugs, bolsters and coloured fabrics covered the floor. The girl lit a brass lamp and the outline of an iron four-poster bed rose out of the darkness, its columns pointing upwards to infinity and down to where its feet rested on four glass ashtrays filled with water to repel invading insects. Overhead a green ensign fluttered like a prospector's claim.

Laura stretched on a *kilim* carpet beside a heap of cushions: 'Our private place,' she said. She poured drinks from a tray. 'It's ravishing,' Sam said, putting his hand to the carpet he was sitting on, in part from genuine admiration, in part from delicacy lest he should appear to be hypnotised by the bed.

'That rug came from India. Milo was there in the war. He sent us things. He and Mama never really lost touch.'

He surmised that Milo was Horatius' father. He vaguely recalled some Indian connection to do with stamps.

'Didn't your own father mind?'

'He was dead by then. Killed at Dunkirk. Anyway Milo was always more like my real father.'

'My father was taken prisoner outside Dunkirk.' She did not react. It was another wrong turning. He seemed unable to resist the compulsion to claim every link, however banal. Cursing himself he went stupidly on: 'He was a Gunner. Royal Artillery. What was your father's regiment?'

'I think it was Scots Guards. Horatius didn't do national service.'

And every turning led back to Horatius. He felt a twinge of jealousy for the incestuous bond between half brother and sister. It was an impossible advantage played against him to repel every advance, excluding him. He was like one of the insects doomed to perish in one of her ashtrays in the vain assault on the impregnable fortress.

He decided to try another tack. Picturing again the strange pair of migrant birds sitting on a bench by the Illbury swimming pool, he asked: 'And were you very close to your mother?'

'A bit too close at times. She used to beat us with a hairbrush. We hid from her. We had secret places even then. We were closer to Milo.'

'Did they get back again together, after your father's death?'

'Oh no. Milo was never really the marrying kind. I suspect that Mother made him marry her in the first place. She usually got her way – first time round, but once bitten twice shy. He used to send us running-away money with instructions not to tell her. That is, when he was flush.'

It was the longest speech he had heard her make.

'Where is he now?'

'We don't ask. The last sighting was Barcelona. But there are gaps. The last one was after some trouble over pictures – to do with attributions. He always had a marvellous eye, but was vague over facts. There was "Pupil Of" and "School Of" and just plain "After". "After" didn't fetch as much. When he was selling a picture he used to ask people straight out how old they wanted it to be. He used to say he was in the antiqu-ing business: he could work wonders with Portobello Road vellum. And frames. He was good at giving things patina. Most of his customers seemed quite satisfied. One or two made a fuss.'

'Like the ambassador's wife?'

It was out before he had time to think. Too late he wanted to bite off his tongue. He had not just confused father and son; he had risked giving mortal offence. To his amazement she did not seem at all put out.

'Oh no. Lady Quicke didn't mind. It was only that Earnshawe trying to show off to the ambassador over the tomato picture. It was really all a storm in a teacup. A fuss about attributions. Again a question of "School Of" versus "After".'

It had been a double mistake. He had not just confused Horatius with his father: he had reckoned without the power of her loyalty. She was not annoyed at the implied accusation against her brother because she did not see it. It was then that he understood that she was quite simply impervious to any suggestion that Horatius could do wrong. Sam felt a thousand miles away.

He could never understand what happened next – perhaps she, too, sensed a defeat? All he knew was that just at the moment when he was preparing a retreat the elusive unknowable creature chose to sound the advance. Casually, almost, the velvet voice said:

'I suppose we might as well make lo-ove.'

23.

He woke to the glory of the morning desert. Through his closed eyelids the silken silver half-light of a false dawn filtered into his consciousness, followed soon by the brilliance of a rising sun. Finally he half opened his eyes: everything round him appeared made of solid gold, the sky, the battlements of the little fort itself, even the uprights of the four-poster bed.

Slowly he drifted back into a dream in which he had been presented with a key of gold with which he would be able to solve the universe. He felt a serenity he had not known since childhood. Then, suddenly remembering where he was, he sat upright. Wide awake now, he put out his hand and felt the bed empty beside him. His last vision of Laura had been of eyes closed neatly in her sleep, her body curled like a cat against his, in repose so complete that his fears melted to nothing in the velvet of the night.

After five seconds of panic, from somewhere below came reassuring kitchen sounds. Soon she appeared, hair twisted into a bun, with two mugs of Nescafé. She was smiling.

'I have word from Horatius.'

Sam pushed aside the unwelcome thought that she was pleased for Horatius, not for him, Sam. This time he was included in her smile; from now on relations were on a different plane. Included. He was included. Sipping his Nescafé, sitting next to her on the bed, he still could not believe his fortune. He had an unfamiliar sensation which he recognized as something akin to happiness.

'Sayid left it this morning. He came by early, directly from Ramada'.
'What did it say?'

'Actually it was five words: "Keep cherries safe send cigs!" They must have taken away his pen, as he normally writes in green. But it's his writing all right.'

'Keep cherries safe? What does it mean?'

'I don't know. As I explained, Horatius thought it best to keep me in the dark. But there's a painting of cherries that used to hang downstairs. It's the one I was talking about earlier. He got me to sew an envelope with documents in it into the back of its canvas. The canvas was double thickness so you couldn't see it with the naked eye. I never gave it another thought. He was always doing that sort of thing.

'I suppose he took copies with him and these were the originals.'

'Where is the painting now?'

'Oh it's quite safe, with the other paintings. Presumably the message means he needs it for some reason. I'd better go and get it.'

'It sounds as if may have to do with what Shehab is looking for.'

She had no answer. 'When do you think you'll be going to see him?'

That depends entirely on Shehab. But pretty soon. He seemed in a hurry. The trouble is, I will almost certainly be searched going in. I don't fancy carrying an envelope full of secret papers. I wonder what happened to whatever copy Horatius took with him.'

There was nothing for her to say. In silence she showed him the note, again on a torn-off strip of a back of a cigarette pack.

'Odd, as he doesn't smoke. But it's definitely his handwriting.'

Sam's eye had caught something else by way of confirmation: after the single word there was the reassuring exclamation mark. Yes, it was from Horatius all right.

Heading back to the hotel in his taxi, Sam felt the surge of a new determination. Thanks to Laura, his courage had grown wings. His moment had come, and he was ready, or as ready as he ever would be, to put it to the test. A demon had been if not vanquished, at least tethered. He would find a way. He would not miss his second chance.

It came sooner than he had expected.

As the taxi ground its way to the hotel entrance, he saw that its flagpole was bare where the Baath party flag had flown until the evening before. In the entrance hall itself, instead of the sleepy policemen in grey uniforms, there was a small contingent of soldiers. The shift of power behind the scenes was beginning to show.

And in the hallway there was Shehab's driver.

'The minister would like you to come at once to his office,' he said. He had been waiting since breakfast time.

From the front desk Sam made a quick call to Noori. The Pakistani was excited. 'Show trials are starting tomorrow and will be transmitted live on the recently established local television network. The minister announced it at his press conference. I have prepared a despatch to London.'

Sam told him to take it to the censor for transmission at once. Then he hung up and tried Timothy Kettle's room. To his surprise there was an answer. Timothy Kettle's only news was that Earnshawe had strongly cautioned him to lie low and catch the next press plane out, so he wasn't planning to leave his room. Sam said he would look in on his way back from the ministry.

On the way to the ministerial office Sam tried to clear Laura from his thoughts. But he welcomed his renewed sense of purpose as he went over the new developments, lending added urgency to Shehab's plans: the nationalisation of the oil companies and announcement of the start of public trials both brought the risk of a new focus on Otway's activities. All too well Sam understood why it was vital for Shehab to dispose of any evidence of his own involvement.

The minister's appearance betrayed no signs of any concern he may have felt. He was his normal self as he shook Sam's hand, his face a mask of impassiveness: a strong man in full control of himself, intelligent, ambitious and wholly untrustworthy.

'We missed you at this morning's press conference. And you missed the announcement of the start of the trials.'

'Noori, the agency's provisional stringer, covered for me,' said Sam. Then, going straight to the point: 'I suppose the start of the trials may not be good news for Horatius Otway?'

'That remains to be seen. He is not a big fish, and corruption is probably not high on the prosecutor's agenda. The leaders of the old regime charged with treason will come first. But just in case, I have arranged for you to go and see him right away. My car will take you to Ramada this afternoon. The military police there have been given to understand that the reason for your visit is to confirm that he is being treated correctly, mainly to satisfy the British Consulate. You may even be allowed to see him unsupervised. The most important part of your mission is to convey to him, privately, that I have ways to have him and his sister put on a plane home once he has handed over to me any documents to do with his past inquiries into the oil pipeline explosion. It is also vital for him to undertake not speak of them to anybody. It seems there are names, even signatures, some forged. Lives could be at stake.'

'Meaning yours,' thought Sam. Then he had an afterthought: 'Also, perhaps that of Horatius.'

'This is a matter of urgency... Your task is to bring me his agreement in principle to the exchange. Then I can arrange for his release.'

Quite how the arrangement would be worked in practice was not explained. Sam thought it best not to ask, but to play along so long as the minister's interests and his own coincided. After that, unless Otway had other ideas, he would have to trust to instinct: perhaps even consult Earnshawe.

After a short pause the minister said: 'My car will pick you up at three o'clock.'

The interview was over.

He found Kettle in his room with the door double-locked. He gave him a brief resume of events, and tried to ring Laura but there was no answer from the little fort. Sam surmised that she had gone to collect the cherry picture. He asked Timothy Kettle to tell her he did not propose to take any documents with him on this, his first visit to Horatius.

Punctually at three o'clock the minister's car arrived and Sam climbed in carrying a carton of 200 cigarettes, purchased from the little gallery of shops on the hotel's ground floor. To his astonishment and delight there was another passenger in the back seat: it was Laura.

'Shehab seemed to think my presence might help persuade Horatius to agree to his proposal.' Indicating the driver with a sidelong glance, she added: 'I haven't brought anything with me.'

The journey to Ramada was without incident. At each road block the ministerial car was recognised and waved through. Meanwhile Sam felt Laura's natural elusiveness return. Although he longed to take her in his arms, he knew he must not even touch her in the presence of the Muslim driver; but her very presence, combined with the warmth of memory, more than made up for it. He was beyond contentment. A certain serenity had settled deeply within him, as if there to stay. However high the stakes, they were in an adventure together. He was included.

Finally they came to a military encampment. The driver spoke to a sentry on guard, who let them into a compound containing a squadron of British built Second World War tanks, surrounded by high barbed wire. They stopped outside a long low building, which gave on to a parade ground; here Shehab's driver let his passengers out, before parking his car under a tree. He did not leave the driving seat. Sam and Laura entered the building alone.

Far from the guardhouse he had been expecting, it turned out to be an officers' mess. There was a reception desk where a uniformed sergeant appeared to be expecting them. There was no question of an identity check, let alone any kind of body search.

'Major Haddid is waiting for you,' said the sergeant, and turned to knock on a door.

'Come along in,' said a voice.

They were greeted in a pleasant drawing-room by a man in his thirties, in a blue blazer with brass buttons, grey flannel trousers and brown suede shoes. He sported both a full-blown moustache and what looked like an MCC tie. Sam had a fleeting vision of a character from P.G. Wodehouse. The man had a turn of phrase to match.

'I think you chaps already know one another.'

At that moment another figure came into view. Sam's eyes turned and there, grinning from ear to ear, was Otway in his white suit, neatly pressed and seemingly none the worse for wear. A change seemed to come over Laura. She ran over to him, embracing him, and in what sounded like a little girl's voice: 'Oh, Horatius, are you all right?' This was something more than love, thought Sam. It was more like worship. He did not know how he could compete with worship.

The tall, gangling figure seemed more than all right. It dominated the room. It was if he, Otway, was in charge of the major, not the other way round.

'Allow me to introduce Major Mohammed Haddid, my keeper. He has impeccable Sandhurst manners.'

The major waved them to a sofa. Horatius addressed Sam. 'I have been telling the major about our school days. He tells me he had always wanted an English education. I told him he had a lucky escape.'

Laura appeared to hang on every word he said. And in his way, so did the major.

'Well I did have a sort of English education. After a tiff with the old man I was sent into the army and went to Sandhurst.'

The outdated slang added to Sam's feeling that Haddid lived in a world that had ceased to exist, either here or in the Britain of his imagination. As to Otway, despite his predicament, he appeared to have lost none of his panache.

'So,' he said, 'you bring news from Shehab, lately turned politician. Tell me all.' This was the Horatius that Sam remembered, already thinking briskly ahead, without the slightest sign of a dent in confidence, always ready with a trick up his sleeve. Sam wondered how much he could say in front of the army officer. As if reading his thoughts, Haddid resolved the problem.

'Well you three have plenty to talk about so I'll leave you till curfew.' He got to his feet. At the door he turned. 'As far as I am concerned, these politicians are all the same: like a bunch of bananas, all of them yellow and none of them straight.'

Clearly pleased with his parting sally, he left the room.

Sam looked at his old friend: 'You seem to have got *him* round your little finger.'

'One of our greater colonial exports was the inferiority complex. We made them either hate us or want to outdo us in Englishness. At all events good old Mohammed has been most co-operative. He seems to have an almost fanatical admiration for all things British. I am of course locked up at night but free on trust when he is around during the day: which suits me perfectly as I would be picked up immediately if I tried to escape. We never talk politics but he has been my mainstay.'

There was a short silence. Sam seized his moment. 'There's been something on my mind, for the past twenty years I suppose, ever since school. You know who betrayed you by telling C-B about your role in the AA?'

'No, but I always rather assumed it was old C-B's son, the odious Stanley that I had to thank…'

'It wasn't Stanley,' said Sam, flushing, 'it was me. I was too cowardly to stand up to old C-B's cross questioning. I owed everything to you and I let you down. It goes without saying I've felt horrible ever since. I always wanted to make it up to you somehow.'

Not for the first time Otway's reaction took him entirely by surprise. He grinned broadly.

'But there's nothing to make up for. When I said I thought it was Stanley I had to thank, I meant it literally. Now I know it was you, I thank you for sparing me another year at that dreadful place. I think of it as a merciful release, not a betrayal.'

With which he waved the matter to one side, and Sam felt the decades of shame that had engulfed him ebbing away. Briskly, Otway went on: 'Now tell me about Shehab. That could really be helpful…'

Sam swallowed his surprise and cleared his throat. 'Shehab wants to do a deal. The oil documents for your freedom. I suppose he wants to avoid any public hearings that could be damaging to him.'

'The documents I had with me in my despatch case were being held here, but Haddid tells me the prosecutor's officers came yesterday to take them away.'

'Oh God,' said Laura.

'It's not that bad. They certainly name names, including senior figures in the present regime, in the official English translation, which has been, shall we say, clarified under my supervision. But on their own they are embarrassing rather than incriminating, embarrassing to a lot of people, including Shehab, who had no right to give (or rather, sell) them to me, but lawyers could argue they are forgeries, especially after my little touch of editing here and there. Fortunately I managed to destroy the really incriminating evidence, a copy of a letter with Shehab's own signature, dated two weeks before the revolution and addressed to Timothy Kettle, authenticating the other documents, which Shehab only signed after driving a hard cash bargain.'

'What happened to it?'

'The original is with the papers Laura cleverly sewed into the cherry picture. I managed to get a note out…'

'Yes we got it this morning,' said Laura.

'I meant what happened to the copy you took with you,' Sam said.

'Will you believe me if I tell you I ate it? Ate it. After we were arrested. Have you ever tried swallowing a whole piece of paper? It was no mean feat, I can tell you.' He smiled at the memory. 'I wanted to protect Shehab as his position was radically altered by the revolution – for the better, as it turns out – even though he took Timothy for quite a ride, financially speaking.'

'What happened? How did you get arrested?'

'I got an urgent message from Shehab to destroy the oil documents as the military police were coming to make a search on an order from the public prosecutor. Somebody in the Defence Ministry had been talking, I suppose. I knew no love was lost between the public prosecutor and Shehab, but I wasn't going to abandon my efforts to build up a decent pension fund that easily. So I took the copy I had made of the documents and the covering letter and headed for the border, planning to show them to Timothy in London with a view to getting the original of the letter to him later on if need be. The border with Jordan is less well-guarded than the Syrian one, so we made for a known gap, but I had the misfortune to have a driver, Karim, who also works part time for the prosecutor's office and he shopped me at a final roadblock. I was held for a day or two and brought here. Luckily our Major Haddid couldn't see what all the fuss was about. He just thinks I just didn't have a proper exit visa, which he doesn't seem to consider very serious, more a parking offence than a war crime.'

'Shehab and apparently the prosecutor take a different view. So does Earnshawe, the MI6 man.'

'Oh him. Not my greatest fan.'

'No, but maybe he can help. It suits the embassy to hush things up while a new oil agreement is being negotiated between our two governments. And Shehab is proposing a deal. He wants your agreement in principle to letting him have all the documents – especially, I imagine, the incriminating letter he signed. In exchange he will arrange your release, and of course Laura's. He wants me to give you his word in exchange for yours.'

'Shehab? Principle? Word? The man was pulling your leg. He wouldn't know a principle if he tripped over one. But of course tell him I accept. I expect we can work something out using a third party. Perhaps even Mohammed here... His father has connections.'

'You know Timothy Kettle is here? He came as soon as he heard.'

For once Horatius seemed disconcerted, but only for a split second. 'That wasn't at all wise of him. If the prosecutor finds out and makes the connection who knows what he may do? Does Shehab know?'

'Yes. And he appeared quite put out.'

Horatius thought for a moment. 'I really think Timothy should leave at once. But first, since he is here, it might be a good idea to show him the documents in the envelope that Laura sewed into the cherry picture. They should be worth a few millions to his firm. He may want to leave them here until a safer way of getting them out is found.'

Already the confident Houdini was back at work.

Sam said: 'I think Timothy Kettle was worried as much about you as he was about the oil documents. Anyway he is due out on tomorrow's press plane.'

'Well, both he and I are safer with him out of the way.'

Sam indicated the carton of cigarettes.

'Laura says you don't smoke but we brought these assuming they are useful as bribes, or should I say tips?'

'Brilliant, my dear friend. My friend here, the brother of Sayid, the New Arab hotel driver, tells me he smokes like a chimney. I am sure they will help to speed him on his way. Although I have to make my messages very guarded. Just in case. The "cherry" message was a bit risky, but I didn't want Laura selling the painting or giving it away.'

At that moment Haddid came back into the room.

'I think you'll have to go now as I am under orders to lock our friend in his quarters at nightfall. I daren't risk upsetting the applecart by turning a blind eye.'

Horatius' final words echoed Earnshawe's. They were delivered in an undertone, addressed to Laura, who had scarcely spoken.

'For Heaven's sake make sure Timothy is on the next plane out. He's a dear fellow, but as the paymaster and instigator of the whole inquiry he risks spilling a lot of beans if they catch up with him. And with Shehab aware he is here you never know what to expect – except that anything he does will be in his own interest.'

Laura seemed cheered by their visit. On the journey home she was more forthcoming about her half-brother's activities. She even managed a joke at his expense. They were discussing the documents in the cherry picture, though with circumspection due to the presence of the driver. 'If those were originals, it's more than can be said of the cherry picture. It is definitely an "After". Not even "School Of".'

24.

The Peoples' Court, adjoining the prison building in the Ministry of Defence compound, was bedecked with the new republic's flags for the opening of the long heralded public trials.

Sam arrived early in the entrance hall. Leaving his portable Olivetti typewriter on a seat, he was summarily searched and given a press pass. When he returned, he recognized the corpulent figure of Colonel Mahdawi, the prosecutor, sitting on his seat, but more to the point, on his typewriter. Along with the world's press, he was waiting for the keys of the courtroom to be found.

The colonel had already sentenced to death an unknown number of officials of the previous regime. Most cases had been heard in private on the grounds of security. The open court was to be a showcase to demonstrate both the rigour and the respect for procedure of the new regime. Sam already knew better. Too many stories circulated of executions carried out within minutes of sentencing, by firing squad in the prison yard for soldiers, by hanging for civilians. There was no provision for appeal. Like his Leader, Mahdawi had blood on his hands. (Little did either man know that their turn would come within a relatively short time, when a young officer called Saddam Hussein would have them both shot at their desks.)

Sam's dilemma was whether to ask the colonel to move or not. It might involve being seized by guards, or it might mean shaking his hand; Sam was not sure which would be worse. He had recently visited the ruined royal palace and shaken hands with a young captain who, he was afterwards told, had personally shot the young king. Sam told himself it didn't much matter but could not suppress a revulsion.

In the end he decided to rely on the relatively sturdy case of the Olivetti until the key was finally found.

The courtroom itself was large enough to hold an audience of a hundred. In the middle of it, the accused stood throughout. The language was Arabic but there was a simultaneous translation into English. Colonel Mahdawi sat at a desk facing the room between two men in suits, presumably legal advisors, who did not speak.

The first prisoner of that opening morning was a senior general who had been close to the king, and was something of a national hero. He was in uniform. He stood with his head held high for the half hour in which he was interrogated. Mahdawi treated him with elaborate courtesy, evidently to demonstrate to the world's listening press, as well as the city's television viewers, that impartiality and magnanimity were the watchwords of the peoples' court.

It did not last.

After an hour, the general was formally pardoned for what was described as misguided allegiance to lackeys of the former colonial power. He left the room a free man.

If that had been for overseas consumption, what followed was a warning to any local dissident that might still be sitting on the fence. Mahdawi looked up to address the courtroom.

'Let nobody be misled,' he declaimed. 'This court is here to remove the cancer of our colonialist past. Some of the accused awaiting trial are guilty of outright treason, others of corruption. Some have taken money to betray state secrets to foreign entrepreneurs and other nations. We have announced that where possible all will be tried in public. However, we have found that where state secrets are concerned justice will be administered behind closed doors. Many of the accused await trial here in custody. However, certain persons walking the streets today, some of the very highest rank, may soon find themselves answerable to us as a result of our most recent inquiries, which are still taking place.

'What you witness here today is part of the story. But it is not the whole story.'

The next accused was also a former officer, looking down-at-heel in a badly creased suit and no tie, accused of high treason for his part in refusing to cooperate with the Kassem regime in its infancy. He was clearly terrified.

Colonel Mahdawi did not speak a lot. But when he did, his voice was loud and rose in anger to contradict the prisoner before him. No, he had not just been obeying orders. He was guilty of betraying his country. The man said nothing. There was no point.

In the silence that followed there was an interruption. A smartly uniformed officer standing in the back of the hall produced a folded white handkerchief, and spat audibly into it. Then he folded the handkerchief with care, and put it into his pocket. From the British press bench came a stage whisper: 'The Voice of the Arabs.' For a reason he could not exactly place, Sam felt a surge of shame for his fellow countrymen. Later he reflected that it was not really the racist overtones that he minded – he was inured to that from his upbringing – so much as the lack of respect for a man about to be sent to the firing squad.

As sentence was passed, the prisoner seemed to crumple. He gave no resistance, made no protest. Grey faced, he was led from the room. He would be taken to the holding cell. Then within a matter of minutes he would be shot either by firing squad or with a bullet to the head. It was the first time Sam had seen a man condemned to death.

A second death sentence, this time by hanging, was passed on a civilian entrepreneur who tried in vain to argue with Mahdawi that he had had in mind only the poor of Baghdad when he had skimmed millions in foreign currency off a defence contract for a building that never materialised, on the grounds that he was diverting the funds to build schools for children.

The rest of the accused that morning were given long prison sentences. They seemed almost grateful to have escaped with their lives. For the afternoon session, the court was cleared for cases to be heard under security conditions.

Sam headed for the embassy.

Earnshawe had evidently followed the court proceedings on television and seemed more immediately interested in the ominous words about secret trials of senior officials than Sam's account of Horatius Otway's relatively luxurious arrangements. But he was alert when Sam told him that some of the documents in Otway's possession had been taken by Mahdawi's agents.

'That means it is no longer just a question of an illegal border crossing. Somehow they are on to Otway and Shehab's project. There has clearly been a change of plan behind the scenes, possibly even as a result. These people mean business, and Mahdawi went out of the way this morning to say so. Not good news for Shehab and his friends. You can count on one thing. Mahdawi will latch on to anything implicating Shehab in corrupt practices. You have seen for yourself what sort of justice is practised here. Mahdawi is prosecutor, judge and all but executioner, rolled into one.'

Turning to the visit to Otway, he dismissed Major Haddid as a harmless lightweight, known to some of the embassy staff.

'However, he comes from a rich and influential family with traditional ties to the army. His father was finance minister for a while under the old regime, but resigned in protest against financial irregularities, which puts him in good odour with the present regime, though he is certainly not part of the inner circle. The family have steered clear of politics ever since. So perhaps the major can be useful in spite of his reputation as playboy and buffoon...

'Talking of buffoons, is Kettle at last keeping his head down? I gather the press flight has been delayed until tomorrow afternoon to allow for the start of the show trials. Let's hope they don't make the connection to him before he leaves. I imagine Shehab is hoping the same.'

Sam thought it wiser not to discuss the plan for Laura to show Timothy the originals of the oil documents.

At the hotel Sam found the Lloyds man still locked in his room. He had one surprising piece of news.

'Shehab rang me. Very friendly. He wants to come and play a farewell game of chess.'

'Surely it would be best to steer clear of him. I am sure that would be Earnshawe's advice.'

'I can't see how I can refuse. After all he is the Interior Minister. Besides, as I said, he sounded very friendly. He said he would bring my exit visa in person. He said it would save me queuing for it at the airport.' He allowed himself a rare smile. 'Perhaps I should let him win. Horatius always did in the old days when he wanted access to files.'

Sam gave up. In common with many people shy by nature, Timothy Kettle had a pigheaded streak.

'Has Laura been in touch?'

'She's coming round tomorrow morning with the oil documents before the plane leaves.'

'I hope you are not planning to take them with you. You may well be searched. And Horatius needs them, too, as a trade for his release.'

'No. But I need to see them to know how strong our case is.'

'They are what Shehab is after. Be careful what you say.'

But the old Kettle was back, white-faced, furtive and yet somehow managing to combine defencelessness with obstinacy.

25.

Something about the knot of people outside the hotel caught Sam's attention the next day as he was leaving for the newspaper office. Groups regularly gathered in the mornings around the main entrance, street vendors jockeying for the best site, party members assembling to demonstrate their loyalty to the revolution, delegations from out of town on sponsored tours. This group was different. It was in an unusual place, outside the wing where the guest bedrooms were. And it had an unusual stillness about it.

Veiled women stood among the men in a half circle, blocking Sam's view. He spotted two of the hotel taxi drivers who would normally be touting for customers at this hour. Nobody spoke, yet there was an air of expectation as if they were all waiting for something to happen. Someone was pointing up to an open bedroom window some six storeys above.

Through a momentary gap Sam glimpsed a figure on the ground, half hidden by an ornamental bush. Hairs rose along his spine. Threading his way through the silent watchers, he could see a man lying on his back. Apparently he had fallen from a window, presumably of his own bedroom, and had landed on the concrete strip at the foot of the building.

It was no surprise to find that he was dead; a halo of blood bore witness to his violent end. It was the first time Sam had seen a dead body; and it was with macabre fascination that he registered that while the back of the head was altogether missing, the upturned face, stone-white and settled in a fixed, vacant expression, was wholly intact. What lay before him was a set of human features, perfectly preserved but in *bas relief*, like an effigy mounted in a church wall.

Except that this was not a church wall, but concrete ground. And it was not an effigy. He looked again at the staring face, and wide open eyes. It was Timothy Kettle.

Sam closed his eyes and took a deep breath to stop himself from fainting. A shock wave ran through his system, detaching him from his emotions. Trying to register what had happened, he was only aware of feeling sick. Now Sam, too, found himself waiting. The reality was too enormous to accept. Standing shoulder to shoulder with other on-lookers he realised that he was expecting the body to move, refusing absolutely to countenance the idea of death. Or that this could be the Timothy Kettle he knew. And even if this was Timothy Kettle's body, Timothy the person was no longer there. He was staring at a facsimile.

A hand touched his arm; he saw the grey of a special policeman's uniform. He looked into the man's eyes: 'Kettle,' he said helplessly. 'Kettle...' He said it again several more times, as much to persuade himself as to inform the man in uniform.

'You knew this man?'

Sam was not prepared for the change of tense. 'We have a lunch date.' He heard himself add, as if to explain: 'We were at Illbury together.'

The policeman took out a notebook and handed it to him, asking him to write down the name. Sam began to write 'Timothy', then stopped. It was wrong, another betrayal even, as if by writing the name, he was closing the door on Kettle's rights. He was being tricked into signing away a human life, issuing a death certificate without authorisation – before he had time to be certain. He steeled himself to take another look.

It still looked unreal. It was as if a gruesome act of magic had framed the dead man's head. Grotesquely large flies formed a black fringe round the coagulating circle of blood. He forced himself to scan the slack mouth and obstinately vacant expression; and this time all doubt dissolved. It was the look that as a schoolboy Kettle had turned on his tormentors, a wolf cub exposing its throat in an act of submission to the pack – the blackmail of the weak that attracted derision but ensured survival. It was the look that he had worn as a shield to ward off a teacher's question in class. It was Kettle all right.

Another rogue thought, unbidden and unwelcome as the flies around the corpse, came into his head. Kettle's blank mask had served him well during his lifetime. Now that he had donned it for the last time to meet his Maker, Sam could not help idly wondering how it would fare with Him.

An English voice, a woman's, was saying: 'It's the young man from the club with the sunburn! I lent him my lotion. All red he was.' There was a pause, then: 'What a waste of a life, killing himself like that...'

More uniformed men were arriving. They had come from a van that had drawn up in the hotel driveway. Two carried a stretcher; another approached with a blanket. As he spread it over the dead man, a corner caught up in one of the hands, in which Sam caught sight of a small dark green object. He bent forward to take a closer look.

His pulses were racing again. He made an immense effort to think lucidly, but the release of adrenalin only added to the confusion inside him. Everything was happening too fast. The only clear idea he could muster was that there was danger and that somehow Horatius must be involved. Another idea, unformulated, was that he must do something: that here was perhaps his opportunity, even a chance of redeeming himself. If so, he had only a few seconds to act, none to think.

He was nerving himself to stretch out his hand when out of the corner of his eye he saw the policeman turn to move in his direction. At the same moment one of the stretcher-bearers lost his footing and staggered sideways under his load and into his path. Momentarily distracted the policeman turned his head. In the few seconds' reprieve Sam stooped and took hold of the dead man's hand. To his consternation he had to force it open using both his own. It took longer than he calculated. He saw the English women watching him. Finally he slipped the object into his palm without using up time to examine it. Besides, he already knew what it was.

Turning back, he saw the policeman looking in his direction. Their eyes met. For a second the other hesitated, then, apparently reaching a decision, he turned on his heel and followed the little procession to the waiting van.

Sam watched until the party had disappeared before transferring his hand to a pocket of his lightweight jacket. He waited until he was in the privacy of his room before pulling out his trophy to examine it. It was a chess knight, carved in dark green malachite, from Otway's set, or more to the point, the set he had presented to Colonel Shehab.

From the start he had dismissed suicide outright as out of character. An accident seemed improbable – the hotel windows were not large. He could picture Kettle sleepwalking, but not fully dressed. What Sam had in his possession was proof of a crude and premeditated act of murder: the black knight, its tiny lance still intact, protected during the fall by the hand clutching it. Shehab was a much more powerfully built man than Timothy Kettle, and bundling him out of his window on the sixth floor would have been be an easy task. And perhaps he had had someone to help him. The body had been discovered by daylight but it must have been lying there for some hours.

'A waste of a life'… As the Englishwoman's words came back to him, suddenly, like a change in the wind, his anger erupted, raging against the Maker whose mysterious ways included destroying His creatures before they had a chance to do anything with their lives. What had Timothy Kettle's been for? Was he just a lesson in the law of the survival of the fittest? Or a casualty recklessly inflicted in a vast flawed experiment called creation? Sam's rage was short-lived, soon tempered by his inculcated fear of blasphemy.

In its place he felt tears welling, and realised that they were as much for himself as for Kettle: the death had violated his safe world of private fantasies and memories; and shaken a comfortable inner conviction, undisturbed since his mother had died, that death was something that happened to other people.

Earnshawe had been right. They, Horatius included, had behaved like schoolboys in a grown-up world. Childhood and adulthood were separate planets. The brutal collision the MI6 man hinted at had become reality in the shape of Timothy Kettle's dead body. The minister had meant it when he had talked of destroying the evidence; he had in more senses than one arranged Timothy's promised exit visa. He had murdered Kettle to be on the safe side, to stop him revealing the source of his information about the oil project. With Kettle out of the way, all that remained now for Shehab to cover to his tracks was the letter Laura was due to bring.

And, of course, Horatius himself.

Now his anger turned full force on Shehab. Kettle's murder had raised hackles he did not know he had; it engendered in him a determination that years of guilt over his betrayal of Otway had made him forget he possessed. He stretched out his hand to pick up his bedside telephone to call Laura, only to find it was ringing with an incoming call. Earnshawe's voice said:

'I think you had better get over here at once.'

Before Sam had time to reply, the MI6 man had hung up: he was well versed in dealing with telephone tappers. When Sam called the fort to tell Laura, her reaction was as he expected: 'We must tell Horatius. He will know what to do. I'll get hold of Sayid.'

Sam hesitated, for a moment unsure of his priorities: to get to Horatius or to see what help he could get from Earnshawe. His decision might literally be a matter of life or death.

'Stop by and pick me up at the hotel. There's something I have to do first. I don't know how long it will take. I don't want to go into detail on the telephone but I will leave a note for you at the front desk in case I am delayed.' He hesitated, then decided to risk the indiscretion. 'It is very important…'

This time there was no waiting for Earnshawe. Sam found him sitting in one of the ambassador's Chippendale chairs just out of earshot of the chancery reception desk. Sam sat down beside him. Earnshawe had already heard from the consulate of Kettle's death, and listened attentively while Sam filled in the detail of the green knight.

'Did you happen to notice the colour of the police uniform on the death scene?'

'Yes, it was the grey of Shehab's own special police.'

Earnshawe grunted.

'You realise you criminally removed a vital piece of evidence. Just as well. Otherwise you may be sure it would never have been heard of again.' He paused. 'You realise also that this puts you in real danger if Shehab finds out. As to your friend Otway, he is the last potential witness left and Shehab will not hesitate to eliminate him. He will disclaim all knowledge of the chessman, and anything to do with chess.'

'And the documents?'

'He will simply disown them, too, as forgeries. Knowing Otway, he may well have a case.'

'There is one that Mahdawi hasn't got. The letter carrying Shehab's signature, certifying their authenticity. I am getting it to Horatius.'

The MI6 man looked exasperated: 'If you want my help, it would really be more useful if in future, instead of holding back information, you kept me fully briefed about what you are up to. This may be Otway's most important bargaining chip.'

Mustering all his forces, Sam said boldly: 'For my own part, whatever the higher interests involved, Horatius Otway's release is my own first priority.'

'I have already told you that Her Majesty's government wants as little to do with Otway as possible. Unfortunately the ambassador is quite adamant about this, to avoid at any cost muddying the waters for future oil negotiations…'

Earnshawe paused to reflect, the way he did when he was coming to a decision. He looked hard at Sam.

'However, I have a suggestion, which I will thank you to keep to yourself. We don't just sit on our hands in the embassy. We have certain sensitive contacts, which we guard closely and use sparingly. Haddid's father is one of them. We have others. We have good relations with one of the two legal military advisers to the public prosecutor. You will have seen him in court. He is the one without a moustache. As you will have realised he is close to Mahdawi.

'My own hands are tied. I cannot approach him officially myself. And you must not tell him I sent you. He may be interested in what you have to say. But if Shehab finds out, and is guilty as you claim, you will be a marked man. You will have watch your back.'

Sam remembered the policeman who had almost certainly seen him take something from the dead man's hand. To his own surprise he felt no fear.

Earnshawe could not resist a parting shot. 'Personally I think it best if Haddid keeps Otway safely under lock and key, so that at least Shehab can't get to him. If it was up to me I would be tempted to throw away the key.'

At least he had got something out of Earnshawe: a contact. Now he knew what to do, and he felt confident he would go through with it. As before, at school, it was in part an act of revenge, with the difference that this time it might not be too late to save his friend. He had no Aunt Olive as an inspiration, but he had Laura: and he had his new-found rage.

He also had a plan.

Short as the visit to the embassy was, by the time he got back to the hotel Laura had collected his note recounting the damning detail of the chess knight, and departed for Ramada.

He considered trying to catch her up in a hotel taxi, and then thought better of it. However much he wanted to be with Laura, he could perhaps do more good in the capital.

That night she called.

'This is a military line normally for official purposes only which Major Haddid has let me use. Horatius is taking a certain action. I am staying here until I hear the outcome. I can't say any more than that for the moment.'

'I am taking a certain action as well. And please let me know what's going on as soon as possible.' Despite the 'official purposes only' for which the line was reserved line he could not refrain from adding: 'I am missing you already.'

'I will be in touch as soon as I can.'

As soon as I can… Sam was sure he detected a note of evasion. Or was this his paranoia, dating from the memory of the day he had badgered his mother to take him away from school and she had gently but firmly put her finger to his lips to silence him?

For the next two days there was no open hearing at the so-named public trials. On the first Sam went with his press pass to the court. Chance had it that the session had not yet begun. One of the two advisers to the public prosecutor explained to him that it was a closed session. The man was alone. He wore a colonel's uniform. He had no moustache.

Sam countered: 'I am not here to cover the trials. I have some evidence that might interest you.'

The other raised an eyebrow. He did not smile.

'Evidence of murder. By a high official.'

The man did not change his expression, nor his formal lawyer's demeanour, as he answered: 'I heard from a certain person that you might be contacting me. He said you had some information.'

So the MI6 man had not been entirely inactive. At least he had secured him a hearing.

'I have a half hour to spare before the court starts.'

Sam had prepared his approach carefully in advance. When he came to the end , the adviser said:

'How do I know you are telling the truth? Where is this chess man?'

Sam looked him in the eye. 'I have it in my possession. I also have a witness, an English woman who saw me take it from the dead man's hand. Timothy Kettle told me the night before that he was going to play a farewell game of chess with the Interior Minister before taking the press plane out next day. They were old business acquaintances as well as chess partners from before the Revolution, when Colonel Shehab was in charge of Defence Ministry archives.'

A gleam in the man's eyes told Sam he already knew a great deal more than he was letting on. There was no question but that he was interested in any information concerning the Interior Minister's activities. It was also clear that for Sam there was no going back. To his amazement, the thought brought a kind of elation.

The colonel repeated: 'I asked: where is this so-called evidence?'

'I can get it to you.'

'You are either very brave or very foolish to come to me with this. You realise you have committed a criminal offence? Why shouldn't I have you arrested?'

'Because I am more use to you outside prison.'

'How so?'

'I can also get more evidence for you of other activity. Of something Shehab cannot deny. A letter he signed confirming the information he gave to Kettle before the revolution. You already have some of the documents, taken from a messenger working for Kettle. But he did not have this letter with him. The police have not been able to find it.'

'So where is it?'

'Again, I can get it for you. But first I have a proposition to put to you. If you will undertake to overlook any minor offence committed by Horatius Otway, who is an innocent party in this matter, it can be easily and quickly arranged. All he did was to try to cross the frontier illegally. And his evidence will be much more persuasive and much more complete if it is given voluntarily as part of an arrangement and not under duress. He can provide the definitive evidence that Shehab was selling Kettle material to help him over an insurance claim.'

'And why would he be so ready to cooperate to convict a man who worked with him?'

'That's perhaps where I can help. Otway was at school with Kettle. They are, or were, close friends from way back. Where we come from, that counts for a lot. I am sure he will be willing to tell you anything he can to convict his killer.'

'And naturally he will be more co-operative if he is given immunity.'

'Naturally... I myself will stand surety for him. You can hold me in his place if you find I am wrong.'

'So you are suggesting a deal.'

'If you like to put it that way. And if you want my motive in all this, I was also at school with both of them.'

There was a silence. 'I will have to consider this matter. You are levelling a very serious charge against a government minister.'

From which Sam concluded that the decision would be taken a step higher up the ladder, by Colonel Mahdawi, or perhaps even the Leader himself.

'It would be best if you stay at the hotel until I contact you.'

'I have no plans to move.'

'Meanwhile I would like to see the evidence.'

Sam persisted: 'And so you shall, as soon as you tell me you agree to my proposition.'

'You should understand that we are not businessmen. We do not do deals. We administer justice.' Earnshawe had warned him that he would get a response of the sort, which should be treated as a delaying tactic rather than a refusal. 'Moreover, I do not think you are in a position to dictate. Withholding evidence is a crime.'

'I am not withholding evidence. I am suggesting it will make it easier for everyone if you get full voluntary cooperation from all parties, including myself, rather than if you use coercion. It will be quicker and more productive if I find the letter for you than if you use other means. And it will avoid an unhelpful and unnecessary international incident. For myself I have no reason to withhold anything from you. I wish only to secure Otway's release.'

The colonel did not answer at once, but watched Sam with his shrewd eyes. Eventually he broke the silence.

'Otway has a sister here.'

'I would want her protected too. Besides, she knows nothing. I repeat: I am prepared to put myself – and my job – on the line for two innocent friends caught up in a matter that seemed normal at the time: investigating an insurance claim.'

'Bribing government officials is illegal.'

'Offering a fee for information received about insurance is normal practice at Lloyds. And quite legal under British law. Otway was merely following Kettle's instructions.'

'Giving secret military information is high treason under our laws.'

'Which was not what Kettle or Otway did. They merely paid for it. Nor did they murder anyone to conceal it.'

Sam's aplomb surprised himself. He was also surprised that the colonel supplied him with a driver to take him back to the hotel. But when he tried to leave next morning to cover the trials, one of the uniformed lobby guards held him back, saying he had instructions to confine him to the hotel. The whisper of fear returned. What if Mahdawi had no intention of agreeing to his terms and was calling his bluff?

Later that morning the driver returned to pick up the chess man. He brought no news of any agreement. After a pause for thought, Sam handed over the malachite knight in an envelope. He had much to lose as it was, but if he refused he stood to lose everything.

Then, on the second evening, Laura appeared. She looked careworn. She said that Horatius' immediate decision when she told him about Timothy's death and showed him Sam's note about the chess man was to hand over the letter with Shehab's signature that she had brought with her. He was ready to testify in court to supply the motive for Timothy Kettle's murder, and ready to accept the consequences.

At almost the same time the prosecutor's office had rung. The authorities had reacted to Sam's intervention with, for them, lightning speed. They had taken the bait. According to Laura, a deal had been brokered behind the scenes: in exchange for his full cooperation Horatius would not himself be prosecuted, but would be kept in custody and expelled after the trial. It was all exactly along the lines Sam had suggested. He felt quietly pleased, but said nothing: this was a private matter between him and his past. He did not want gratitude from Horatius: he wanted peace from his conscience.

An official car had taken Horatius to the capital. Laura's concern was that the prosecutor would not keep his word. Sam was able to assure her everyone concerned wanted the matter hushed up.

Laura and Sam were having dinner when one of the lobby guards came to tell him the ban on his movements had now been lifted. There was no explanation for the suddenness of the move.

That night Laura stayed with Sam at the hotel. Still anxious, she asked him not to make love to her, but just to hold her; her fear for her brother was real enough, and Sam could feel her shaking in his arms until sleep brought its kindly relief.

Another unexplained event next morning was both a relief and a concern. Shehab did not appear as usual for his daily press conference. Seeing Timothy's killer posturing to the world's press was a prospect

Sam had not relished; but his absence also made him wonder with alarm whether Laura was right and Shehab was devoting his energies and all his considerable resources to getting to Horatius.

In his place at the press conference a stand-in confined himself to reading out official statements in a monotone, and did not accept questions. Most of the correspondents, due to catch the afternoon charter plane out, read nothing into Shehab's absence. Only Noori appeared to scent something unusual in the air; the editor of *The Desert Times* had his contacts, not least the official censor.

While the world's press was piling into taxis to head for the airport, there was a knock on Sam's hotel door. It was Noori. In his hand he held the latest edition of his newspaper, fresh off the press.

'I thought this might interest you.'

Sam looked at the front page:

HANGED FOR HIGH TREASON

Under the banner headline and occupying most of the rest of the page was a picture, a week or two old, of the Interior Minister. An official announcement followed:

> The Public Prosecutor's office has issued the following statement: 'Colonel Ahmed Shehab was today convicted of high treason by reason of activities which came to light during recent investigations. These investigations revealed that the minister had sold military secrets for his personal gain, including classified state documents, to agents of a foreign power during his period as an official at the defence ministry.
>
> 'The traitor was sentenced to hang by the court under the jurisdiction of Colonel Ahmed Mahdawi in a private session this morning. The sentence was later carried out. His replacement as Interior Minister will be announced shortly.'

Noori continued: 'The censor brought the statement and we made up the page together. He refused to allow any further comment. I also sent the story to London with your by-line. I hope that was all right.'

On an inside page was a brief report of the death of a British businessman staying at the New Arab Hotel and found dead, having apparently fallen or jumped from his bedroom window.

Before leaving, Noori appeared embarrassed for a moment. 'The censor also told me my accreditation has been confirmed. Which means…'

'Yes Noori: the Alwiya Club. I haven't forgotten.' A look of sheepish triumph suffused the Pakistani's face.

It had all happened with brutal despatch. The trial had taken place and the sentence carried out that same day, presumably to prevent Shehab's political allies mounting a protest. In passing, Sam observed that death by hanging underlined that Shehab's rank was not a military one: it did not just bring Shehab his just deserts; it also symbolized the final defeat of the politicians in the struggle for power within the military regime.

Clearly Horatius had carried out his part of the agreement to the letter by testifying convincingly in court. The magician had lost none of his magic, and none of his nerve. Clearly, too, he had not lost his taste for playing with fire. As to Shehab, in killing Timothy Kettle he had made a miscalculaton: he had clearly misjudged Horatius' personal attachment to him and the risk he was prepared to take of being prosecuted himself.

At the fort that evening Sam said: 'So, Horatius finally turned the tables on Shehab.'

'Ye-es. It was rough justice. But after what Shehab did, I have no pity for him. I was only worried the authorities would not keep their side of the bargain, but it looks as if they intend to, if only because they are anxious to keep things quiet about their part in the oil pipe incident. I had a call this afternoon from Horatius. He is back at Ramada.'

Sam said nothing. His own part in the affair could wait.

'Does all this this mean you will be leaving?'

'Not only leaving, but leaving tomorrow. The embassy rang to offer to send our things on. The deal was that we leave at once and say 'nothing to the press.'

'You realise that includes me? But never fear. I have given my word to be discreet to just about everybody, including Timothy, not that it did him much good.'

Two questions were burning his tongue, but he held them back.

Quite what had Earnshawe done behind the scenes? It looked as if, despite his antipathy to Horatius, and against the strict orders of his own ambassador, the MI6 man had privately played his part in oiling the wheels, risking his career by going against the ambassador's orders. Unwittingly Laura confirmed this version of events. 'I think one of the lawyers in court knew Haddid's father. He spoke to Horatius outside the court. He was very insistent on everything being done by the book, and on absolute discretion.'

Sam had no difficulty in guessing why: Mahdawi didn't want the Leader to think that his real motive in prosecuting was to destroy his rival in the struggle to be number two on the Revolutionary Council.

Then there was a second and less savoury question that Sam scarcely dared formulate, concerning Horatius' role in forging documents, which Sam decided to shelve for the time being.

His thoughts came back to Laura.

'And shall I see you in London? Noori's accreditation has finally come through and there is no reason for me stay.'

'That would be nice. But I am not sure where Horatius wants to go next.'

Sam's heart sank a little. 'Nice' was not the word he was hoping for. For him the thought of seeing the light his life again was more than 'nice'. Just then it was the difference between the prospect of a happy life and emptiness. But, as ever, Laura was tied to Horatius. He, Sam, was an outsider once again, a dispensable appendage.

'For the rest of the evening I have to pack up. I leave for Ramada first thing tomorrow. If you would like to come and help please do, but if you are out after curfew you will have to stay: you can always sleep in the bed Horatius uses downstairs – more comfortable than the floor after we have dismantled the big bed.'

It sounded like an invitation to help arrange his own execution.

EPILOGUE

It was one of those London clubs with high stone portals where the name was not written up anywhere; you were supposed to know it. Sam Cork turned over the postcard in his hands as he waited for his host in the entrance hall.

Horatius Ariel Otway… In the distant days of prep school and surnames he had not given much thought to the Ariel. Now, like Shakespeare's mischievous imp he had finally been released from his bondage…

The card was the first news he had from him since he and Laura had left Baghdad and vanished into the ether. It was written in green ink and simply read: 'I see Godonay did his work – finally! Talk of Delayed Action!! Hope to see you soon! Will you be going to old C-B's memorial service?' There was an Indian stamp and no return address.

Sam had not at first fully grasped the reference to Godonay, except to recall that as schoolboys they had invoked his powers of black magic to strike down the headmaster. The card was signed with Otway's name in full with a flourish of exclamation marks. Under it, in spidery writing: 'See you soon L. Love.' (Was the 'love', written after her initial, an afterthought? Or was it just unusual, like herself? Or else his own paranoia at work?)

He had hesitated for a long time about attending the memorial service for Mr Canterbury-Black. There would have been no question of going but for the chance of seeing Laura, assuming she had accompanied Horatius. The card left everything open.

Finally fate had taken the decision out of his hands. Aunt Olive had rung to say that his father had died, and the funeral was to take place on the same morning as the headmaster's memorial service. Sam's self-effacing but obstinate parent had intruded as little as possible into his family's life, but when he did his timing was faultless. Aunt Olive had said: 'I hope you'll come to the house after the funeral. I'll be making sandwiches…' It was her way of dealing with difficulties, imposing order: on Judgment Day while humanity awaited the terrible verdict she could be counted on for sandwiches for all, sheep and goats alike.

Like Aunt Olive, another old Illbury boy, Tom Mott, the diminutive but once subversive son of the tyrannical KC, had invited a few old Illbury boys to his club in the evening after the service. Sam was hoping Horatius would be there, ideally with Laura in tow.

He kept his eye on the hall porter in his glass cage conducting his own version of Judgment Day, admitting some, casting others out. A man came up, evidently among the saved: the porter pointed to where Sam was sitting. A moment later he was heading towards him across the elegant stone flagged floor.

'Sam Cork!'

Sam realised he had been staring at Thomas Mott without recognising him. Now there was no mistaking the short figure, portly now and with slightly thinning hair. He still somehow had the walk of a small man willing himself to be taller. There was a slight puffiness about the cheeks, hardly surprising after all the years.

'Sorry to hear about your father. We missed you at C-B's service.'

The handshake was confident.

'Is Horatius Otway here?' Sam showed him the card.

'My dear felllow, he's not a member here!'

'I meant is he coming? With the others?'

'Oh no… I haven't invited Otway. I don't think that would have been suitable. Anyway he wasn't at the service, I don't think.' Sam swallowed his mounting indignation as Mott went on. 'I asked you early so we could chat privately. I wanted to ask if you could shed any light on the terrible business of Timothy Kettle. I think you were out there at about the same time. But first, some tea, or a drink?'

He led the way to the club's big sitting-room and signalled a waiter.

'I'd really like a scotch.'

Mott looked at his watch. 'Splendid. A little early for me.' Too early, too, for the main topic of discussion. 'Do you have a club? I find it useful, especially at weekends when I come up for the day from Surrey.'

Up for the day. Out to the Middle East. Down to the country. And perhaps, every now and then, over to the continent. The conventional

English phraseology reminded Sam that he had always his reservations about trusting Mott: despite his interest in black magic, he had always been the first to trim his sails to the prevailing wind.

Sam waited for him to bring up Kettle's death. He was not disposed to hurry him. He had not yet made up his mind how to react.

'I was thinking during the service,' said Mott, approaching his subject from a fresh angle, 'that there has been quite a holocaust among us old Illburians, apart from old C-B himself, that is. First poor old Tom Jellicoe.'

'Why poor? What happened to him?'

'Surely you knew? He was killed during his national service. Another terrible affair: blown up by his own hand grenade during practice. He threw it and apparently something went wrong.'

The news ran through Sam like a knife. As he took a sip of his drink, he pictured Jelly bowling, letting go too soon, the ball floating high into the air and landing almost at his own feet. A sudden rage seized Sam. 'Bloody fools!' he said, half under his breath.

Startled, Mott said: 'Who?'

'The army. They should have known he couldn't throw. Anyone could have told them...'

'Ah well! All that was a long time ago. I say, you really have been out of touch. Everyone at the memorial service was asking after you. You seem to have slipped from view.'

'Yes.'

'Stanley's the new headmaster at Illbury, you know. He's turning out really very well. Had to take on the job at short notice, too.'

'No, I didn't know.'

'Poor old C-B. Awful way to go. Did you hear?'

'Just the card from Horatius Otway. Someone said something about an accident. I only saw the bare announcement in the papers.'

'Oddly enough that was an explosion too. Were you at Illbury when there was talk of an unexploded bomb, after an air raid? Well, it finally went off – how many years since the war is it? Nowadays of course they have a regular electricity supply from the grid. Old C-B must have disturbed it when he was clearing out the spinney round the old electricity pump, and...' His hands parted eloquently.

Sam took another long sip. His anger of a moment ago had yielded to a surge of unholy joy. 'Of course! That's what Horatius meant: Godonay! So it worked!' He picked up his empty glass.

'Would you like another one?'

'I wanted to raise a glass to Godonay.'

A furrow creased Mott's brow. Sam leaned forward:

'Remember? Paramaribo…'

'Wasn't that where Otway was born? I remember him telling us.'

Sam was waving the glass now: 'AA! Anarchists Anonymous! Remote Control! Godonay! And Delayed Action!' He looked straight into Mott's eyes. 'Your *Book of Black Magic*!'

Slowly the mist cleared from the face in front of him, then seemed to close in again. 'I say, you really do have a good memory,' Mott said, stroking his head.

'For certain things, yes…'

There was a short silence. 'Anyway after the accident Mr C-B seems to have lost his memory. He just sat in a chair and stared at the wall.' Mott's voice changed as he went on: 'You know, it wasn't such a bad school really, when you come to compare it.'

It had all gone. He had forgotten. Everything.

Sam leaned forward again: 'C-B was a sadistic old brute.'

'Oh I don't know. He wasn't such a bad chap. And at least we didn't have bullies at Illbury.'

'Except the headmaster. At Illbury the bullying was done by the headmaster.'

Mott chuckled, a confident chuckle. 'Well, it didn't do me any harm. And you look pretty good on it yourself, if I may say so. I've put my boys down. I'm confident they'll be in good hands with Stanley.'

Mott was smiling. Mott was unmarked. Only the unhealthy clung to their inconvenient memories. Sam thought: it is necessary to forget the past so that it can repeat itself. It was a Mandarin law of survival. The establishment closed ranks round the authorised version. Mott was free, free to repeat the errors of the past. He, Sam Cork, was, at least until recently, its prisoner. He framed the words in his mind to say to Mott: 'You survived. I didn't…' then thought better of it.

'We must get together some time and talk about the old days,' Mott

said, his tone contradicting his words. Finally he got round to his reason for asking Sam to come early: 'Timothy Kettle was missed too, of
course, at C-B's service. Horrible story. Found dead after a fall from a
hotel bedroom window. I wondered if you could shed any light on it,
as you were in those parts. He had no known reason to take his life.
Plum position to take over his family's Lloyds syndicate. Heir to a bar-
onetcy. But you never know. He always played his cards very close to
his chest.' Mott stopped; then a new thought seemed to come to him.
'Oddly enough he had hired Otway to do a job for us, on the side, I
think to help him out. In the Middle East.'

'Us?'

'The Kettle syndicate.'

'I thought you were all set to be a barrister?'

'Well I did read law but now I work as a Lloyds underwriter. The
Kettle family very kindly took me on. Even takes me out to the Middle
East a bit. That sort of thing. It has worked out really very well. Now I
find I am increasingly having to take on Timothy's workload.

'But back to Timothy himself. I'm not sure exactly what he was
doing out there. As I said, he played his cards close to his chest. I know
it was to do with an old insurance claim, a really big one, and I am
checking to see whether a statute of limitations may apply. But what a
time to choose to go!'

'Did it never occur to you that he might have been concerned for
Horatius Otway?'

'I rather doubt that was the reason. Between ourselves, Otway
never was a very reliable sort of fellow. I think we made a mistake
doing him a favour. Always was a strange sort of cove. Remember
what he was like at school? I see from the stamp on his postcard that
the Indian connection is still alive. Tea, I think. But it's not what it was
in his father's day. I gather he's selling up. In fact he rather made a
hash of things altogether. He was dabbling in the art business too. All a
bit dodgy. Not natural Kettle territory.'

There was a long pause. Sam felt his resentment rising to the surface again. It was in part the criticism of Horatius to which he took
exception; but it was equally the phrase 'taking on Timothy's workload', the words of the dissembling opportunist. It would have been

more to the point if he had said 'filling a dead man's shoes', which he clearly intended to do. Mott's barrister father would have approved. Stepping over dead bodies for advancement ran in the family. He couldn't help thinking that Kettle's death suited Mott's career – but perhaps the whisky was at work on his overwrought imagination.

Watching silently as Mott started stroking his head once more, another thought came to him. In the end Shehab had been convicted of treason, not the murder of Timothy Kettle, which gave rise to the uncomfortable question: were the documents which sent Shehab to his death in part, or even wholly, forged by Horatius Otway? Sam was not sure he wanted to know the answer. Either way Shehab had got his just desserts. At all costs Sam was determined not to give Mott any ammunition that he could use against Horatius. Who knew what he might dig up once he began investigating? It was a matter of loyalty, part of his amends to Horatius.

He made up his mind. Holding other man's gaze, he said: 'I'm sorry. I'm afraid I can't help you.'

There was another pause, shorter this time. 'Of course. I quite understand. I hope you didn't mind my asking. Another scotch? I think I'll join you.'

Mott looked round for the waiter, seeming to welcome the interruption. He seemed almost relieved.

'Tell you what: stay on for a bite. The food's quite good if you stick to the steak and kidney pie. And you'll meet the others. Old familiar faces. I'll just go and ask if they can do an extra place for dinner. Hang on, I'll be back in a second.'

He watched Mott as he made his way upstairs to see about dinner, rounding the confident sweep of the stone balustrade, pausing to greet a fellow member, passing the marble deities and statesmen presiding from niches at each turn, beside two figures hand in hand on the upper landing labelled Goodness and Mercy and known to members as 'Good Mrs Murphy'. In the other direction the steps led down to the echoing tiled chamber that he had visited while he was waiting, with great porcelain urinals bearing their makers' name and the wrought iron hooks where members left their great coats. Order, grace, permanence. Mandarin territory.

While he waited, Sam had time to go over the role of Horatius in Shehab's demise. Earnshawe had explained it in detail to him before he had left.

His version fitted the facts: determined to make the charges against Shehab stick, Mahdawi had opted to rely on treason rather than murder. Sam's discovery and rescue of the chess piece in Kettle's dead hand, seemingly watertight proof of murder, might not have held up in court. The senior echelons of Shehab's own police – who already resented being placed under military control – might have been only too happy to protect him by testifying that he had never been in Kettle's hotel room. And there was only Sam's word, possibly backed by a foreign witness, that the knight had been found in Kettle's hand, while the rest of the set could have easily been disposed of.

But the key documents implicating Shehab in selling military secrets held good, especially when supported by Otway's evidence in court against his former helper turned killer. Not only that, but they were serious enough in the present climate to earn the death penalty.

The whole issue placed Horatius in a moral league outside his own. He, Sam, came from the professional middle class, which he had been taught was the real moral backbone of the nation. Whether he liked it or not, he was imbued with his father's values. These did not include faking evidence, however worthy the cause. For his father the end did not justify the means – otherwise civilisation ceased.

All of which led to the further question for Sam: in Horatius' place would he, could he, have done the same?

He had no answer. Except that he was not in Horatius' place, and had not been called on to decide. Only Horatius knew if they were dealing in forgeries. One of Aunt Olive's sayings came into his head: man's humanity lies not in his strength, but in his vulnerability. If Horatius had a vulnerable point, it was a weakness for taking the law into his owns hands. If, to avenge a friend's murder, he had resorted to forgery, he, Sam, was not going to pass judgement on him.

Horatius and Laura lived in a world of different values, ultimately based on patrician banditry. Now, like the pair of exotic visitors to the pool at Illbury, they had migrated back to a planet beyond his ken. Could he in real life cope with a Laura so blindly, unconditionally loyal to her sibling, himself the embodiment of a patrician bandit? Just then Sam didn't care: all he wanted was to hold her in his arms.

Against his own expectations he had found the courage to take his second chance. He had played his part, beginning with retrieving the malachite knight. It had set off the chain of events leading to Horatius' release. And he had thought up and proposed the deal. Perhaps after all he was destined for the unexpected, too, in the wake of his lightning passion for Laura; or was he unalterably conditioned by his past – when he had pined for the mother of an infancy he could never recapture – and destined for all time to yearn for an unattainable ideal rather than to love the real, with all its flaws?

The old question wouldn't leave him alone: could people change, or was everyone shackled for life to an innate character? On reflection he decided it was the wrong question. It was not a question of change. In his moments of courage he had not acquired any new characteristic that did not exist before. On two separate occasions – at school and then again two decades later in Baghdad – he had uncovered an existing one that invested him with the power he needed to prevail. Pious souls had taught him that love drove out fear. It was a lesson with a difference, the difference being that in his case the driving force had not been love, but hate; and hate in turn had generated a thirst for vengeance that stilled all fear. It was not quite the noble virtue he would have liked it to be; but it was what it was. It had twice done the trick. It was good enough for him.

He wondered what home truth Aunt Olive would have to offer on the subject of change: something commonplace but sound, no doubt. He could hear her words now: 'Give change a chance.'

Meanwhile he would have to sit it out and wait for the migrating season to come round again.

Mott and the drinks arrived together. 'Look, dinner's fine. I hope you'll stay.'

Sam had warned Aunt Olive he might not be back for supper. She had planned Welsh rarebit. Welsh rarebit had become the nearest thing in his life to a running saga. Once, long ago, he had gone out of his way to praise her Welsh rarebit in order to conceal his extravagant dislike of the dish; ever since she had made a point of preparing it specially for him. All of a sudden – perhaps it, too, was the effect of the whisky – he had a sudden urge for Welsh rarebit. Besides, there was no point in staying. He had come to see the magic show and the magician wasn't there.

He knew the lines. 'Alas, if it's all the same to you, I am expected at home... I must really be getting along...'

They were returned in courteous, warm Mandarin tones. 'What a pity... Well, now that we have met up again we must see more of each other...'

'Yes. Of course. Absolutely...'

Mandarins liked to keep their lines open: you never knew.

Sam turned to face the infinite prose of the grimy London evening. A pall hung over the capital. Perhaps somewhere, up, out, over there, the magician was still at work. Homo ludens, Ariel released, a free spirit above the clouds. Across the pavement an evening newspaper vendor chanted his headlines, reminding Sam of ones he had heard a few months back that were to change his life: 'Coo di ta in Middle East! King assassinated! Coo di ta! English nanny butchered!'

He headed for the blue half-light of the Northern Line underground sign, expiring to black where two bulbs had been smashed. If he hurried he could just catch the fast train in time to face Aunt Olive's Welsh rarebit.